E. ARNOT ROBERTSON

(Eileen Arbuthnot Robertson) was born in Surrey in 1903, the daughter of a doctor. Her family moved to Notting Hill, London, when she was fourteen. She was educated at Sherborne, and in Paris and Switzerland. In 1927 she married H. E. Turner, general secretary of the Empire and Commonwealth Press Unions, later to become Sir Henry Turner, CBE. Her first novel *Cullum* was published in 1928, followed by *Three Came Unarmed* (1929), *Four Frightened People* (1931) and *Ordinary Families* (1933) the latter two both published by Virago. Her other novels are *Summer's Lease* (1940), *The Signpost* (1943), *Devices and Desires* (1954), *Justice of the Heart* (1958) and *The Strangers on My Roof*, published posthumously in 1964. She also wrote *Thames Portrait* (1937) and *The Spanish Town Papers* (1959), both with photographs by Henry Turner, and a children's book, *Mr Cobbett and the Indians* (1942).

E. Arnot Robertson was a broadcaster, lecturer and film critic; she was at the centre of a famous lawsuit when she sued MGM who had tried to stop her attending screenings as a result of her 'hostile' reviews. She lived with her husband and son in Heath Street, Hampstead: ardent sailors, they would frequently cruise to France, Belgium and Holland on their yacht. After 34 years of marriage, Henry Turner was killed in a boating accident on the river, a loss from which E. Arnot Robertson never recovered. She committed suicide in 1961.

D1458188

FOUR FRIGHTENED PEOPLE

by

E. ARNOT ROBERTSON

with a New Introduction by

POLLY DEVLIN

Published by VIRAGO PRESS Limited 1982
Ely House, 37 Dover Street, London W1X 4HS

First published in Great Britain by Jonathan Cape Ltd 1931

Printed in Finland by Werner Söderström Oy, a member of Finnprint

British Library Cataloguing in Publication Data

Robertson, E. Arnot
    Four frightened people.—(Virago modern classics)
    I. Title
    823'.912[F]   PR6035.0548
ISBN 0-86068-280-3

CONTENTS

INTRODUCTION

Four Frightened People, E. Arnot Robertson's third book, was published in 1931 to general acclaim — indeed rapturous acclaim might be a more accurate description — and she became, at the age of twenty-seven, a literary sensation.

She had already built up a substantial and astonished following with her first two novels, *Cullum*, (published in 1928) and *Three Came Unarmed*, which appeared a year later. Both were full of nervous passion, scintillant descriptions and scrutiny of accepted mores, and both seemed to have enraptured or dismayed reviewers in almost equal measure. *Cullum* especially, published when she was only twenty-four, was much exclaimed over because of its extraordinary maturity, depth and sexual candour, although this last was thought perhaps a trifle unbecoming in such a young lady. Indeed harsher things were said: 'Miss Robertson is to be congratulated on a first novel of unusual promise,' wrote one reviewer,

. . . but there is neither need nor excuse for treating sex matters with such crude realism . . . It isn't that I am shocked, she need not hug that flattering unction to her soul. I am merely sorry that she could have let herself down by giving so unmistakable an exhibition of the inferiority complex. It is all very well to be outspoken, but there are some things which are better left unsaid and *Cullum* is full of them.

This first book, written as she said with 'a pencil in one hand and a tiller in the other' (for although she pro-

fessed a dislike of boats she was a great sailor), deals
with a man who weaves fantasies around his life, which
is itself a lie, with such vivid veracity that the truth of
what he is saying and doing seems unquestionable.
Only when it is too late is all revealed to be fake, and he
a cheat. It's a desolate and romantic story, charting with
a vixen-like acuteness the birth, betrayal and death of
first precious love – precious in every sense of the word.
But the preciousness is blackened with typical Arnot
Robertson zest and humour (gusto, in fact), as well as
with the exquisite *mise-en-scene* descriptions of land-
scape, sailing and bird-life for which she became re-
nowned, and which were as jewelled, detailed and
down-to-earth as an illustration from a medieval Book
of Hours. Indeed they made some earnest reviewers recommend her books to ornithologists and yachtsmen.
Because of these passages, too, which form the unam-
biguously 'pure' background in all her books to the
more dubious human goings-on in the fore, she was forgiven much by her predominantly middle-brow readers, some of whom seemed to regard her insistence on
the same clarity about human sexual relations and activity as aberrant or perverse lapse of good taste.
Three Came Unarmed was stronger stuff – a tragedy of
manners based on one of those themes which run like a
heart-beat through her books, the theme of the noble
savage or innocent and his or her inevitable besmir-
chenment in negotiation with society. Again she was
attacked, this time for having such a romantic idea of
nature and humanity.

'This is in fact the old "noble savage" nonsense, so popular in the later part of the 18th century,' rebuked J. B. Priestley. 'These creatures do not really come from Borneo, they come from Rousseau and cloud-cuckoo land.' And once again her sexual candour shocked reviewers, although it's hard to know why.

Yet she never did subscribe to the Rousseau-esque ideal of the noble savage, she was too conversant with everyday ignoble behaviour; and she never did wish that her characters could journey backwards to a never-never time of primitive simplicity. The most vulnerable and natural of her heroines is usually worldly-wise to the point of cynicism, and has a quivering nose for up-wind society stirrings. She did however believe that the elemental and primitive side of nature waited, marking time, behind the flimsy barriers of modern civilisation before crashing them down, and one can't but feel she was praying for the day.

Four Frightened People catapulted her out of the cult into the best-seller class, and into fame. In it she unwove the theme, theories, devices of the two earlier books, turned them round, and sent four sophisticated people, two men, two women, refugees from a small ship stricken by bubonic plague, unarmed save for a good line in chat, into the deepest Malay jungle, and fantasised with astonishing verisimilitude about the results. Here nature is malevolent, baleful and erotic, and takes a revenge which is described with an explicit authenticity that makes the Malayan jungle alive and livid, a place sliced with screams and infested with fear;

and the savage, far from being noble, is almost sub-human.

With this book she gained not only a wider audience (the book went into reprint after reprint, a Penguin edition, and was made into an abysmal movie), she also gained her full confidence, amounting almost to arrogance, and through the endearing and often irritating voice of her heroine, a young doctor, Judy Corder, one can hear the tones of the author's voice, quizzical, amused, sometimes abrasive and wholly unsurprised.

The story is pure fantasy but the authenticity and authority is such that it reads as a documentary or a chronicle of what happened – a vivid recollection of experience terribly suffered. The jungle stinks, the predators stalk, the civilised people crawl – and retired colonels wrote telling her that, having lived in Malaya for 50 years, they too knew every inch of the ground she had covered, and enclosed hand-drawn maps with x (crosses) marking the spot. They also remembered meeting her at the Residency for tea. In fact she had never been to Malaya in her life and had done all her research in the British Museum.

'I back the British Museum Reading Room against travel,' she said at the time; 'it's much easier to keep a sense of proportion about flies, heat and smells for instance, from a distance than when living among them.'

'A foetid gale surprisingly reminiscent of the London Tube Railway passages after rush hour was blowing across the swamp' surely bore the mark of experience rather than research. But it was a measure of her art as a

writer and a measure too of the strength and accommodation of her imagination, this conversion of acquired
knowledge into stuff, although one can't help suspecting that in weaving her own authenticities she was aware
of a kind of fakery that excited her own disapproval.
But here was another of the questions or themes that disturbed and preoccupied her, all her life: the question of
literary morality, of immense deceit and intense insin-
cerity, of where truth ends and deception begins. It was
the theme of *Cullum*, and she returned to it again and
again in lectures and broadcasts, as though some childhood voice was ringing in her head warning against the
wickedness of telling tales. 'Do you remember,' she
wrote indignantly in the *Daily Herald*,

how adults expected us to believe things which they obviously did
not believe themselves? the importance of truth, for instance? Be-
wilderment was added to the sense of insecurity. Half a dozen
times a day we heard them lie, socially, brazenly or by implication.
But if we had – THAT was different.

Although her stories explored the human psyche,
examined motives and desires, they can all be read on
the level of thrilling yarns like those of Rider Haggard
or Conan Doyle's *The Lost World*, and she used venera-
ble plots, stock situations on which to hinge her astrin-
gent and often original view of the society in which she
lived and had been brought up. For all of the four of the
title, *Four Frightened People* is still about the eternal
triangle and the fate of the fourth member of the party,
Mrs Maybrick, occasioned excited comment from
readers and critics who thought such behaviour very

unEnglish. Exactly the sort of sentiment E. Arnot Robertson enjoyed demolishing.

Mrs Maybrick, too, is a woman of the kind she enjoyed demolishing. It is a barbed and accurate word-picture, that never sinks into caricature, of a certain kind of garrulous well-meaning woman who drives her listeners almost frantic, and is supposed to be based on her mother.

Many members of her family are supposed to have been the originals for her characters but she said:

You can't take characters wholly from life. Even if you could it would not be desirable. Actually we are all a mass of inconsistencies and the novelist's job is to distort characters by selection, impression and emphasis into some kind of continuity. Even if you knew your brother, for instance, as well as you think you do, you would find that you couldn't successfully put him whole into a book because of his artistically deplorable habit of talking at times exactly like some other totally different character, whose conversation you also wanted to use. Life is rarely artistically probable . . .

In *Four Frightened People* she took artistic improbabilities and made them not only possible but real, and took artistic risks with passionate nerve and flair; but it's hard to know why she was so castigated for being sexually shocking.

'Rather too full blooded', 'Clever, but crude' and 'Appalling sexual candour'were some of the caveats used to warn unwary readers, and another warned against 'Strong meat as broad as anything in Smollett or Fielding'.

It wasn't even that she was any more frank than many

of her contemporaries. Perhaps it was because her heroines were like the daughters of her readers, conventional in their demeanour, their well-brought-uppishness, all that gels from the shires should be, with nothing in the least distancing about them – nothing greenery-yallery, or bogus, or Bloomsbury (indeed E. Arnot Robertson often had a go at such things). Yet these ridin', huntin', fishin', bird-watchin' heroines talked uninhibitedly and raunchily about taboo or sacred subjects – the Empire, established religion, the old. But about sex and passion she often wrote with a modesty and a reticence that makes the sudden sexual passion in her stories live in the shadows until suddenly it flashes to the foreground, blinding even the clear-eyed participants.

It is hard to credit how readers could be shocked:

This is love, to my thinking: not the endowing of another person with alien beauty –I never considered Arnold Ainger as good-looking as Stewart, who was himself nothing out of the ordinary – but the flowering into significance of their most ordinary attributes, as wonderful as the putting on of leaves by a bare tree: so that it would be sacrilege to credit them with more loveliness than they possess, for the marvel is that they exist, just as they are.

This is from the school of Holy Writing rather than Smollett, and her heroine Judy Corder is both a 'new' woman and an old-fashioned one – looking back at the Edwardian values of her parents with scorn but holding on to basic decencies.

Fidelity, monogamy is at her marrow, as part and parcel of her code, but in a famous passage, which was considered as shocking as any and was much parodied (best of all by E. M. Delafield) she considers which of her two male companions she will eventually sleep with:

I realised detachedly, as if this only affected someone else, that should we reach conditions primitive enough, both men, irrespective of my attractions (if any), would want me as a woman, and I should want one of them very strongly, and not the other. I looked round, wondering which of these two I should be hungering for soon.

Judy Corder, in many ways the leader of the expedition, tells the story with a dogged honesty and in so doing reveals a good deal of ambivalent thinking about women and sexual roles.

What often emerges is an arrogance and certainty about her own qualities and any woman who deviated or differed was damned. Poor Mrs Maybrick: – 'Until this journey,' Judy says, 'I had always been glad of the tremendous physical courage of unimaginative woman: it made my work easier. I have not felt the same about it since knowing her.'

Miss Arnot Robertson shares many of the attitudes and attributes of her heroines, the passion, courage and speed but her impressive intelligence was tinged with conceit, the intellectual impatience that very intelligent women often have.

She wrote about the herd, the race, 'the mass' of people, with a contempt that bleeds over into her treatment of women. Indeed it is hard not to feel that she aligns herself on the side of men, and was at heart that terrible concept, the tomboy and that she would have liked to have been an honorary man.

But as long as I could remember, even at the time of my deepest content, I had been preoccupied with books and theories and the like, though in a rather practical way, and not with the cares and interests that make up the lives of the satisfied wives and mothers I have known. I wondered whether I had been born without much chance of the less intermittent forms of human happiness. There is a spiritual arrogance, it seems, in choosing the great, far-off deities to worship; lesser gods of hearth and street and market are offended and take toll of simple things. It is not wise for woman to go whoring after beauty and truth: theirs are the jealous little household gods, made to their measure, ready to be kind if given allegiance; and most women chiefly desire kindness in a god.

She always gave her heroines their sexual due and recognised that their desires and needs were at least as strong as any man's, but her pronouncements contain many paradoxes: and although she believed that her writing was apolitical, almost every line carries a message and reeks of her politics as much as of her place. She fought her corner, but there is an undercurrent of rage throughout her books. She once confessed that 'an enthusiastic hatred for many things and people is not the best qualification for anyone trying to produce a work of art but this is what made me start writing'.

Part of the rage comes from being a woman. For her, locked into her time, women in the mass were inferior to men, yet individual women were nearly always superior – or better still, equals; and one can't help feeling that to achieve this equality they had first of all to tally with Miss Arnot Robertson's idea of herself, and also had to renounce something of themselves. That something was attachment to, and feeling for, other women. It was almost as though she felt that by apprehending fully her womanhood she would become diminished.

This ambivalence mixed with her utter common sense runs through her life and broadcasts. In 1935 in an unrehearsed broadcast debate between herself and Rose Macaulay she said,

The trouble with all discussions of women, unfortunately, is that facts are apt to be denied because it would be so terrible if they were true . . . Now personally I think that most of the facts about the majority of women are deplorable but one of these unfortunate facts is that the burden of responsibility for themselves . . . is a very heavy one. There is something very fundamental with women, their spiritual need of dependence. I don't think you will ever be able to educate it out of them. As a matter of fact I think if you did the human race would stop!

Her work is often tainted with this kind of snobbery about women but it it is hard not to forgive it when one relates it to the patronising attitudes of the time. For example, a typical review written in 1934 in *Queen* magazine and placing Virginia Woolf and Pearl Buck in the front rank of women novelists and E. Arnot Robertson in the second, began with 'A very average member of the reading public – neither a cynic nor a misogynist – surprised me the other day by remarking in reference to modern literature that he had never yet read a good book written by a woman.' Another, also reviewing her work, wrote,

I notice that week after week I have been selecting as the best novel of the week books by women . . . their quality has been unmistakable. For years women have been prolific writers of novels, now they are getting very close to the leading place. They have not yet reached the first place, will they ever do so? But in the second rank they are crowding out the men . . .

He ended his review by saying that Miss Arnot Robertson's book was a master (sic) piece. Another wrote:

. . . the subject chosen is an exceedingly difficult one. The theme – although I shall probably bring down coals of fire upon my head at the hands of the feminists for saying so – is really a masculine theme. Yet Miss Arnot Robertson has faced it as a man might face it, with all that almost bald statement of certain facts, which however are robbed of anything nauseating simply because they are not mixed up with that sex-starved sentimentality which usually makes so many women's novels a rather horrid mixture of scent and drains . . . I cannot convey to you the remarkable way in which Miss Robertson develops her theme. Hers is the masculine touch all the way through . . .

It was against this kind of prejudice and atmosphere that she was battling, asserting herself and her heroines' rights, and battling too against the deceit and hiding of things that had been part of her background. Her writing must have been as deeply shocking for some of her family as for her readers, for like her heroines she was impeccably well brought up, born and bred in Surrey, the daughter of a country doctor who hacked about his country practice on his horse and who, when she was fourteen, moved to Notting Hill.

As so often happens to children who are suddenly removed from their first place, the secret rooted palpable world in which they have nurtured their souls, absorbing and observing nature in an illiterate, wholly intent way, E. Arnot Robertson seems to have kept a delicately detailed, crouching, living world of nature in a crystal ball in her imagination which she could shake and see again, plainly, the world of childhood. She drew nourishment and light and air for her mind from this world, as well as material for her wonderfully delineated nature stories in her books, but she was not above parodying herself observing its magnitudes with minute fascination.

But much of the anger that runs through her books springs also from childhood memories – the cruelty and deceit inflicted on children by spiritually defunct adults. 'Blackness was never again so complete,' she wrote in an article, 'or so hopeless seeming, once one had got through the worst of childhood into the early teens . . .' And all her life she harboured bitterness about the pain she had experienced at the hands of female relations, teachers and mentors. 'I have never yet met a woman in charge of children who is spiritually fit for the job,' she wrote. 'They are resentful against the youth they have lost and sentimental about it for the same reason, and they will always gravitate towards it unless prevented by emotional tests which we are at the present unable to devise . . .'

Perhaps it was because of these childhood experiences as well as the press of history that made her admire men so extravagantly. That and the fact that since she was

twenty-three she had lived with, loved and was married
to one man, Henry Turner, general secretary of the
Empire Press Union, whom she had met sailing. He
was her best critic, her touchstone, and when he died in
a boating accident after 34 years of happily married life
her own remaining life was not, for her, worth living.
She committed suicide and the coroner brought in a
verdict of accidental death. It might have been the final
twist to one of her own plots.

Polly Devlin, Gloucestershire, 1982

To, and in reproof of,

HENRY ERNEST TURNER,

my sailing partner, who said:

'The trouble with you is that you're a prematurely
mouldy intellectual, and at the touch of your pen
romance goes rancid.'

ROUNDING ORFORDNESS

Lordy, but this is something like a day!
You have not bungled, as You mostly do,
Spoiling fine seas for pennyworths' of blue,
Letting the wind come foul, or die away.
We've 'all plain sail,' and rainbows in the spray,
And – when I'm starving! – bread and cheese and
  beer.
We've saved our tide, too; flood makes south from
  here.
Drenched, and with love thrown in, 'Too rich!' I
  say.
God, I could cry, such joy is close to sorrow.
White rings of bubbles, as the sleek bows lift,
Run widening past to join the wake we've made.
Lord, I will be more reverent to-morrow;
Could You expect, in flinging such a gift,
That I should feel a stranger and afraid?

FOUR FRIGHTENED PEOPLE

CHAPTER I

THE SHIP WHERE THINGS WENT OVERBOARD

'The trouble with you,' I said to my cousin, who was trying to sink into liverish sleep again in the sweltering heat of the promenade deck, 'is that you are a prematurely mouldy intellectual. You haven't an ounce of normal adventurousness in you –'

There was a confused noise of Chinese voices raised excitedly, just audible above the throb of the engines from where we sat, aft by the rail. A small dark patch appeared in the edge of the wake where the disturbed water, as though flattened forcibly by the heat that pressed like weight on all of us, smoothed itself out precipitantly into the quiet glittering sea. From the crowded main deck, where five hundred indentured Chinese coolies were herded, someone had flung overboard a sleeping mat: but one's eyes could not bear to look at it for more than a few seconds against the blinding radiance of the sea.

It crossed my mind to wonder, without interest, why the sleeping mat had been discarded: its almost certain lousiness could not have been a sufficient reason, or nearly everything belonging to the miserable Chinese would have followed it.

'– I suppose you worked it all out of your system messing about alone in small boats at an age when you ought to have been in the nursery, only playing at sailors,' I went on.

'Sh!' he muttered, making a commanding gesture with one hand without opening his eyes, 'I'm preoccupied.' He slipped back instantly into the heavy torpor from which I was kindly trying to rouse him, because sleeping intermittently before lunch in this terrific heat ruined one's digestion and temper for the day. We were steaming down the east coast of the Malay peninsula, accompanied by that tropical pest, a light following breeze which robbed the ship's movement of any freshening effect on the stagnant air.

'– till now,' I persisted, 'you wouldn't recognise Romance if you met it. You've been in love with me, off and on, for years, and you do nothing about it –'

Stewart stirred and suffered himself to be dragged from the slough of sleep in which three-quarters of the occupants of the deck-chair line were now wallowing, to their subsequent discomfort. 'Damn you, Judy,' he said with reluctant gratitude, and resigned himself to staying awake, and waiting for the bell to call us to a fly-blown meal which, if it was anything like the previous day's lunch, most of us would feel unable to eat. 'I wonder why you, who are more squeamish than most people about straightforward lying, should exaggerate so much worse than anyone I know! I was never more than half in love with you, even at my most impressionable period, when I was about fifteen, and then it was only because I'd saved your life and it seemed the proper thing to be.'

On the other side of Stewart a middle-aged woman, whom I had hoped soundly asleep, suddenly became wide awake, leant forward clapping her fingers together noiselessly in a girlish way she had, and cried, 'Oh, Mr. *Corder!* Did you really *save* Miss Corder's *life?* How thrilling. Tell me *all* about it!'

She was a Mrs. Mardick, whose bounding vitality and animal spirits would have made both of us avoid her at any time. At a temperature of 107 degrees in the purely hypothetical shade – there was no real shade on deck, for the glare from the rippling water danced into every corner, under one's hat brim and between one's narrowed eyelids – her unquenchable vitality became personally offensive. She made the handful of young people in the ship feel weaklings by constantly reiterating her liking for the heat – 'Nice!' she said maddeningly when we grumbled. For ten days she had been the life and soul of a dejected company that would have been tempted to barter both for peace and a breath of wind. Few are more unpopular on board ship in low latitudes than those who set out to brighten the lives of their unwilling fellow travellers; and none remain more blissfully unaware of the loathing they arouse.

I looked daggers at Stewart for waking her; he looked daggers at me for being the indirect cause of her waking, and the tall, lean man on my other side, who had his arm in a sling, no one knew why, woke up and glared at all three of us before immersing himself in a book.

Stewart gave Mrs. Mardick, without enthusiasm, a brief account of how he and I had capsized a dinghy in the days when he, only son of the editor of that clean, healthy paper for boys, *Young England*, was full of its sterilised ideas of chivalry, modesty and unobtrusive courage: the paper can never have had a more devoted reader than Stewart at fifteen. We had been certainly not more than a hundred yards from shore, in calm water, at the time of the accident. I, being much fatter, could swim as far but not as fast as he could, but he insisted on rescuing me. Knowing from practice that if one kept quite still, Stewart only held one's head under water intermittently while life-saving (a struggling victim had a devilish time) I stopped swimming when he first pushed me under by his grip on the back of my jersey, and allowed him to tow me ashore. I was ten, and did not realise that this was a momentous occasion. I chattered all the way home of other things, but the hero, lost in dreams of being now on an equality with the chief character of the current serial, heard little of this irrelevant, womanish babble. Just before we reached the house belonging to his parents, with whom I also lived, he said gruffly with an effort, 'I say – don't tell them anything about this at home.'

It was exactly what Dick Barton (of *His Honour or His School?*) would have done: but in his case someone would have blabbed suitably. I looked up in surprise; 'Rather not, you ass,' (they might not have let us use the dinghy again), 'I wasn't going to.'

And I did not breathe a word of it. He missed his only chance of getting the coveted *Young England* medal for gallantry. It was enough to make any enthusiastic supporter of that paper a mysogynist for life. Instead, the incident, which I forgot in a few days, gave him a tenderly protective feeling towards me for some weeks. He even wrote to me twice from school the next term; it was the summer term, and cricket was not his star game. In the autumn romance died, and I relapsed into my old position of holiday fag.

Mrs. Mardick greeted the tale with little shrillings of delight. She leant forward across Stewart and addressed the distrait person on my left. He was the only person who had so far evaded with complete success her efforts to make us all one happy body of intimate friends during our three weeks voyage to Bahila.

'Oh, Mr. *Ainger!*' (She had discovered his name from the passenger list, and that was as much as

17

anyone knew about him.) '*Did* you hear, Mr. Corder saved Miss Corder's life once?'

He did not catch what she said above the slight hubbub that broke out then, for a moment, on the lower deck, or if he did he was too far away in spirit to realise instantly what was said to him. She repeated the sentence more insistently, and he looked up from the book on his knee with hostile and in-attentive eyes. When addressed unexpectedly, this man had a habit – very disconcerting until one knew him well – of tilting his horn-rimmed glasses on to his forehead by one earpiece and staring at the speaker for a second or two as though he could not believe that anyone had really uttered such a remark. All that this withering look meant, as I learnt later, was slight absent-mindedness and defective sight. He did this now.

'*Once?*' he echoed vaguely, giving the word no more emphasis than she had done, but in his unemotional voice this raised it to the importance of italics. '*Once?* Really! Well, of course, one could hardly expect him to make a habit of it, could one?' Before returning his attention to his book he gave Stewart and me, to our surprise, a fleeting hint of a grin. Mrs. Mardick, for the first time in our experience, was entirely at a loss and remained silent for quite two minutes, looking from Stewart to me to know how she should take this. We gave her no lead, hoping that she would go to sleep again if conversation languished.

To straighten my face at which laughter was pulling, I glanced astern just then: another small pliable object, presumably a second sleeping mat, had been flung over-board and now floated, black and inexplicable, against the intolerable shimmer of the sea. There were always minor disturbances breaking out among the coolies, herded like animals into inadequate quarters in this small and dirty ship. Two or three orders were shouted angrily in Dutch at this moment, and the noise stopped.

I did not understand Dutch; apparently the man beside me did: his strikingly light blue eyes lifted from his page and stared unseeingly at the heat-crawled seams of the deck. It was the startled movement of his head that caught my attention: I should not have noticed it but that with low curiosity I was trying, as I turned back towards the rail, to see what he was reading. It was Greek, modern Greek at that, and as my expensively futile classical education had stopped five years before I had already returned, like most people of twenty-six, to semi-illiteracy from the academic point of view: but something familiar in the form and the heading of the pages identified the book for me. The man's face remained expressionless as he waited, listening intently for something that did not come: there were no further sounds from the lower deck, and in a minute he went on reading.

To the handful of idle passengers Arnold Ainger had been a welcome source of interest and conjecture.

While nearly all the rest of us, in the enforced intimacy of small ship life, had told one another in ten days more about ourselves than we should have confided to acquaintances of six months' standing on land, he had disclosed to no one what he did, where he was going when we reached Bahila, nor – most interesting of all to me – what was his ostensible reason for travelling by this disreputable boat. I had been amused to find that nearly all the passengers felt impelled to concoct different explanations of their presence in her. She was ill-found and uncomfortable, and wandered from port to port instead of going straight to Bahila like the bigger liners; but the difference between a passage in her and a second-class ticket in one of them was only seven pounds. We were, however, a company of impoverished-whites-out-east, who are among the most carefully-genteel of all classes: so far Stewart and I were the only people who crudely admitted, whenever the subject cropped up, as it did nearly every day, that we had not got that seven pounds to spare in order to save ourselves a fortnight's grilling. This was regarded as rather an unpleasant admission on our part: one hardy liar on board even claimed that he liked this trip in the hot weather and would not care to shorten it; some found the smelly little ports 'so quaint;' others preferred travelling in a small ship that had only one class to going second in comfort in a big one – 'so much more sociable.' I felt that if we could find even one other person who admitted without hesitation that he could afford nothing better, the social side of this voyage would not remain as deadly as it had been hitherto.

Because Arnold Ainger volunteered nothing, interesting rumours were passed round about him. He was a rather distinguished scientist – he was something quite important in Government survey work – he was a professor of history. The last was Mrs. Mardick's theory, founded I suppose on the fact that the books he read all day appeared from their bindings to be old as well as learned. In any case here was her chance to prove it. She ignored his last remark.

She leant across Stewart and said playfully, 'I'm afraid our frivolous conversation has been disturbing your reading, Mr. Ainger?'

'Not at all.' The tone would have deterred anyone but Mrs. Mardick from going further.

'I can see you're taken up with something frightfully deep; is it – er – historical?'

Her bird-like head tilted on one side enquiringly, with that underlying purposefulness with which a robin flirts about a worm too near the gardener's spade: even Mrs. Mardick lacked the nerve to ask him outright what he did for a living. As she seemed determined to talk across us, Stewart and I flattened ourselves uncomfortably farther and farther back in our chairs.

Ainger sighed and looked down speculatively

at the book in his hand. 'I'm afraid I have really no idea,' he said politely, and attempted to read on.

'Well, *I* think it's *splendid* to be able to concentrate so well on a ship. I'm afraid I'm not exactly a *highbrow* –' her youthful giggle interrupted her. Mrs. Mardick's laughter, like that of so many girls of the age she played at being (with no real intent to deceive) had no relation whatever to amusement. '– but I'm always meaning to do some *serious* reading, and of course a voyage ought to be the *ideal* time. I travel a great deal, you know; my husband's work takes him *all over* Malaya and I join him when I can, though funnily enough I've never been down *this* coast before, so I said I must do this trip this year even if I just *roast!* – he's in Singapore, you see – and I brought a lot of really *good* books with me and I haven't opened *one*. Isn't it awful of me? And yet one just picks up a 'thriller' like this,' – she indicated the book on her lap – 'and can't put it down! My husband teases me – he's always reading, but only technical stuff: he has to for his work, of course; one so soon gets behind the times in forestry – he says, "There you go, just *wasting* your time on some triangle drama." But I don't expect you read fiction, do you Mr. Ainger? I mean, men don't as a rule, do they? Your book –?' The predatory robin's eye came round to it again.

He lifted his glasses again and stared. 'Just another triangle drama,' he said after a second, thinking to choke off her interest. But he did not know Mrs. Mardick.

'Oh, goody!' she cried with her pretty, noiseless hand-clapping, 'And here I was thinking you *so* learned! Tell me what it's about!'

'The Father, the Son, and the Holy Ghost,' said the exasperated Ainger, getting up and walking away with his Greek testament under his sound arm as the bell rang for lunch.

The disturbance, as everyone who could face the oven-like atmosphere below decks pushed back their chairs, saved Stewart and me from a prolonged discussion on the spot of all the interpretations that, given time, Mrs. Mardick would put on his last answer, in order to conceal from herself the incomprehensible fact that he had not been a willing participant in the conversation.

She hurried along behind us when we tried to escape. 'Miss Corder! One minute, Miss Corder! My dear, *did* you hear that! *What* a thing to say in answer to a plain question. I knew there was something extraordinary about that man. Did you happen to see what he really *was* reading?'

'Gospel of St. Matthew in Greek.'

'*Ah!*' said Mrs. Mardick with the happy air of one who solves an important problem at last, 'then he's either *mad* or a clergyman. Anglo-Catholics make that kind of joke, you know. To prove they're men of the world – *so* silly of them: as if it took in *anyone!*'

23

Stewart stood back to let her pass down the companion way, from which a gentle breath of oil fumes of two varieties, engine and cooking, rose up to caress our damp faces. But nothing put Mrs. Mardick off her food.

'Heavens, Judy, I can't face it, can you?' Stewart said over his shoulder. 'What about going back and waiting for dinner?'

The cooking-oil smell, borne on the heavier kind, had just reached me: it seemed rancid; we had suspected yesterday that it was. I agreed with relief and we went back to the line of chairs, taking up the footling conversation that we had just started when Mrs. Mardick first interrupted us: the heat inclined one to slightly bellicose argument, but made one too stupid to argue intelligently. We talked desultorily, consecutive thought was an effort when the pores of one's skin, intensely irritable from over-stimulation, felt as though each had a separate life of discomfort to itself. It was easy to get ruffled over the most trivial matters in this weather: about ten per cent of the passengers were no longer on speaking terms with others.

'I may be a desiccated highbrow – no, mouldy was the word, wasn't it?' Stewart, who was a journalist and playwright, said pointedly after a while, 'but anyway I'm not a dam' supercilious one!'

'Meaning, I suppose, that I didn't properly appreciate Miss Hales' *ingénue* scientific interest yesterday evening?'

I was surprised to see Stewart, who was fair and coloured easily – to his mortification in earlier years – beginning to turn pink at the ears in response to this shot in the dark.

'She really was interested,' he said shortly, and then laughed. 'You are a brute, Judy! It's awfully lucky for me, as a lazy person, that you were born a woman, otherwise there'd be so many occasions when honour would require me to exert myself and strike you. This would be one of them.'

Stewart was the only young man on board who could possibly be called handsome by anyone, even in a ship in the tropics, and he was not particularly good-looking. As relics of an air smash in France he had scars on the temple and jaw; I imagine that these were his chief attractions. The softly pretty Miss Hales and a stalwart young mathematical mistress, on leave from a Malayan Government school, were sweetly competing for his interest. He had given no sign before that either had been successful, and I had enjoyed the contest, favouring, if either, the less clinging teacher; she had the better figure, and I preferred good bodies to good faces. She was one of those close-cropped gruff girls who are so much more aggressively boyish than any normal boy: she missed few opportunities of impressing on one how hard her rather small hands were, how muscular her not-too-developed calves. This kept every man in her vicinity aware of her essentially female presence and was, as Stewart said, hitting below the belt, even hers, which she wore drawn tightly round her hips, in order to make their narrowness apparent. What, in fact, it chiefly accentuated was their entirely unmasculine contour and bulk.

It is odd to look back on that voyage, with the knowledge of what was happening in the ship at the time, and to remember how closely one's attention was focussed on such trifles as this three-cornered flirtation. Miss Hales had gazed up at Stewart with wondering dark eyes, while he and I and the two girls were chatting in the bows the previous evening, watching the green fire of phosphorescence paled by the ardent bluish moonlight to a hueless radiance, as the sharp stem flung back the water in high white wings.

'Why does the moon make only such a narrow sort of fairy path on the water, instead of shining all over it, Mr. Corder?' she had asked dreamily.

Reverting to childhood I had kicked Stewart gently on the ankle: as a rule we were at one in amusement at this flatter-his-vanity-by-her-ignorance method of enticing the male: but on this occasion he had not responded.

'Angle of incidence same as angle of reflection!' snapped the other girl swiftly, so that Stewart looked at her in astonishment, partly because of the challenging tone in which she proffered the obviously unwanted information, but chiefly, I think, because he had long ceased expecting such

26

positively human intelligence from personable women of her age. A strapping young creature with her head tilted back provocatively, she would have made a not ineffective contrast to the gentler girl but that she despised tangible feminine wiles, such as powder, as wholeheartedly as she evidently did those of flattery: the angle of incidence was disastrously equal to the angle of reflection where her hot face caught the light from the fo'c'sle companion lamp, and this was not a climate where women out for admiration could afford to be as boyish as all that.

'Er, yes, that's right – at least – ' Stewart had said, returning his attention entirely to Miss Hales, to whom he amplified the explanation hazily in terms which, judging by her pleased nods of comprehension, made the theory of reflection beautifully lucid to her. They conveyed nothing to me.

It must have been at this moment that Miss Hales made her unsuspected conquest, I thought now, recalling the events of that evening – the last enjoyable one we spent in the ship, or, indeed, anywhere for several weeks. Listening to Stewart floundering and enjoying his floundering, because the listener's ears were so well shaped if not receptive, I had been as happy then as I had felt at any time during the past year: life and all the charming absurdities of sex were delightful, I was gradually rediscovering, if only one remained the disinterested watcher.

27

But I was mildly repentant, this afternoon, that I had unwittingly avenged the defeated contestant on the spot by asking Stewart, in a tone copied from Miss Hales', a string of innocent-sounding questions of the same semi-scientific character. Stewart had a newspaper-man's smattering of physical cause and effect, which was even scantier than mine. He was aware of this, and could have wrung my neck for showing him up.

I admitted to myself, while we went on arguing pointlessly about our respective forms of intellectual snobbishness, that he was quite right about my superciliousness: a turn in my affairs of which Stewart knew nothing – though how much he suspected I could not tell – made me seem irritatingly superior at times towards the silly and entertaining and pretentious side of sex, which I had enjoyed at one time as much as he did still. My defence, which I could not offer, was that this was preferable to growing bitter, and I think there was no other choice for me just then. I was not superhuman, and some memories were still agony when they broke loose, in my weak moments, from the will's control.

There had been a man who had preferred someone else: I could not even wonder at it, for she was charming. That is all the story, except that we had been lovers at the time he found her, which made it slightly – not much – worse for me. It made it possible for people to say, 'Never see you and that

nice friend of yours – what was his name? – together
now! What's happened?' And I would have to
answer indifferently, 'D'you mean Hugh? Why,
nothing. We often meet,' (this was miserably
true), 'only of course I've been busy lately, since I
scraped through my finals.' (Curious that it can be
such pain to be forced to say carelessly a name that
is always in one's thoughts anyway: curious, too,
what cruelty well-meaning elders practise on the
young, in spite of personal experience of the suffering which surely no one escapes entirely in youth?)
But our being still unmarried made it possible for
him to leave me without much delay – without a
long effort of loyalty which would have made him
my lover when inclination had ceased to do so. That
is the thing which, in retrospect, I think I could not
have borne – No, I say that, but it is not true:
there is no torment or humilitation of mind and
body that mankind cannot bear if need be: the
fragile fibres of our flesh and spirit are bound
together with an endurance which is pitifully,
magnificently beyond bounds (for death is not a
limit in this sense but only a possibility of escape,
which makes almost all sorrows bearable). In my
own case, I think I had less passive courage than
most women, for I had run away from trouble. It
was not present in my mind now at every minute.
I had reached the stage when I could realise that I
was the richer for having known him. For choice,
I would not have been spared that experience.

I smiled placatingly at Stewart and got up. 'Well, you can't be so innately mouldy after all,' I said lightly, 'if "a pair of sparkling eyes" has worked such rapid havoc with your sense of humour – "happy man, etc." as the song says (particularly remember the etc.-bit about keeping "if you can"). The skipper is casting eyes in the same direction, and if one overlooks the surrounding oiliness, his eyes leave yours nowhere. Besides, he wears gold braid.'

Prepared to make the most honourable amends possible, I waylaid Miss Hales' unattractive mother as the two emerged from the ordeal of lunch. The girl was badly parent-ridden: unaware that her charms had faded and that, like her daughter, she had nothing else to recommend her, Mrs. Hales followed the pretty little thing about with a lovingly jealous eye, spoiling, with the best intentions, every *tête-à-tête* the girl began. I piloted the older woman to her usual place, sat down by her and insisted on talking to her until drowsiness overcame her. The daughter secured my empty chair by Stewart and began chattering to him eagerly, I noticed out of the corner of one eye, while I kept a conversational grip on her ponderous mother, and thought respectfully of a mahout I had once seen restraining a restless elephant: but he seemed to do it without effort; twice I thought Mrs. Hales was going to escape me and succeed in joining them.

As soon as she was stertorously asleep I moved.

The afternoon heat seemed to be increasing: sweat and the misery of prickly heat started wherever one's skin pressed against something: a bare arm, though weighed down by its own indolence, shrank from contact with the hot wooden side of the chair: where damp clothes were forced against the body the slight pressure became intolerable after a time. As I walked aft on my way to the lower deck the air seemed to solidify into a suffocating barrier on every side, opposing all movement. I heard my heart thumping from the effort of strolling, and yet this change of discomfort was preferable to sitting still, at the moment.

None of the other passengers, except a jolly little boy born in Shanghai who was always slipping away from his parents to talk to the Chinese coolies, went down to the lower deck as a rule. They missed a sight worth the energy required to penetrate into this other world, the real life of the ship. At all hours of the day two or three or more of the Kanaka stokers – supple, sinewy fellows with golden skins that made one forgive the unrelenting sun – sprawled half naked on the deck outside the stokehold, waiting to go on shift or recovering, dead-beat for the moment, from a spell below. The appalling heat of the furnaces, unendurable for white men in this climate, merely polished these lovely bodies: and as the men coming off duty filed out and flung themselves down carelessly to cool, sleek-muscled arms and legs and powerful shoulders shone mattly,

like fine silk, through the powdering of coal dust
that ran off them leaving streaks of clear, wet gold,
as though such tempered skins were unsoilable.
They were beautiful and I, though born with little
sense of reverence, could always be held awed and
content by the splendour of good flesh, whether
human or animal. A cat jumping, horses in full
gallop, slim girls with superbly balanced bodies,
a young man using his strength – these set the world
in flower, humbling for a moment the lasting
fairness of inanimate things before the transitory,
breath-stopping graciousness of life.

The Kanakas were as unaware that they were
worth observing as they were of the lavishness of
their display, so that they took no notice of me when
I passed by to gossip with the old Portuguese chief
engineer, who liked to talk English – he was always
practising in the hopeless hope of getting into an
English ship – 'Oh, but they have the engine
there! Beeg – much power – *efficaz* – what is that,
not ever go wrong ?– jus' like God." He was a
dull man, but an excuse for standing near the after
well-deck, watching both the coming and going
of the brown men and the multifarious activities of
the Chinese coolies. These last were not a pleasure
to the eye, but they were entertaining with their
endless quarrels and cooking, earnest confabulations
and prayers.

The faint air from aft, gaining on the ship for the
moment, wafted the smell of their rice concoctions

and of their close-packed humanity towards us. The Chief and I retreated forward, he in deference to my northern bred fads since he smelt nothing, and as we passed the indifferent, statuesque natives, he politely intercepted my view with his decorous, paunchy figure. I was thinking idly how physically unworthy of the thin-flanked, hard grandeur of the young male is the utilitarian female in almost all forms of life – plants and fish excepted – when a voice called my name peremptorily from the promenade deck companion-way. Arnold Ainger was standing there.

'Yes?' I said; but he waited for me to come to him. His 'Miss Corder!' had been so urgent that I left the Chief and joined him. He gave no explanation of this curt manner, turning on his heel as soon as I reached him, so that I found myself accompanying him back to the promenade deck.

'You're a doctor, aren't you?'

'Yes, but how did you know that?'

'I thought you must be; you passed a pair of blunt-ended bandage scissors yesterday to someone next to me who was barbarously slitting up the pages of a book with his fingers –' (the offender had been Stewart, I remembered, but at that time Ainger had not paid sufficient attention to either of us to know that we were related, or even that we were close friends). 'I could have proposed you a vote of thanks: that's one of the practices of the illiterate, like wife-beating, which no decent man

33

can watch entirely unmoved. I've never known any woman carry, from commonsense alone, something that cuts effectively, so I supposed that it was a professional habit, and you were either a doctor or a nurse. You don't look like a nurse. Well, I'm sorry to have to ask you to work on holiday, but the ship's doctor is ill – have you met that interesting specimen of the Dutch medical service, by the way?'

'No, I haven't.'

'It's not surprising; I've had the greatest difficulty in seeing him on two occasions by appointment since we left Rapi, though I told him when we started that I'd want my arm dressed at least once a day. I only secured his attention then through a fluent knowledge of colloquial Dutch, and on both occasions I wished I hadn't, while he was treating me. Anyway, I wonder if you'd mind renewing the dressing; my arm's getting unbearably painful, and I can't even live in hopes of making the fellow see to it now; he's gone down with – dysentery, I'm told.'

I think I noticed at the time that pause before the word; I am not sure.

So many small things that I record of this day, as having been observed at the time, may have slipped past my conscious attention when they happened, and delving in my memory afterwards for significant facts, I have retrieved them from the odd pigeon-holes of the brain where all experiences are stored, and more or less lost, unless the conscious mind soon returns to claim them. At the moment I know I was chiefly aware of thinking that if he had already waited several days for a dressing, surely he could have had patience until I had finished my talk with the engineer. But the man himself interested me.

'Certainly I will. What is the matter?'

'Blood-poisoning after *kurap*.'

'*Kurap!*' My slight resentment vanished instantly. I had only been in Borneo three weeks and had not had a chance to see a case of this virulent skin trouble, which is carried by one in six of the natives in the interior. There must have been a trace of ghoulish professional elation in my voice, for Arnold Ainger smiled at me sardonically.

'Sorry to disappoint you – the *kurap's* over. I caught it when I spent six weeks in an outpost rubber station in Sarawak, like a fool, much too soon after typhoid: it gets you when you're out of condition, you know. Two of the Murut boys there had it already. When I was nearly through with it a half-healed patch on my arm was torn open by *lianci* thorns, and some tropical germs seem to have got in – wonderful how energetic they keep in this heat; I wish I had half their vitality.'

'You must have a good deal of vitality yourself, to have survived blood-poisoning on top of *kurap* on top of typhoid,' I said. 'You've really no business to be alive at present.'

'Neither business nor pleasure,' he assented gloomily, and when I examined his arm, fighting down giddiness brought on by the stifling heat of his cabin, I was ready to believe that existence had little value for him at the moment. Round the new scar tissue a considerable area was badly infected, and under the incompetently applied bandages the whole of the fore-arm was so inflamed that he must have been suffering torment. Looking back on my first meetings with Arnold Ainger it is odd to remember that I was disappointed to find that he was right about the *kurap* being over: he had only local poisoning to contend with still.

'You'd better let me dress this again to-night,' I said. 'I wish you'd mentioned it before; it's done it no good to be left so long untouched.'

But in the delicious coolness of the evening the indefatigable Mrs. Mardick got up a treasure-hunt, with wildly misleading clues placed in various cabins. No one else knew where they were, and she herself was too busy hounding on the laggards in the search to remember for certain what bathrooms or cabins were immune from the inrush of crypto-gram-hunters.

We waited until about half-past eleven, and finally he suggested the boat deck, which was for once as deserted under the close bright stars as it was in the day, when the vertical sun poured down on it. Mrs. Mardick caught us sneaking away from all the fun and frolic.

'You *slackers!* Well, I'll let you off *this* time, but not on Thursday, mind!'

'Thursday?'

'Fancy dress *essential* for dinner – to celebrate reaching Pedagor, that's just half way to Bahila, you see; we're supposed to get in about midday. I've got the captain's permission, so I'll have you in *irons* if you don't produce something, you see if I don't – oh, it's ever so easy, really, because it doesn't really matter what you are; I mean, you don't have to *be* anything. Not *really*,' she added, in concession to the unresponsiveness of our faces. 'Just something pretty or funny. I could make *you*,' she said magnanimously to Ainger, 'into a brown paper parcel. The sailors'll have heaps of rope.'

'Oh, God!' said Ainger softly as we went on up, but whether this was drawn from him by Mrs. Mardick's plans or the throbbing in his arm I did not ask.

The changing of the dressing was painful because of the general infiltration of the whole infected area. When I had finished we stood for some while leaning against one of the boats, luxuriating in the freshness of the air. We talked little because even out here on the water, which is changed less than the land by the coming and going of the sun, there was the secretive, menacing feeling of the Malayan night about us, holding us still and expectant, somehow a little on guard. One waited for nothing, and yet waited intensely, so that when a fish-eagle called suddenly, mournfully, from the direction of the darker horizon where the coast lay, both of us started and, unable to see each other clearly in the deep moon-shadow cast by the boat, turned to one another with an unspoken reassurance that day would not have prompted.

Spreading out from the nearly invisible land came the sense of ancient evil which tropical earth exhales at night: all land, even that which has been conquered and enslaved, becomes hostile and strangely different when light has died some while; it grows older and stronger in spirit, as old and potent as the primitive jungle that we were skirting, and regardless of man save as an enemy. He is dull-nerved who can walk across his empty, friendly English garden at night and believe it still empty and friendly. In the dark hours we are no longer masters of the soil, and at the back of my more-or-less practical mind I have suspected obscurely since childhood that the earth is aware of this.

Away to starboard, about two miles off, loomed the tropical forest swamp, where at every second the soil gave off fresh, rapacious life, and as silently and persistently as though we waited for something to come out of it to us, we watched its dim outline sliding by against the stars, undulated sometimes by little hills, and broken twice by the gleam of rivers.

Once someone came up on to the boat deck, walked round and went down again without seeing us or our seeing him; we were between the boat and the rail.

It must have been a few minutes later when quiet steps padded over the deck below us. Instinctively I made no sound as I moved forward to look. The moonlight streamed down on to the face of the man who walked there, and I recognised one of the ship's officers. He stopped and looked sharply all round, glancing up directly at us, but the deceptive light was brilliant, so that the shadows were blue-black and impenetrable. We were only dark, unmoving patches against the detailless gloom of the boat He listened, but there was no sound above the throb of the ship. He spoke softly to someone behind. Other feet shuffled forward and two men, slightly drunk to judge by their gait, came into our view, carrying between them something whose shape could not be entirely disguised by the disinfectant-reeking sheet with which it was covered. They tipped it overside with an effort and went back out of our sight. Another body was brought out, so light, as some of the undersized, ill fed coolies were, that the bearers had no difficulty in lifting it to the rail, where they rested its limp weight for a moment before letting it slip over. The green fire smouldering in the dark water woke and leapt up at it, eagerly it seemed, and surrounded it with strange radiance for a second before it sank.

We waited for a long while then in the strained, brooding silence which was emphasised by the steady pulse of the ship under our feet: I could not even hear Ainger breathe. I put out my hand convulsively, without thinking, as the quiet shuffling of burdened men returned, and he winced as my hand struck against his arm, but neither of us moved or spoke. I thought at the time that it might have been some trick of stars and moonlight, a reflection on wet material from the 'narrow sort of fairy path' on the water, but I believe now that as the reek of creosol came up to us again I saw some slight movement of the thing under the saturated sheet. They had more difficulty in swinging it over the rail. Afterwards one of the bearers, who was my steward and a lad of about nineteen, leant back against the rail as if he were faint or sick for a moment: the smell of disinfectant had been almost overpowering even where we stood, about twelve feet above, but it dissipated quickly in the off-shore night breeze which was blowing athwart the ship, to the great content of the passengers with starboard cabins.

The officer handed a flask to the boy, and he drank and pulled himself together, handing the flask on to the other man. There was no suggestion of officer and subordinates in their bearing, they were three men working secretly together for a strange and horrible cause.

They went away and we remained where we were for some while – ten minutes perhaps – but nothing happened except that the moon, looking huge and red now through a rising mist, set behind the shrouded land. The serrated edge of the forest, softened out of individual tree shapes by the white vapour, ate up into its bright core, till at a certain moment the remaining light seemed to ebb suddenly from the water and rush upwards and out of our world, away behind the brooding jungle, as the thin rim of the moon was cut in two by some giant growth there, probably a group of monstrous ipoh trees, which blotted it out altogether in a few seconds. The two shining edges seemed to fall suddenly behind the forest, and the star-relieved darkness felt cooler.

It was as if the moon's going set us free to move again. I heard my hard-held breath escape in a long sigh. Arnold Ainger stirred and said in a low, matter of fact tone: 'I wonder if the last was the doctor? He was a big chap. I've been expecting this – overheard something. There's bubonic broken out among the coolies, and they don't know it yet. Officially those' – he jerked his head towards the dark water rippling softly astern with green points of light dancing and fading on it – 'are in the sick bay with dysentery; and they'll remain so until we're past Pedagor.'

'Why?'

'Because for one thing the skipper's also part-owner of the ship and has a share in the profits, and we have a consignment of stores to unload there. He doesn't want that stopped, and the ship held up for quarantine and disinfection in an out-of-the way spot where the whole business would be twice as expensive. But the main reason – and I'm with him in this; he's a fat scoundrel but he has sense – is that he's got only seven or eight whites in the crew and five hundred Chinese on board. They'd panic and clamour to be rushed ashore if they knew. He can't land them here, or he'd lose his trading concessions. I've seen a crowd of Chinese go mad with fear; I daresay he has too. There'd be no stopping them if they tried to seize the ship. I think I needn't elaborate, to you, the points in favour of our continuing to act the unsuspecting passengers: news like this would take about five minutes to spread right through the ship. As it is, there's a thin skin of discipline and deception between us and large-scale murder.

'I'm not sure there hasn't been murder already,' I said, 'Technically at least: the man was probably dying.' We were talking in whispers, although now there was no one to hear.

'If you mean that one of them was still alive, yes, I saw that too. But' – he suddenly gave his very quiet laugh – 'I really meant my murder, which has always seemed the worst form of that crime and, since the War, the one thing to be avoided at all costs. At Pedagor, I think, no-one will be allowed ashore – fever in the port given as an excuse: it's only a tiny rubber station: they'll dump the cases on the quay, and the skipper will see to any business alone. Palimbang's the next biggish port. This is only guess-work, but I've no doubt the skipper intends to get an armed guard there, and give the coolies a good look at the rifles before he announces quarantine.'

Hardly aware that we had moved, I had walked with him by now the length of the boat deck. We began descending the steps to the promenade deck.

'Now I expect you understand why I was a bit curt this afternoon, when I wanted to get you away from the lower deck – and I don't see why, Muriel,' he went on without a pause, but in a slightly louder, sulky half-whisper, as we came down, 'you want to go making friends with some damned engineer. The fellow's old enough to be your father, and of course you must please yourself, but personally I should have said it was a bit undignified. Still, if you really prefer his company –!'

The captain stepped out of the shadow thrown by the companion way, into the glare of a bulkhead light. I had not seen him till he moved. The look on his face stopped us where we were, standing a little above him on the narrow stairway. Fear and a desperate kind of anger were surprised into his expression. The amiable, juicy fellow, whom I had always disliked, was caught entirely off his guard for a moment.

'How long haf you been up there?' he demanded.

He made no attempt to conceal his anxiety. Possibly he was quick-witted enough to have realised that it was useless to try; if we had seen anything we had surely seen too much – among other things, the movement of a dying man who was probably shark's meat already. If we had seen nothing it mattered little what we thought of his behaviour. But he believed, because he was afraid, that we had seen.

Into both Ainger's mind and mine came, unreasoningly, a feeling of danger, perhaps only the illusion of taut nerves, for what could this man do to hurt us even if he knew for certain how much we had discovered, and he was beside himself with fear? It was fantastic, but it was real, the sense of imminent risk that, comparing notes afterwards, we found born in both of us at the same second, the instant that he stepped forward, one hand in his coat pocket and the other shaking with his usual cigar between his fingers, so that the glowing tip threw tiny concentric circles of light on the white cloth of his jacket. I watched these stupidly, while Ainger answered.

'How long? Well, I don't know. How long have we been, Muriel?' (There flashed through me cold, irrelevant amusement that he should have chosen for me at random, in the stress of the moment, the christian name that I had most reason to dislike. If I had been 'Muriel,' how little all this would have affected me personally, save as a possible obstacle to my home-coming, for one's mind is almost invulnerable, armed with such joy as I should still have had.) 'Ten minutes or a quarter of an hour, I suppose,' Ainger was saying. 'We went up to see

the moon set and nearly missed it. It was quite
spectacular; did you happen to see it?'

'I haf been here, about this deck, an hour perhaps.
You did not pass in this time. I should haf seen.'
His tone made the statement almost an open accusation: where the man's face was picked out by the
light from the lamp it was pale and shining with
sweat: he looked ghastly.

'You were standing over there,' said Ainger
carelessly, pointing, 'and spitting with remarkable
accuracy over the rail.' This was one of the captain's
accomplishments. Ainger's voice was perfect: it
held the slight insolence of the man with nothing
to conceal who will resent further questioning,
pointless though it seems. No doubt the captain had
been standing about here, save for his excursion to
the boat deck, for well over an hour, keeping guard
lest any passengers came to disturb the work of the
only four men on board whom he dared trust.

'Why do you want to know?' Ainger added irritably, and squeezing past me, walked down the last
few steps towards the motionless figure that stood
in our way. Over Ainger's shoulder I saw the
skipper's hand stir convulsively in his pocket as I
followed. The tension, greater for us because we
must not show it, increased unbearably for an
instant. At the last second the skipper moved back
a step. He took no notice of the question.

'You stay a long time after the moon is not there!'
he said slowly, still unpleasantly.

Ainger's curiously soft laugh sounded suddenly again. He glanced at me and then at the skipper. 'Well, good heavens, man,' he said impatiently, coming down brilliantly to the other's level of humour and mentality, 'who wouldn't, in the circumstances?'

The skipper laughed gaspingly with the relief of sudden conviction; and as his amusement was even more uproarious than this type of pleasantry normally evoked in him, we laughed obligingly too.

'Don't tell my brother!' I said slyly with an effort. Reaction was upon me, I was beginning to feel sick.

This, also, was received with gusts of laughter. The man was almost hysterical with the lifting of part of the weight from his mind: we had seen nothing.

For some reason he had insisted from the first on referring to Stewart as my brother, though both of us had corrected him. Probably he did not believe in our mere cousinship anyway, and thought it nicer for us to be travelling together with some more unassailable claim of consanguinity.

'Ho, no! I do not tell him! So it is "Muriel," so soon, eh?' He looked at Ainger meaningly; his manner had grown intimate and ingratiating again. 'You do not waste moch time, I think! Voyage too short for you, eh?' He took his right hand unobtrusively out of his pocket and caught hold of my arm above the elbow, running metal-chilled fingers, colder than his palm, up the bare skin.

46

Detesting this handling, I almost respected him at the moment: there is something vaguely admirable about a man who can contrive, shortly after conniving at murder, to express by his looks and voice undiluted humorous suggestiveness.

'You shall haf a drink with me, yes!' He had us both jovially by the shoulder now and was urging us towards the smoke-room entrance. 'Not in my cabin: it will not look good so late, and we must not forget that brother! Ha, ha!'

'Very kind of you,' said Ainger disengaging himself with a skilful air of accident, 'but the bar's been shut some time.'

'It is no matter,' said the pinnacle of the ship's discipline airily, taking a deep chest-breath to enable him to dig into an inside waist-pocket, 'I haf a key, see?'

CHAPTER II

THE LONG DAYS

A RAT ran, with its head strained back so that the sharp nose pointed upwards, across the brightly lit alley-way between the purser's office and the cabins nearest the dining saloon. It knocked blindly into the cabin partition wall and ran along it for a few yards, with that obscene wobbling of the hind-quarters with which all rats move; the breath whistled, surprisingly loudly for so small a beast, in its taut throat. Collapsing suddenly, it twitched for a few seconds before it died.

Miss Hales, who was going in to dinner with Stewart just in front of me, gave a little squeal of disgust and drew back. The young mathematics mistress striding along beside me pushed her way forward and bent over the animal curiously, stirring it with her toe. 'All right, it's dead!' she said, with faint contempt, to the girl who had recoiled. 'They're poisoning them, I suppose. Obliging of this chap to die in the open: they don't generally. Must be strychnine they're using, don't you think, Miss Corder? – look, it's quite rigid.'

'It looks like strychnine poisoning. I shouldn't

treat the corpse with such disrespect, if I were you,'
I said, trying to make my voice sound casual.
'They're nearly all full of fleas, rats.'

'Oh, I'm a hardened ratter,' she said gaily, still
prodding the thing with interest. It had died in the
strained position in which it had run, and the
muscles were now relaxing, so that the head began
to droop forward. 'No, see, it can't be strychnine.
Arsenic, perhaps. We had a plague of rats in the
school last year — those wopping big black chaps
that come in from the jungle — and when I put
down arsenic they used to crawl away into places
I couldn't get at, and take revenge by stinking us
out.'

Stooping in the narrow passage, she was in the
way so that none of the rest of the little group could
pass, but she continued to stand there, considering
the dead animal, having the consciously unfeminine
woman's delight in investigating anything that other
women disliked.

The lad who was my steward ran out of the
stewards' room with a dish-cloth in his hands,
pushed her aside unceremoniously and picked up the
rat in the cloth. There was an open port-hole handy,
and he flung the animal and cloth out together.

The other passengers went on to the dining saloon,
remarking that somehow one never thought, in the
ordinary way, of rats being all round one in a ship;
yet they probably came into the dining saloon at
night. Their voices died away, for I had made some

excuse to go back to my cabin, where I sat for a long time with my head in my hands, weakly unable to face the usual gaiety of dinner: the high standard of jollity set for everyone by Mrs. Mardick at our table seemed specially unattainable.

It was the need for pretence, a pretence of normal cheerfulness that must not be relaxed for a moment, which made these two days before we reached Pedagor seem endlessly long. This incident of the rat's death, on the day after our discovery of the outbreak, was the only other unpleasant happening which I was actually to witness on board, but I knew, because Arnold Ainger had told me when I was dressing his arm earlier in the day, that two more of the coolies had died or were dying. Getting from the sick bay steward the boracic lint that I wanted for his arm, Ainger had talked to this white-faced, haunted looking man who had admitted that yes, dysentery was increasing among the Chinese.

Unlike the people who had gone on to dinner after watching the rat die, I had no difficulty in imagining at any time the proximity of those hidden watchers which infest nearly every freighter, the rats, on whose bodies bred the fleas that carried the disease. Soon, as the means of infection multiplied, this would spread like a flame through the ship, like an evil emanation from some uncheckable source, killing at random, in a few hours.

Later in the evening I heard with a sickened lack

of surprise of the sudden illness of the funny little boy who used to squat solemnly, for hours at a time, in front of one of the older coolies, listening to Chinese legends. The symptoms, inconclusive enough in other circumstances, pointed only to one thing now.

I did not know what to do. The child's parents had been told that the ship's doctor was ill himself and unavailable, and as I never mentioned my profession if I could help it (people with imaginary ailments wanting free consultations are a pest to all doctors travelling) they did not know that there was another doctor on board. But if I offered to see the boy now I could not allay the parents' anxiety, which was mild at present, and there was nothing that I could do to ease the brief, terribly certain suffering ahead of the child; nor could I tell them the truth and prepare them a little for their probable loss. There was nothing of any use in the ill-equipped sick bay; I had already discovered that: because the only disinfectant on board had been used too freely at the first scare, the ship had even run out of creosol.

I wrote a note to the mother eventually, saying that I was ready to come at any time if she wanted a doctor, and then did not send it, for what was the use?

As the time crept on long past midnight – sleep was as much out of the question as it had been the night before, so that I did not undress for several hours after the other passengers had retired – I tried to shut out of my mind the vivid picture of the boat deck as it would be now, black and silver with moonlight and deep shadow, and of what I knew must be happening within sight of it at the moment. I dragged at my thoughts, striving to fix them on the children's clinic job waiting for me at home, which meant a great deal to me; on my father's recent death in Borneo, which meant nothing at all because neither I nor my mother had seen that charming but irresponsible person since I was a child; on books and friends and small sailing boats, all very important things. I clutched at any train of thought that would serve me as an escape, save the one leading to the two people in England with whom my thoughts stayed most easily, against my will. But failing the courage to think of them, I saw whether I closed my eyes or kept them open, the shuffling burdened figures passing below me, and the phosphorescence leaping up avidly to clothe the things they let fall. I saw that scene for hours, over and over again, all through the night.

I had avoided being with Stewart as much as I could during the day without doing it obtrusively: we knew one another so well that sustained pretence between us would probably be impossible; he would see that there was something wrong; and though one could trust Stewart with the truth it would be no kindness to share this knowledge with anyone else while we were all equally helpless. But the next morning I could not so easily keep to my own company. 'I'll hold a place for you,' he said as he got up from breakfast. With the fierce morning sun slanting in under the awnings, there was, for about two hours, only one even moderately comfortable spot on board while the ship headed south-west, as she had been doing for the last four days. This was a wooden slat seat (cooler than a deck chair because it only touched the body in places) at the after-end of the promenade deck, and it held five people. There was great but politely hidden competition to get to it immediately after breakfast. It was understood, in the curious way in which unspoken rules establish themselves in any Briton-carrying ship, that securing that seat in the dawn till breakfast period, the pleasantest part of the day, did not entitle one to keep it for the sultry morning session when it was particularly desirable. The first comers after breakfast had the right to it. Stewart's unrivalled talent for conveying food from his plate to his stomach with scarcely any perceptible pause on the way stood us in excellent stead here. Having finished breakfast while the rest of us were still looking askance at our unidentifiable fish, he usually put my book and cigarette-case down in an empty place by him and explained blandly that 'My cousin is just coming back,' to would-be forestallers. They knew that he lied and that I had not appeared since breakfast, and he knew that they knew: but so far, even with tempers running as high as they did in this heat, no one had had the nerve to defy that shadow of prior right, a moral claim that, except in the matter of colonising, has always been particularly effective in controlling the British.

But to-day when I came on deck I found that in spite of his invitation, he had not managed to keep a place until I appeared. Miss Hales had sauntered up and paused pensively in front of the empty seat: Stewart, sweeping my things aside, had unhesitatingly sacrificed my comfort to hers: she was the sweetest looking girl on board, and the thermometer had been at its present height for many days.

On my way to discover this comprehensible breach of faith I almost overtook Arnold Ainger, who was strolling very slowly along the deck, reading as he walked. Stewart, seeing me close behind him and feeling slightly guilty I suppose, got up to greet me just as the lean, lanky figure drew level with the coveted seat: Stewart and I did not stand on this kind of ceremony with each other as a rule. Seeing something move, in the corner of his field of vision, Ainger half woke up from his Greek testament and tilted his glasses on to his forehead for a moment: narrowed by the strong light, his eyes assumed again, accidentally, the look of contemptuous incredulity with which I have seen pathologists regard inoculated guinea-pigs who have not developed the disease allotted to them.

Seeing a space empty on the seat, 'Thanks,' he

murmured to no one in particular, sat down in Stewart's momentarily vacated place, and went on reading.

In a few seconds he grew aware, even through his concentration, of the astonished looks turned on him by Stewart, who was left standing awkwardly beside him, and by Miss Hales and myself as well as by a most unpleasant Dutch boy of nine years old, who, with his tutor, was sitting next to him. This spoilt and adenoidal urchin had a habit of sniffing and an irritating way of goggling at everyone with his mouth hanging open: next to Mrs. Mardick he was the worst neighbour to have in the ship. Ainger looked up and took in the position with a grin which made one forget that he was still obviously a sick man, it altered his grave face so completely. He obliterated it instantly and turned on the staring little boy. 'Why don't you get up and give that lady your seat, eh?' he demanded severely, indicating me. 'At your age I should have jumped at the chance.'

Too much dazed by the suddenness of the attack to be master of his actions, the child took the suggestion, and the disconsolate, conscientious tutor leapt up and followed him as he wandered away.

'That's better,' said Ainger comfortably, 'Now we can all find room,' and he resumed his interrupted study.

It did not go on undisturbed for long. Mrs. Mardick was right in thinking concentration on a book almost impossible in a ship. Stewart, talking to Miss Hales, was absently cutting with his fingers the pages of a cheap German paper-back edition of *The Case of Sergeant Grischa:* the price of a book had nothing to do with Ainger's dislike of this habit, a feeling I shared. I saw him casting increasingly annoyed glances sideways. He stood it for about two minutes and then said abruptly, 'Miss Corder, whose life I understand you saved, has a pair of bandage scissors which I'm sure she'd lend you again as a small return for that service. Or I have a penknife if you'd care to borrow it as a paper knife?'

Stewart looked blank for a moment, and Ainger added in a conciliatory tone, 'I think that book's likely to be one of the most lasting things the War has produced – I hope it is, anyway. All my worst instincts are being roused by seeing you add a copy to the world's store of mutilated things. You might pander to a convalescent's fads and cut it decently. Have you reached the barracks part – the unforgettable scene – the man fooling with his guards – rifle and bayonet fighting – when his sentence is announced?'

Stewart had. The two thawed to one another at once in the community of appreciation, and I found what I had not expected (because, whatever your tastes are, it is too much to hope for from ninety nine per cent of strangers) that Arnold Ainger spoke exactly the same language as we did. This has always seemed to Stewart and me one of the most exciting discoveries that one can make about another person. It is possible to talk from the first in mental shorthand with such an acquaintance, certain of comprehension: and this is to have found the makings of an intimate friend.

We must have spent a good three minutes reminding one another unnecessarily – which can be an enchanting as well as a tiresome kind of talk – of the series of deeply etched pictures in *Grischa* before Miss Hales was able to make out whether Stewart liked the book or not. In the end, she asked him, to be quite sure.

With the exemplary patience shown by intelligent men to the obtuseness of only the prettiest girls, Stewart broke off to explain that indeed we all considered it a remarkable book, though what she wanted to know was only whether *he* liked it, and should she read it? He immediately forgot her again; Grischa's Babka was a rival that could not be disposed of by an upward glance and a couple of artless questions. This interruption of hers probably saved her life. Had she not made it, Ainger might have agreed to taking her with us when we left the ship (in which case I doubt whether any of us would have survived). As it was, she was one of the seven upper-deck passengers who went down with plague after we left, and one of the four who recovered from it.

Evidently feeling that listening to any more of

this dull conversation about an unknown book, which seemed likely to go on indefinitely, was too high a price to pay for a comfortable seat, Miss Hales drifted away to rejoin her mother. The fond woman had remained all this time hovering in the background, waiting for her anxiously. A grey-moustached, red-faced, white-haired ex-cavalryman called Colonel Chayning immediately pounced on the vacant space between Ainger and a brother officer, equally fiercely tinted, who had previously beaten the Colonel in a dignified walking-race to occupy the fifth place. Both were ruffled by this apparently unconscious contest, and exchanged only polite monosyllables, though they were, as a rule, inseparable cronies. Gazing fixedly ahead to avoid one another's glance, they made me wonder irrelevantly, as cavalrymen have before, whether there can be anything contagious, over long periods, in the supercilious expression of well-kept horses? I had had long, unescapable conversations with both of them on other occasions, from which I had gathered that their minds must have reached their apogee at about the beginning of the century, and now, though no longer at their apogee, they were still at nineteen hundred – this was the period, incidentally, when the cult of personal courage which the War killed ('How can man die better Than facing fearful odds –') was at its height as the well-bred Englishman's religion.

On no other morning was there so much shifting

about in the sought-after seat, to which everyone clung like a limpet as a rule once they had achieved a place: but Arnold Ainger, who was largely responsible each time for the voluntary relinquishing of the position, was unaware that the two old men, the war-graduates of South Africa and the Indian frontier, at once began listening with detached professional interest to the exchange of more recent War memories, to which talk of Grischa had led him and Stewart. From previous experience of the old and of the gulf that can yawn suddenly between my generation and theirs when they make some cheerful, wholesale condemnation of cowardice, or some deification of sheerly insensitive bravery, I wondered how much they were taking in of the talk of these two unsentimental civilians, to whom courage and cowardice were the reactions of the same man's nerves, when they were untried and young in fear, and when they had been worn down gradually, less by the dread of death than by the strain of continuing to exist in conditions which the old men understood only officially.

Ainger broke off reminiscing for a moment to say, 'By the way, are either of you in a hurry to reach Europe? – I particularly want to be in Geneva on the 15th of next month, and that doesn't allow much time for getting connections at Bahila and Colombo –'

'We're probably much more worried about time than you are,' I said. 'We're running it closer.

I'm supposed to be taking up a resident job at a new clinic in Croydon on the 11th, and by that time, if we aren't in London, Stewart'll have overstayed his leave from his loathsome paper for a fortnight, so he's particularly anxious to get back.'

'Believe me he is not in the least "anxious" to get back,' Stewart corrected gloomily, 'he's merely forced to, as soon as possible, by degrading financial pressure.— I ask you, who would be anxious,' he said, turning to Ainger with a rueful smile, 'to get back to running a two-thousand-word chat column called "Interesting Facts About Interesting People" in a stunt daily?'

His job was a very sore subject with Stewart, whose ambitious play, his one chance of escape from the toil of cheap journalism, had failed thoroughly just before we were called out to settle the affairs of my happy-go-lucky father who had died at Jesselton.

'Good heavens! Is that what you do for a living?' said Ainger, and surveyed Stewart with the awed sympathy that one accords to sufferers from rare and curious diseases. 'Well, if you have got to go back to it, why don't you both fly from Bahila to Singapore and so save two days? There's an air mail service just starting. Personally I can't afford it; I'm coming back broke from a six months' holiday. If I wasn't I shouldn't be travelling by this boat.'

Had we not guessed before that we had found a

congenial spirit we should have suspected it then; here was someone else admitting the only valid reason for using this ship.

'Not even if we could afford it, which we can't, either,' said Stewart the ex-airman decisively. 'Beastly dangerous thing, flying, and I always have hated taking risks.'

The Colonel and his friend sat up and seemed to bristle. They gazed meaningly at each other with their disagreement temporarily overlooked, and then stared at the slightly disfigured young man who had not, in their eyes, earned the right to be openly afraid. Their thoughts were almost visible – *What was England coming to when her young men publicly owned themselves cowards?*

'Of course your lot had a fouler time on the whole than mine,' Ainger was saying, back on the War again and still supremely oblivious to the listeners. 'Shorter expectation of life, and very little chance of a nicely proportioned wound, which was the hope that kept most of us going towards the end. I was curiously lucky, though: except at certain moments I never quite *believed* in this war, if you see what I mean. Realised that it was happening, but couldn't think of it as real. Except for languages, which are what I came East to study, the Napoleonic Wars have always been my main hobby – I went straight back to those properly comprehensible campaigns when I was demobilised, and before that, even at some of the worst times, they seemed much more credible than the idiotic nightmare which was actually going on round me. That was definitely an advantage – gave one some sort of mental alibi – made me a surprisingly brave man on the whole – surprising, I mean, to me, looking back.'

Colonel Chayning made an indescribable sound in his throat. He and his friend rose as one and left us, their difference forgotten – what was England coming to when her young men *publicly proclaimed themselves brave?*

It was impossible for them to realise that, unlike themselves, these two survivors of civilised combat were no longer in a position to be diffidently hopeful or modestly doubtful about the suffering capacity of their nerves.

It was now about eleven o'clock and the other passengers, stewing in discomfort elsewhere, had sunk into the morning lethargy: no one disturbed us by wandering round to see if any of the cooler seats were unoccupied, because in the ordinary way – when Ainger was not there – they were always full up at this hour.

Screwing up his eyes against the glare, Stewart said, 'There's a reddish sort of headland on the horizon: wouldn't that be the cliffs on the other side of Pedagor?'

'Yes,' said Ainger, hesitated for a second and then gave his almost inaudible laugh. 'I feel like Noah, deciding which pair of animals to save – will you two have a shot at leaving the ship with me at Pedagor?'

'Leaving the ship – ?'

Stewart and I echoed this, not quite together, and in very different tones. In his there was only astonishment; in mine, I think, an eager grasping at the hope of escape, or at least of action, as a relief from the passive anxiety that had been eating into my nerves not only on personal counts, though I was frightened enough, but also because my hands were tied, professionally, by the need for secrecy, in circumstances in which I ought to have been of use; I was as helpless and as useless as the other passengers, and I had the burden of knowing it, which they had not.

Ainger explained the situation on board to Stewart, who said nothing at first, and then asked some question about the length of quarantine. Knowing Stewart's quick imagination of old I did not think, as I could see Ainger did for a minute, that Stewart had not realised at once the horror covered by Ainger's unemphatic words.

'A fortnight from the time of segregation,' Ainger told him.

'That's ridiculous,' I said, surprised. 'A person infected with plague comes out with it in three or four days as a rule. Seven days at the outside.'

'The quarantine period varies all over the world. And here it'll be a question of clearing baggage, where I believe the infection can hang on longer,' Ainger said. 'In any case, once the ship is in quarantine, it'll be a good three or four weeks before

we get away from Palimbang, with all the red tape
there is attached to clearing a vessel. I can't possibly
afford that delay, and I suppose you can't either,
quite apart from the fact that the thought of spending another three days in the ship in these conditions
is pretty well intolerable. My idea is to leave all the
luggage on board to be sent after us – we should
be given no choice but to wait for it in Palimbang.
If we take nothing but the clothes we're in (and if
we survive the next four or five days of course),
there's no need to worry, we can't infect anyone
else. Kintaling, where we can get a passage on a
freighter to Singapore, is only about thirty miles
up the coast. I know a certain amount of Malay
which ought to help us.'

We talked for a long time, discussing every
eventuality that we thought might arise. It all
sounded admirably simple. Hubbub, breaking out
again for a few minutes among the sweltering
Chinese, stopped our discussion. I felt that tightening of the throat which fear always brings me:
each time that one of those clamorous disturbances
had broken out among the coolies during the last
thirty-six hours I, and Ainger too, no doubt, had
listened intently for a new note of discovery and
panic to sound in the angry voices: now Stewart was
listening with the same anxiety.

The Captain walked aft to glance down over the
rail behind us at the after well-deck. The man's
full, moist face looked as nearly haggard as was

possible for him while in good health: his excessive amiability had become an effort.

'The brother and the lady and the friend make company together – oh, that is good, that is!' His heavy cheeks creased with merriment that did not affect his eyes. 'Three not a crowd, eh?' He listened for a second to the shrill voices rising from below, but the noise began to subside, to our intense relief, and he went up to the bridge.

When retreating steps were no longer audible Stewart said, 'That rat that died yesterday near the dining saloon, Judy, was that plague?'

'Yes.'

'Did you know it at the time?'

'Yes.'

He gave me then, backhandedly, the most effusive compliment that I could remember receiving from this life-long companion. 'Good God! You have missed your vocation, my dear; you ought to have gone on the stage!'

'I suppose we couldn't take –' he started again and stopped, blushing gently from the ears forward and glancing back along the deck from which Mrs. Hales and her daughter had disappeared.

'Who?' said Ainger, and, 'You're quite right, we couldn't!' I said. 'Pull yourself together, Nookie!' (This was an old term of affection, Stewart's pet name for himself as a child.) 'Plenty of clean, healthy sport in due season, and so on, but one must draw the line somewhere. It may be only thirty miles to Kintaling, but we have to walk it, remember. What about the mother, who couldn't do that anyway, and couldn't be trusted to keep quiet for five minutes about the reason of our going if her darling was taken and she was left behind? If you can't travel without a harem of some sort, better take the schoolmistress — grit, gristle and girlish charm combined. She does look capable of lasting the distance.'

'No, thank you!' said Stewart, and looked at Ainger for the casting vote.

'D'you mean, take the girl who was sitting here this morning when I came along?'

Stewart nodded and muttered something about '— only crossed my mind — three already, so one or two more wouldn't make any difference,' which was unnecessary as a disclaimer of personal interest because Ainger had not noticed his attentions to Miss Hales any more than he had noticed our constant association until I told him of the relationship.

'Well, no, I'm sorry,' he said firmly, 'but I'm not really fit myself for thirty miles of bush-whacking, and I definitely don't feel up to doing it with someone who doesn't gather by the end of a longish conversation what the talk has been about!'

Exactly how we should get away from the ship we could not work out beforehand: if, as Ainger surmised, no passengers would be allowed ashore at Pedagor it must be by one of the small boats that clustered round the ship at all her ports of call. The circumstances must decide the means.

For half an hour or so after the decision was made I was conscious only of an extraordinary feeling of lightness and relief. I had not realised, until the possibility of escape lay within a few hours' purchase, how great had been the strain of these long days and nights, when I had felt the thin walls of the ship, the planking under my feet, even the stagnant air, to be instinct with the infection that was spreading among us. An ascetic looking Italian priest, Father Gerrari, had not appeared that morning, being indisposed with some trouble that his wizened sister told me 'seem fooney, but not bad, I t'ink — dis heat not good for eating, and my brot'er, 'e 'ave never eat enough.'

I went to talk to her, as a means of keeping in check my growing excitement. She was not, as yet, more likely to be a carrier of the plague than any one of us, or anything I touched. I learned that this devoted and half-starved looking couple were returning from Kandon, their birthplace, where they had seen consecrated a Catholic mission church built largely through her donations — she kept the shawl shop opposite the historical old church in Florence into which he, as officiating priest, refused to allow American ladies with uncovered arms. The hire of a shawl for an hour to amplify their costume was five lire, besides a two lire tip to the guide, who procured it for them from the shop and afterwards, I gathered from the proprietress's naïve lamentations at the greed of guides, came back and claimed another lira as commission from the shop. Some generous but interfering American sightseer had once bought a shawl outright and bequeathed it to the vestry for the use of her countrywomen, but apparently it disappeared at once – given, Signorina Gerrari said, to the deserving poor. 'We have such poor – ah, so many; it is terrible!' And the shop continued to prosper: but, beyond the cost of their return ticket to Kandon, the priest and his sister had kept none of the money they had made between them, she told me: it had been given in love to the furtherance of the work of the Church which smiled on their co-operation with such admirable understanding of the tortuous ways of the human mind. Like many people who are congenitally incapable of any religious faith, I had always had profound respect for that most remarkable achievement of man's genius for organisation, the Holy Roman Church; its ends are so breath-stoppingly holy, its means so superbly Roman in their ruthlessness.

It had been a shock to hear that the priest had been stricken. Even after the sickening of the boy who made friends with the Chinese, I had hoped against knowledge that the disease would not pass from one to another among us as quickly as among the close-packed, dirty Chinese. But the heat poured down from the sky, percolating into every corner of the boat, and the rats crept up from below, marauding at night, and with them came the constantly increasing danger.

The father of the sick boy passed by, and the priest's sister asked him how the child was doing. From the man's almost unconcerned description I imagined that his son had reached early and easily the stage of coma – 'sleeping nicely, thank you. Seems better – has got his colour back again, I'm glad to see.' Poor middle-aged fool, he should have learned enough in ten years engineering in the East to suspect that bright flush. I got up suddenly and went below, all my momentary elation wiped out by intense depression: surely what we intended to do would not turn out as easy in practice as it sounded in theory? People did not work such simple confidence tricks on their ill luck and get away with it, in my experience.

Down in my cabin, I caught sight of the reflection of my hands in the looking glass as they collected one or two handkerchiefs, all the Malayan money I had, and a pocket comb, and poured quinine into a smaller bottle – we could take only such things as could be crammed into pockets – and my hands surprised me absurdly: they looked steady and assured, like the hands of someone else, having all the confidence that I had now lost. Through my porthole, if I half shut my eyes, I could see the land, or rather the jungle which hid it; behind the thin fringe of casuarinas on the shore one saw no land, nothing but vegetation so thick that it was impassable to the eye, a monotonous, fierce fertility that even under the sun seemed hostile. My hands, directed by habit, finished for me the job which my brain had little leisure to tackle of choosing between necessities – we were almost at Pedagor and did not know when our chance would come. I was thinking with a sinking heart of the jungle as I had seen it not far from Jesselton, in a nicely conducted party, from paths laboriously hacked out of it, and in such broad daylight as the close-growing trees allowed: and even then it had seemed overwhelming. But we should be spending more than one night in it on our way to Kintaling, – several nights probably, because we could not take the danger of infection into another settlement – and in this part of the vast primitive forest there were only natural tracks and the paths the natives made from them.

It was as Ainger had predicted at Pedagor: notice was given out that no one except the crew of the boat landing stores was to be allowed ashore, because of a reported epidemic of some sort. Restless and anxious, the three of us waited for the little sailing boats that had greeted us everywhere else with insistent clamour, their owners standing up and gesticulating wildly, to the danger of the more collapsible craft, as they shouted up preposterous prices for their wares.

We were to remain there at anchor until eight o'clock in the evening: there were only a few crates to unload, but the Dutch crew were a leisurely lot, and the captain himself was going ashore to transact the business connected with the shipment.

An hour passed and no boats came. We watched the village, a small natural clearing between the everlasting casuarina line and the headland that merely interrupted it for a mile or so; beyond, the thin green fringe between shore and jungle stretched on again to the horizon. There were a handful of huts and a couple of big go-downs, but few signs of life discernible even from where we were, hardly a quarter of a mile from the small harbour entrance.

A flutter of grey-brown appeared between the harbour arms at last, but it turned out to be a big fishing canoe setting out for the night's work: several more followed, and we grew almost apathetic with disappointment and the gradual weakening of hope. The boats were tacking with the tide against a light head wind, making straight for us and then going-about under our stern. Because escape seemed so close and yet so impossible the idea of remaining in the tainted ship became more unendurable. None of the three of us, lounging together by the rail, cared to mention our renewed hopes when one boat stood on, farther than the others, until she was abreast of the ship. Seeing that there was only a fat old woman in her, with a boy at the steering oar and no fishermen, I said softly to Ainger, 'If she stays on that tack any longer, shall Stewart and I go down the gangway and begin

71

to bargain for something so as to attract her there, where you won't have to shout your conversation with her?'

Before he had time to answer, a group of passengers, headed by Mrs. Mardick, closed round us. 'I *must* have a sarong,' the familiar voice was saying excitedly, 'and if you guess from that what my costume's going to be you'll be *wrong*, so *there!*' Ainger gallantly gave up his place by the rail to her, stood behind her for a few seconds looking as nearly murderous as his unexcitable face allowed, and then disappeared below; she continuing for some time to throw over her shoulder to him conjectures as to whether the boat was really making for us or not; though by now there was no doubt of it: the ship was already blanketing her and the boy was sculling over the stern towards us.

The woman in the boat began holding up knives with ornamental handles, coarsely made sarongs and huge nuts from the jungle with faces and figures carved into them: she cried unlikely prices in some almost incomprehensible mixture of Dutch and English (these Dutch ships were the only passenger vessels that called here: where she had picked up her English it was impossible to conjecture from her extraordinary accent, which sounded like a poor attempt at broad Scots.)

I did not know at the time what Ainger was doing, nor what line Stewart and I had better take: Mrs. Mardick and her chattering friends, stationing herself round us at that moment, upset everything. As she never tired of proving to us, by using native words for products of non-Malay origin, she knew a certain amount of the language too, probably not much, for a whisky and soda was not merely a *stengah* to her, and the Chinese coolies were not only *sin-keh*, both were always pronounced as though she only thought of them in inverted commas: but we could not risk relying on her limitations.

As I learned later, Ainger was at the moment trying, from my cabin porthole, to make the native woman bring the boat nearer the side of the ship, away from the hanging gangway, at the top of which Mrs. Mardick and her friends were clustered. He dared not raise his voice, not knowing who might be in earshot, nor how much they would understand if they heard. But the boat woman was already within bargaining distance, with her attention divided between him and the group of women: she saw no reason for risking the light boat against the iron side and, from where she was, continued to cry her wares. When Ainger shook his head, calling to her urgently to listen to what he wanted, she brought down a little the unwarrantable sum she was asking for some carved paddles and went on clamouring, giving the paddles to the boy to pass to him through the porthole: the boy himself, with a permanent grin on his face, seemed to be a half-wit. The woman would not speak Malay but only this bastard Dutch Scots-English, so that he could not discover which of the many dialects she understood.

'*Sayaha trada mahu bli apa-apa.*' – He tried several, he told us later. 'I buy nothing but I give you money – much money – look, all this I give – if you come back at sunset – not before, not after, but exactly at sunset. You understand?'

'Herr tak' *durian* – eh, leetle money!'

Mrs. Mardick went down the hanging gangway and began bargaining for her sarong. Here was a real customer; the boat woman transferred her interest entirely to her. One of the Dutch officers hurried down the gangway after Mrs. Mardick and explained politely that in view of the reported epidemic ashore it would be wiser not to buy from the boat. He told the occupants to be off, and Ainger threw a handful of small coins at the stupid looking boy, showing him others. The officer shouted at the boy, who obediently put over the steering oar and hauled in the sheet of the palm leaf sail: but seeing the money in Ainger's hand he changed his mind before the boat got way on her, and sculled back towards the ship.

Noticing that the boy's attention was caught once more by someone we could not see, who was probably Ainger, Stewart and I turned to the officer as he was about to become peremptory with the pair in the boat, and we plied him with questions about the seaworthiness of these Malayan fishing boats, which, as we knew already, are so rigged that they capsize whenever they gybe, unless the bamboo mast breaks first. We spoke as an observant couple knowing nothing of marine matters, and it is a universal human trait to enjoy imparting superior knowledge – both Stewart and I will cheerfully bore the uninstructed for hours with the technicalities of small boat sailing if given the chance. The steamship man explained to us shortly, and very badly, as much as he knew about not only the local rig but also the theory of sail, using the little fishing boat to illustrate his dissertation. He must have thought us the most intelligent landsmen he had ever met, from the encouraging rapidity with which we picked up the idea.

Meanwhile Ainger, speaking as slowly as he dared, knowing that his chance might be over at any moment, hammered home to the pair what he wanted, stopping and trying again in a different idiom whenever the blank brown faces grew blanker. He did not know, when the officer finally sent them away, whether they had understood or not. Asked to repeat instructions at the last moment, both had grinned and said nothing.

It was maddening to have to spend the next hour and a half uncertain as to whether the boat would come back or not, chatting to other people, pretending to be fixing up a costume for the evening. As things turned out, there was only about half an hour in which we should have a chance of getting away unseen: after dark fell and before the ship sailed at eight o'clock.

Sunset came and passed and there was no boat, but Ainger had been reckoning on the Malay temperament when he specified this hour; it would have been too early.

When the darkening water was invisible more than fifty yards away from the ship she stole up to us suddenly, making no sound in the still water stirred only by the long shore swell, and scarcely noticeable in the gathering dusk with her dun sail and low freeboard, save where the phosphorescence lit brilliantly round her blunt bow.

The other passengers were nearly all below, as we had hoped, borrowing safety pins and burnt cork from each other in obedient efforts to look funnier than usual, or sweeter. Leaving the ship was in one way easier than we had expected, for the captain's boat was still ashore and the gangway was over the side. (We had reckoned on the difficulty of getting out through a porthole, which would have meant a short drop into the water because the roll of the ship made it too dangerous to bring the boat alongside. Sharks, though not particularly plentiful hereabouts, were numerous enough to make it unpleasant to be forced, as we should have been, to avoid all splash and therefore all haste while in the water.) Somehow, though, this unhoped-for smoothing of the path by the convenience of the gangway increased my forebodings over the whole business.

Going first, I chose a moment when the one or

two people still on deck were on the other side of the ship, to slip through the break in the rail on to the gangway, safely in the shadow of the hull, below the level of the lower deck. Then we heard the voice of Mrs. Mardick sergeant-majoring the truant few who were enjoying the first breath of cool air instead of dressing up.

'You wicked people!' Her mock-scolding of Stewart and Ainger rang out with a horrid carrying quality. At any moment some strolling passenger or an officer would come into sight and earshot, and remain there after she had gone. 'I believe you're trying to escape,' she said, and came to the rail and saw me. 'Why, Miss *Corder!* What *ever* –' the jolly tones rose shrilly.

Ainger seized her by the arm, and shook it slightly: it was always hard to get her attention away from a humorous point on which it had fastened. 'Listen,' he said,' fifteen people are dead or dying of plague in this ship. We are leaving, and you'd better come too, now. There's no time to fetch anything; you'll get your baggage sent on later. Get into the boat.'

It was an enormous risk to take on a second's decision, knowing her as little as we did, for I should have expected her to make some commotion or delay that would have lost all of us our chance: she might even have screamed. But as we found later, she was an exceptionally brave woman. She said nothing, but nodded, gasping. Ainger's action was the best thing – probably the only effective thing – that he could have done at the moment. He and Stewart, seeing that though agreeing, she was stupified beyond movement for the moment, pushed her on to the gangway and followed her down.

She had recovered herself a little by the time she reached me, and began to ask questions in a half-whisper. I shut her up brusquely with a gesture.

From the portholes near by, cone-shaped beams of light cut and intensified the gloom around us, the voices of passengers in their cabins were audible as we waited for the scend of the swell to lift the waiting boat towards the stage where we stood. Ainger took the first chance; I pulled Mrs. Mardick forward to go next, but there was no opportunity for a few seconds. Miss Hales' voice was saying confidentially, only a few yards from us, in one of the cabins, '*So* do I, dear; just the same. Isn't that odd? I mean, I always say food that's meant to be hot *ought* to be hot. I mean I like things iced as much as anyone, but if something's intended to be hot let it be *really* hot, that's what I say.' The boat lifted on the swell towards us, and I tried to pass Mrs. Mardick to Ainger, but she was totally unused to small boats, and a chance went by. 'Half cold soup going greasy – ugh! And I'm just the same about *frappé*. Things being *really* cold. I'm funny that way.' Stewart shoved me aside as the outrigger swung in again, lifted Mrs. Mardick and dropped her in. 'Oh, so am I,' agreed the voice of the mathematics mistress, a little distrait and muffled, probably because of pins held between the teeth, or possibly, now that Stewart's preference had become marked, she was not feeling so chatty as the victor. This dialogue comprised the last words we heard from civilisation for many weeks. As such they remain engraved on my memory. It is a pity, perhaps.

" 'Interesting Facts About Interesting People' " I murmured to Stewart, saw my chance to jump and took it. 'My God,' he whispered back when he had landed anyhow in the boat after me, 'To think I'm making all this effort in order to get back sooner to running that!'

We missed the captain's returning boat by about five minutes, for we crossed it on our way to the shore, but the crew saw only a Malay fishing boat, out at night as usual.

One of the crew hailed friendlily, and the boy, sculling over the stern (the woman had not come this time; and a dead calm had fallen) made no answer, turning to us in the dark and giving, I suppose his usual vacant grin. Ainger replied with a soft Malay salutation, thinking that silence might arouse their curiosity, and the boat passed on. Crouching in the deep narrow well, as we passed to leeward, we could even smell the captain's cigar.

When we dared to talk, remembering how voices carry over water, Ainger could get next to nothing out of the boy, who either did not understand his questions or was too nearly an idiot to be able to answer them: the dialect spoken here was one of which Ainger had only a smattering. After all our anxiety Mrs. Mardick turned out to be a broken reed in the matter of Malay.

One remark let fall suddenly by the boy Ainger greeted with his curious laugh, which Stewart and I came to hear with uneasiness later on, after we had learned that his sense of humour was generally impersonal so that laughter from him meant, as likely as not, that providence had gone out of its way again to play some specially low trick on us.

'Curious coincidence!' he said. 'The captain was telling the truth in all innocence – by accident, of course – when he announced trouble at Pedagor. This fool says, "*Ha-a, oran put' mateh*" – he must mean "*Hawa, orang puteh mati*" – "Cholera. White men dead." As far as we're concerned, this is one of those master strokes of misfortune that are rightly described in insurance work as "Acts of God," because no mere blind force is likely to pile it on so thick. I believe there were only three whites here, but I was counting on getting a guide personally recommended to us by one of them. Malays have an amiable habit of offering a guide to you, for a consideration, to places they've only heard of vaguely, hoping to meet someone *en route* who does know the way.'

He asked the boy further questions, and elicited

something about a half-caste who was still alive, but the boy mentioned him with disdain. Beyond this we could get no information of any kind, for as we slid neatly down the face of a sleeping wave between the rough wooden piles of the harbour, the boy would only repeat anxiously over and over again the sum of money that Ainger had promised him.

Having made the boat fast to a cluster of others before we landed, he ran away into the darkness without a word when Ainger paid him. We might have been the only human beings for miles, judging by the silence and darkness of the village behind us, as we stood hesitating on the beaten earth quay. Away in the jungle that crept down to the village clearing, tree frogs and cicadas were still keeping up desultorily their unearthly evening chorus. For me, in view of to-morrow's enterprise, this weird concert was anything but a heartening sound. Trying to recapture the feeling of relief that had come with nothing more than the hope of escape, I reminded myself that we were safely clear of the ship now. Our absence would not be discovered for certain until after the ship sailed, when it would be too late to bother about us: even if we were missed before, the captain, warned by our move of how much we must have known all along, would not send a boat to fetch us. Having gone ashore without permission, as he could explain satisfactorily to the other passengers, we had only ourselves to blame if we missed the ship. But my elation of the earlier part of the morning would not return.

'I don't know what you feel,' Ainger said, 'but I'm against knocking up any of these folk to get a night's shelter. It's not fair on them, for one thing; also I'm ready if unwilling to start dying of bubonic plague any time during the next three or four days, but to pass out with bubonic plus cholera would be definitely redundant.'

'Sort of medically rococco,' I suggested. It seemed essential to keep at bay somehow, by pointless jokes or any other means that occurred to the uneasy mind, the overpowering feeling of the solemn, indifferent, many-eyed night around. Soon we would be in the jungle, and there would be no fighting any more against the overwhelming feeling of the night, but meanwhile let us stave it off as long as we could.

'Not in the best traditions of artistic restraint. I think so too,' said Stewart. 'But maybe I'm just "funny that way". We'd better wait here till the moon rises in about two hours' time, and then find some natural shelter from this wind, which is going to get damnably cold later on.'

It did: Malay nights can seem bitter after the devitalising heat of the day. As an amateur in physical discomfort compared with the men I found the night miserably long, though later I was to look back on the bed of a dry runnel we found in the moonlight as a resting place of comparative luxury, since it was fairly safe, not damp, and we were not even particularly hungry. Mrs. Mardick, who must have been new to this kind of thing too, determinedly made light of it. How light she made of it! It was not until she had been doing so intermittently for about an hour that I realised just how uncomfortable the river bed was.

'Anyway, this is better than being made into a brown paper parcel,' Ainger said with unkind satisfaction as we sat down, and Mrs. Mardick protested with gay astonishment. She was indomitable for hours on end, observing cheerfully, whenever one of us complained of the hard ground, that we mustn't grumble, everything might have been *much* worse. This encouraged in all three of us a darker frame of mind than we should have been in otherwise. She gave us a taste of her quality that night: nothing upset her equanimity or made her waver in her determination to keep up our spirits. She was an admirable woman in many ways, but they remained unsuspected ways for some time. I came to dislike her in the early hours of that night far more than I had done on board. Then she went to sleep, which was beyond any of the rest of us. She slept like a child. Nothing short of physical violence could disturb her: sleeping was one of her talents, and in these circumstances I disliked her easy repose even more than I disliked her personality when she was awake.

I remember that Stewart and I tried to start a

discussion, to fill in the time, about the influence on contemporary literature of Aldous Huxley, whom Stewart, like most young writers, regarded as a kind of elder brother who had won them all the latchkey. This was the kind of topic that would generally keep us going for hours, but now none of us, I think, paid much attention to what was said: we were listening, unwillingly, to the lively silence that succeeded the jungle's evening clamour. Into it evaporated as quickly as we made it the sense of human companionship and support which we strove to create.

This was after we had watched the ship sail, a thing of such beauty in the night, jewelled with tiers of light, that it was hard to believe that she carried the pollution and wretchedness we knew to be aboard. She was not far from us, but before we heard the rattle of the cable coming home we saw the phosphorescence, a thin ghost of fire, a milky radiance just discernible against the black water at that distance, light faintly under her stern and drip from the stem as the anchor came up. I have never seen this living gleam in the water, before or since, as brilliant as it was that night. On the quay near by, where the slow breaking swell splashed up at intervals, bright points of green light shone like stars on the salty earth for seconds at a time as the waves flung up and stranded them.

The deep-water channel between the sandbanks off the coast was close in shore here: we could almost have hailed the ship, she passed so near; and as she gathered way her bows were wreathed in opaquely shining water. Forward along her side, where the thrust of the hull turned the sea aside, and in her wake, the water glowed, as though incensed at her leaving.

Even her defects were made lovely: as her ill-designed hull drew up a quarter wave, this grew into a swirling mound of soft light. It fell away into a trough of dead water under her stern, hampering her way: but here, too, was fire. She was so enchanted, this ungainly craft from which we had at last managed to escape, that like all lovely things she tore one's heart for a second by her going.

CHAPTER III

DEOTLAN AND WAN NAU

BEFORE dawn came, the voracious world about us knew of its coming and stirred in the darkness. The jungle, its nocturnal life stilled for some while now, woke again with its myriad shrill voices of the early dawn at the same time as a light wind, which blew away the mist between us and the still undimmed stars. On the ground the morning damp clung clammily, penetrating to our bones. Slight, unseen movements all round us, more sensed than heard, set our tense nerves on edge, but at the same time I was deeply thankful for these disturbing signs that the long night was nearly over.

A dog howled in the village and another echoed it, and then from far behind us the jungle answered, though whether the high, long drawn cry that sounded like a mocking imitation came from a bird or a beast I could not tell. The dogs grew silent at once.

Here, day was not the decorous successor to night known to us at home, lazily resuming sway over a drowsy world when the darkness thins and

86

dies, bequeathing its lost kingdom to the unwilling light. This struggling, sun-born life in forest, swamp and teeming air was too urgent and too ephemeral to wait for the going of night before resuming its unchanging day-labour of growth, fruition and exhaustion once more. Day extended its reign into the darkness, stealing precious time from the night, and when the sky paled perceptibly at last the feeling of full day was already abroad on this impatient earth.

Soon in the grey half-light men stood blinking at the doors of their huts. As in most Malay villages, these fragile leaf-thatched dwellings were raised on posts, and several women appeared at the top of their ladders carrying water-pots and sleepily twisting in and securing the ends of their sarongs as they stepped down with the light grace of their race from the platforms before the doors. Looking at us over their shoulders, they went down the slope on which the village stood, towards the stream that had once run in the wide ditch we had found on higher ground. Now, having shifted its course, as Malayan water-ways will for little apparent cause, it formed at its mouth the small harbour which was still thickly shrouded in mist – the lovely morning mist of these lands in which are dimly foreshadowed, when the sun rises behind it, all the colours of the burning day to come, and its gorgeous close. Torn from the tops of the jungle trees and the bare ground near the village, the mist still lay in the hollows, and the women, threading their way between the tall clumps of reeds to the stream, stepped down into this pale, luminous sea of vapour and disappeared.

We went to meet them as they emerged with their crocks on their shoulders, and Ainger spoke to them, but they avoided us sullenly. The boy who brought us ashore, idiot as he seemed, had somehow warned the village of our coming, for no one appeared surprised at sight of us. The epidemic was still at work here, though it was slackening. Some of the huts stood empty and others had already been burnt. From a few of the rest no one emerged that morning; and as the women passed they spoke of these, gesticulating to each other, calling a name and sometimes receiving an answer. The water carriers kept their distance from one another, only members of the same family and so occupants of one hut walking together.

The men, like the women, would not enter into conversation with us, going back into their huts or moving away when we came into the village street to speak to them. It was not hard for them to guess that it was some serious trouble which had brought whites ashore secretly at night from a passing ship: the exact nature of our trouble they did not want to learn; they had enough of their own.

'This finishes any hope of getting a guide, even a self-recommended one,' Ainger said, 'or a gun.'

We turned away, I remarking with a fatuous

cheerfulness (for which Stewart, always an early morning pessimist, glowered at me discouragingly) that anyway the unapproachableness of the Malays made no difference to our food problem. This was now looming large in our minds. With cholera in the place we could not have risked buying their rice had they been willing to sell.

Running feet thudded softly behind us, and we swung round together at the first sound of them – in any case before I was conscious of hearing them: it is remarkable how soon one's nervous reactions quicken in such conditions.

The man who caught up with us, panting, was small but thickly, almost clumsily built for a Malay, and dark, but not with the usual olive tint: evidently the half-caste of whom the boy had spoken. He had a handsome, over-mobile face: his manner was excessively eager.

'Tuan do business with this man, Deotlan,' he said. 'I the most-white man of this place. No one speak English only I. I see ship's captain to-morrow.' (We never managed, in our long association with Deotlan, to rid him of his verbal confusion between 'yesterday' and 'to-morrow' in English – both words only meaning 'another day' in his particular dialect – but this was an almost endearing mistake compared with the average Malay's inability to distinguish between 'to-day' and 'to-morrow' in any language in business matters.) 'I make all right for you. Yes, by God. What you want?'

Stewart questioned him about Kintaling, asking
how far off it was, which we already knew, and
roughly what lay between us and it, and if it was as
big as Pedagor, which we knew it was not; in order
to find out, before discussing the matter of a guide,
whether the man had been there or not. But his
knowledge of English turned out to be disappoint-
ingly slight: he said 'yes,' politely to every question
he did not understand, and it was some time before
we learned that 'Yes, by God,' picked up from a
white man he had respected, was his only reliable
affirmative. He had learned his glib greeting
phrases to us off by heart.

As soon as he gathered what we wanted, the man
appeared anxious to come with us but unwilling,
for some reason that Ainger could not discover,
that we should go to Kintaling: he mentioned hope-
fully, instead, the names of several other towns
further north along the coast, but gave in, again
without explanation, when we insisted that unless
he could offer some good reason, our destination
must be Kintaling.

Ainger warned him that we were possibly bubonic
carriers when suggesting a sum for his services, but
the man accepted the price eagerly and waved the
danger aside: was there not *penyakit*, 'the thin sickness' in his own village? And yet it was not for this
that he wished to leave at once. He urged us to
start before the sun grew hotter, and we moved on
towards the lower slope of the headland, where a

stream ran above the village and was therefore, we hoped, unpolluted.

At his frank explanation of the real reason for his anxiety to leave home, Ainger's serious face lightened. 'Deotlan's wife has got his gun,' he told us, grinning broadly, 'and won't let him back into the hut or cook for him, because she suspects him of philandering with a woman who has now developed cholera. He's deeply aggrieved about this. Says it's unfair because really he's been making love in quite a different quarter for the last week. He's told his wife so, too, but she still threatens to put a bullet through him if he comes back – she is, he says, a very unreasonable woman.'

Deotlan, who sometimes understood much more English than one expected, and sometimes much less, nodded at the last few words.

I tried on him sympathetically the one Malay expression I had picked up in Borneo. '*Sakit hati*', that most useful description that can be supplied to anyone obstinate, ill-tempered or for any reason in a bad way, though all it means literally is 'a hard liver.'

'Yes, by God,' he agreed with simple fervour.

'But you – you, a man – are not afraid of a woman, are you?' Stewart asked curiously, slowly enough for the other to understand. We had not yet made acquaintance with that startling Malay truthfulness on the subject of fear which brings forcibly to European notice the extent of our own traditions of pretence about it; and – what is more serious to the average European, who is not interested in the holes in his intellectual honesty — makes it impossible to shame these normally stout-hearted people into displays of courage which they do not feel.

'Natural' afraid.' Deotlan said reasonably. 'Woman — *sakit hati* — have gun. No gun, I beat her, and woman afraid. Wai!'

We learned something of Deotlan's history during the day. As a youth he had left his far-off southern village and gone to Singapore, full of pathetically high hopes of enlisting the interest of white relatives. Of what happened in the short time he spent there he never told us anything: some humiliation still rankled: but as 'dirty native' had remained his most vehement form of abuse, it was not hard to fill in some of the details from imagination. He had lived at Pedagor ever since, with his unrecognised white blood burning his veins.

It appeared that we could not, as we had intended, skirt the coast to Kintaling. The wide, marshy delta of a river lay between us and it. None of the little Pedagor fishing boats would undertake to sail us so far, Deotlan said. They were on fighting terms with the delta fishermen. We should have to go the overland way.

Behind the village lay a stretch of untilled padi field rapidly turning back into secondary jungle.

'If only this were the rainy season,' Ainger said

gloomily, as we made our way round the overgrown ground, 'There'd very likely be minute fish – come from God knows where – in the mud puddles. Like whitebait.'

'Well, it isn't the rainy season,' Stewart answered, 'so for heaven's sake shut up with this mis-timed Malay Family Robinson stuff.'

Said with a shade of difference in his tone this would have been a mildly good joke: as it was he spoke with a surface amiability under which lay a little more than the normal suppressed irritation of a breakfastless man reminded of appetising food when he has had no dinner the night before. For each of us but Mrs. Mardick the previous day's tea was only a painful memory of the refusal of unpalatable food which would not have seemed anything like so unpalatable now. Yesterday's lunch was our last meal, and not a large one at that. But Deotlan had just told us, to our immense relief, that he could get rice for us; good safe rice; a small quantity of it at any rate: so that our immediate anxiety about food was allayed – though rice was not, at the moment, what we would have chosen. It occurred to me to wonder whether Stewart would have made this remark in just that short tone if things had been going less easily with us: almost certainly not, I thought. As matters stood, we were merely in uncomfortable circumstances, not in hardship. I saw Ainger glance at Stewart sharply under lifted glasses. He started

an answer and thougdt better of it, turning it off
into a question to Deotlan.

We were all three nervy from the strain of the
night spent in the open, to which we were not
yet accustomed, and aching with stiffness due
to the damp, the earlier cold and the hardness
of the ground – Stewart had previously confided to
me cheerfully that he thought he had a touch of
rigor mortis, and when pressed anxiously and
humourlessly for details, said that he felt like a
Huddled Shape, which entirely reassured me.
None of us was in a normal mood. Without the
irritant of hunger, or in more arduous conditions,
Stewart would not have resented Ainger's tacit
assumption of leadership as he did now: obviously
the other man knew more about the country than
we did, though he knew little enough. Mrs.
Mardick only knew Singapore and the European
aspect of a few other districts. Ainger at any other
time would have been indifferent to the slight
annoyance in Stewart's tone, which seemed to
have nettled him now. I knew that, constantly
on the watch for the first slight symptom of infection in any of us, I, too, was keyed up to a state
in which I was over-sensitive to everything, so
that there occurred to me, only vaguely ·then, an
idea that must have gone on working itself out in
my brain during the day, though I was not consciously thinking of it; for it returned, developed
a stage further, in the evening – now I realised

only that we three (Mrs. Mardick was always irrelevant to the party) would be excellent companions in civilisation, to which we spiritually belonged more than most people, and probably also in exceptionally adverse physical conditions, which would be so alien to all of us that we might share them almost detachedly, as an intellectual experience: but for a long period of mild discomfort we should be ill-chosen associates. These two men would agree only intellectually, on subjects with which they felt at home. Away from their common interests – books, humanity in theory, and the world of abstract ideas – they would come up against the knots in each other's character – Ainger's rather high-handed intolerance which I had already sensed once or twice, and Stewart's obstinacy which I knew of old. There was a strain of hardness in Ainger which was not in Stewart, the more sensitive and artistic, the less purely intellectual of the two: Ainger had a cold academic brain which Stewart had not: I was the only practical person here, and the material quality in me would annoy both men in certain circumstances as much as their lack of it might irritate me. Altogether the expedition was not starting auspiciously.

We knelt at the stream, drinking as much as we could while we had the chance: it might not come again for some time. Having short, unsuitable hair that unless treated with severity fell into fat Victorian ringlets of a grossly improbable kind, I put my whole head under water when we washed afterwards, and shook off most of the depression of the previous day and night, shaking the cold water out of my ears. The world seemed considerably brightened when I could see it again; partly because the sun was beginning to climb free of the horizon. Moving almost visibly up the sky, it gilded the tops of the tallest forest trees with a glow that, even though we were still in the dew-soaked shadow, sent a feeling of warmth running through our bodies, under our chilled skins. In a sudden improvement of spirit Stewart, who had no voice whatever, tentatively produced under his breath a few bars of synthetic bathroom song: but this half-conscious defiance of the still radiance around us was a failure. The unmusical notes thinned out into the shining emptiness of the morning and he stopped abruptly, disconcerted by the vast quiet that reigned everywhere now that the breeze had died and the morning chorus was over. Even the swiftly running stream barely stirred the bent reeds through which it passed without bubble or fret, muttering almost inaudibly under its banks.

Clumsily, because his right arm still hurt him to move, Ainger pulled off his shirt before washing, with an unconcern for which I was thankful, considering that for the next four days at least considerable intimacy between us would be unavoidable: in the circumstances any show of self-consciousness would be unforgiveably inept, for it would have

made our journeying together awkward, which at
the moment it was not. Stewart, as I knew from
years of sailing with him, was happily immune from
attacks of surplus modesty, like most small boat
owners. I could not imagine, offhand, anything
more embarrassing than to spend several days
working through the Trenganu jungle in the society
of a physically shy person, situated as we were,
with only one moderately efficient weapon (Ainger's
revolver), among four people; so that the one chance
of safety in a land of remarkably variegated menace
lay in remaining together, waking or sleeping. But
it struck me as extraordinary that we three should
by any means have got ourselves into a position in
which such apparently trivial things could become
one of the main standards of friendship. Mrs.
Mardick remarked with bright unconcern, as she
undid the neck of her dress an innocuous couple of
buttons before washing, that fortunately she was
not one of those people who minded this kind of
thing. Two of us glanced at her in mild surprise
(Ainger being far away in thought, as usual: more
often than not he missed remarks not directly
addressed to him. At the moment he was improving
his Malay with Deotlan, which was typical of him
at such a time.) In the circumstances it seemed an
odd thing for her to say, but we accepted the statement for what it appeared to be worth until by a
series of modest wriggles, designed to displace her
dress but not her camisole, she had followed my

example in exposing almost as great an area of skin as she showed in evening dress. From then on, until her toilet was complete, we were left under no possible apprehension as to how much Mrs. Mardick did not care about this kind of thing. It even became noticeable to Arnold Ainger. Rarely can any stressing of unconcern have made three originally unconcerned people feel more indecorous. Deotlan, not understanding her unreticent modesty, was imitating Ainger – for was he not also the possessor of white blood, and therefore a washer-by-principle? – He stripped a little further, and she took this steadfastly as a matter of course, even refraining from looking away, which for her would have been the natural thing to do.

I attended to Ainger's arm as well as I could without renewing the dressing, having only enough lint for two more changes; and before leaving the stream we ate the biscuits and chocolate which were all that we had brought from the ship. Deotlan led us through scrub and high *lalang* grass past several clearings planted with coco-palms, among which stood the outlying huts of the straggling village. He stopped a little farther on where the path forked, the beaten track turning towards the jungle and Pedagor's precious patch of durian trees, and a faint trail leading to a well-kept patch of padi by which the last hut stood. He looked round, but there was no one in sight but ourselves, and he took the second track. A small, slight woman, not old but already growing bent with work, straightened herself with an effort from digging round the roots of one of her few struggling fruit trees. She stared expressionlessly at Deotlan, not at us, as we approached: it was as if she did not see us: but he hardly looked at her.

He glanced back along the path and all round us again, listening attentively, but the high grass hid us here from the other huts and there was no disturbing sound. Making a sign to us to wait he walked up to her as she stood beside the hut, and at his coming, though her melancholy face did not alter, she let the heavy two-pronged fork she carried slip from her hands, and stood with them hanging limply by her sides. One hand, I noticed, was short of a joint on all fingers.

He spoke to her urgently, but for a moment she continued searching his face with wondering, magnificent, dark eyes, uncomprehendingly. He repeated something quickly, and she ran without a word into the hut. Seeing them together one noticed the white strain in him. Beside hers, his skin showed pale, and lip and nostril lacked the spread flatness that for the first time I saw in her face in attractive form. She was purely Malay, of a refined type which I had not met before, and unusually charming-looking for a native woman, to our eyes: they made a handsome couple.

She brought out to him a small quantity of rice, and some dried fish; he examined it and argued, apparently about the amount, but she shrugged her weary-looking shoulders and said nothing. Hitching the container she gave him on his back in the uncomfortable native fashion, with a line over one shoulder and under the other, he left her with a nod and hurried back to us.

'This food is safe,' he said in Malay to Ainger, who translated 'This woman, Wan Nau, does not often go to the village: she has not been now for a long while.'

'What about paying for the stuff?' Ainger asked as Deotlan prepared to lead us back towards the forest.

'There is no need,' he was told. 'It is a gift. You can give me some money for it, perhaps, and she will have something when I come back.'

'We'd better pay her something now,' Ainger said, stopping, 'unless it would offend her.' It was more in our minds than in Deotlan's, apparently, that travelling with people off a ship with bubonic on board he was not certain of his return.

'She will be glad,' he made Ainger understand, 'She is very poor.'

I took a dollar back to her: I was interested to see the formation of the curious stump-fingered hand. She had not resumed her digging but stood staring after us.

She took the money in her small, perfectly formed left hand, keeping the other behind her, and did not thank me. Instead she gave me a long look, the sudden fierceness of which I remembered later, when I realised that to this sad, humble mind, misled by Deotlan's big talk in former days, we were 'his people,' the white folk, who had unaccountably refused to recognise his kinship before, but were now travelling with him as one of us. And I in particular was a young woman of his race, in whose company he was going through the jungle, to some place outside her ken, going perhaps for ever, as indeed he was. Yet without hesitation she had given us a good deal of the scanty store of rice which would have to last her until the next season, because Deotlan, as he had shamelessly explained to her, was without his gun owing to his wife's well-founded if ill-directed jealousy, of which Wan Nau was not the cause. He could not shoot game: she must provide what she could, he had told her.

The sun was blazingly hot now: through our thin clothes it scorched our shoulders and backs, making the thought of the jungle ahead of us pleasanter to me than it had been.

Walking by Deotlan I said in slow English, explaining as much as I could by gestures: 'That woman's hand – like this – is that natural?' Judging from the way he treated her she was of so little account to him that I thought I could not be treading on delicate ground in asking this, and from the careless tone of his answer it was evident that I was not.

'Natural,' he nodded. 'She is a Wan, married *pantang*' (forbidden).

I did not understand, but Ainger who had not noticed her hand looked up with interest. 'Was she disfigured in some way?' he asked, and I told him.

'It was always like that? All her life? When she was born?' I persisted with Deotlan. If so, it was an extraordinary malformation: it could not be an accident, for the thumb, which would have escaped an injury to the fingers, was also short by a joint: but there are curious rotting diseases of the tropics of which I had heard but knew little.

'Of course, always, no. Or I have no marriage with that woman.'

'But that's not your wife!'

No, Deotlan was not now married to Wan Nau, it appeared, though he had been once: Ainger translated laboriously, putting in parenthetical explanations of the bare, wretched narrative when he could. Or at least Wan Nau thought that Deotlan had been married to her; he himself had never been sure, for she was a Wan, a member of one of the countless families of semi-royal blood whose men may marry anyone they please, since they raise a commoner to their own rank by an alliance, but the women can make recognised unions only within their own caste. The honour of the rajah or sultan to whom they are distantly related lies in their keeping, though he does nothing for them, so that though sometimes desperately poor these unlucky women dare not form a liaison with one of the villagers among whom they live, which would at least secure a man's help to supply their needs. A royal relative is prompt to avenge the shame of his neglected family, and in the unfederated states his power is absolute.

Wan Nau had thought that marrying one who was half white, as Deotlan represented himself to be, she married an equal, so that her marriage would be recognised. It was not so; she was ordered to leave him, her elderly cousin Wan Daud, who lived in a neighbouring village, assuming authority in the absence of the rajah – Deotlan, in his account of the affair, avoided naming or referring to this great man directly, according to custom. Wan Nau, bred from the finest fighting stock in the province, sent back an insulting message and persisted with the liaison which she proudly considered marriage. In view of this she was fortunate in escaping lightly, compared with many similar offenders, from the consequences of a powerful relative's wrath. What happened to her was in the nature of a forbearing second warning of the fate that came without warning to others. Deotlan had been away fishing when this earnest of future punishment was meted out to her, or he would have been ham-strung or krissed by Wan Daud's sons. Had he returned to her afterwards, this would inevitably have happened to both of them, but he was too cautious to consider such a course for a moment when he heard the news. In any case he had no strong inclination to rejoin her by this time – they had been together for some months, and his was a light and roving disposition. And now, as he said with a rueful laugh, he was married again and sorry again, and this time it was the woman who drove him away. Deotlan was good-humouredly prepared for open amusement on our part over all his matrimonial mishaps; even inviting it by his way of presenting his tale. Like most Malays he made up a little for what he totally lacked in compassion by a keen if crude sense of humour, which did not fail when the joke was against him: he seemed a little disappointed that we did not laugh.

Much of his light-hearted tale we missed because Ainger could not yet understand the clipped Trenganu Malay, but from what we pieced together I gathered that he and Wan Nau had lived on for two years at Pedagor at opposite ends of the long, straggling village; he because he was a fisherman and knew the water thereabouts too well to move – besides, he saw no reason for going – and she, because there was nowhere else for her to go: but they did not see one another. Until to-day, they had not set eyes on each other for many months, he said. But remembering the way she looked at him I thought that probably, from the higher ground by her patch of rice, she must have watched sometimes for the going out and returning of his boat, and have seen him pass, unaware of her, in the distance.

Ainger translated something else with an impassivity equal to Deotlan's; he was not easily moved by suffering. Of the three of us only Stewart showed what he felt about it, by the angry frown that always came when he visualised pain in others. Wan Nau's rice would not hide *'penyakit itu'* – 'this affection' (one must if possible avoid calling cholera by its name during an epidemic) Deotlan assured us again, because she had told him before giving it to him that Wan Daud's son, Dris, from an uninfected village, was the only person who had been in her hut for a period of days longer than Chipa (the djinn of this disease) can live without drinking blood. She did not like Dris, nor the cause of his visits, but she dared not refuse herself to him when he wanted her, or, jealous, he would say that her lover had come back to her.

'He comes often, the man she doesn't like?' Stewart asked – Yes, he came often; had the Tuans not noticed the face of the woman, it was considered pleasing? – This had gone on for over two years, we found.

I could say nothing, being sickened suddenly, through the realisation of another woman's misery, by the old fret and weariness of spirit from which I had been freer of late, the resentment felt, I think, by most unhappy imaginative people at the uselessness of all suffering. It is a selfless jealousy of wretchedness, this feeling that though life brings forth so much sadness, and one's own is so small a part of the sum of sorrow, still it is enough to fill the whole earth with its helpless longings: why must the sorrows of so many others be added to a world surcharged, it seems, with one's own pain? To all who suffer angrily in mind, not only in heart, the bitterest part of this waste of spirit which is human pain is the knowledge that it is futile, without value either to the sufferer or to others.

To Stewart, who was irritably depressed by this incident because of an innate gentleness that turned savage before cruelty, I could not say anything of what was in my mind at the moment. As a rule there was no impersonal trouble that could not be lightened by discussion with him; but Mrs. Mardick was in earshot, and because we must bear with her whatever she said I was afraid of what she might say: she was the sort of person who thought Christianity an adequate result of the sufferings of Christ, and would talk easily of vague compensations for Wan Nau, and of the shorter memories and less enduring emotions of the lower orders of life. We went on in silence.

'Natural – she is a Wan.' Certainly that mutilation was natural enough, I thought, here in this callous and lovely land. The pitiless sunlight streaming down on us, the fiercely fertile ground over which we made our way, and the clouds of humming winged life into which the dancing air about us steamed as the heat increased – these aspects of the safer, open ground took on for me a new quality of malevolence, toughening my nerves for the dark of the forest, which could be only a little older in iniquity than this conquered ground, where men tormented each other through brief lives.

Inadequately armed as we were, I was relieved when the green gloom of the trees closed round us, shutting out the daylight as completely as if dusk had fallen in a few seconds. It would be easier to put out of mind the eyes of the woman as she watched Deotlan.

'It's empty here!' I thought, astonished first by the all-pervading hush, the unexpected absence of movement and colour noticeable as soon as we had pushed our way through the creeper-crossed, scarcely perceptible opening in the solid wall of the jungle-edge, into a low tunnel of matted vegetation.

With the superb inconsequence of his people, Deotlan muttered softly into the straining quiet the sonorous '*Ya illa —*' following the Mohammedan affirmation of faith in one god alone by several propitiatory incantations to the all-powerful spirits of the country's earlier animistic cults, over which the invading religion is thrown like a transparent ceremonial robe above an indispensable garment. There could be no doubt from his voice which set of words carried Deotlan's greater faith, but probably he would have devoutly beaten the man who questioned his allegiance to the prophet.

Here was a hush against which one could not with dignity put up a defence of human voices, as we had tried to do during the night in the open: it seemed to grow more insistent, heard through our words, and we ceased talking with the same self-consciousness with which Stewart had stopped singing by the stream. Yet in the crowded jungle there could not be absolute quiet but only the precipitate of many soft sounds, making up an oppressive peace. Once that morning a troop of baboons fled whooping overhead, startling us with their shattering din: but there was no room for echo in the forest; the closeness of the foliage muffled all noise, so that the composite stillness of tiny insect hummings and far-off bird calls and the whisper of monstrous growths sucking at the dank earth seemed to leap back afterwards, obliterating the outrage.

The going grew slower and more laborious as we came to soft ground. Even in the drier places where our feet did not sink wearyingly, requiring an effort at each step to free them, creepers and thorny tendrils clutched and hindered us. Walking sometimes with a protecting arm before our eyes for a few steps, we stumbled over dead branches and roots hidden in the lush growth underfoot. Ainger looked done-up after we had gone little more than three miles. By then we had been in the jungle for four hours.

Nowhere, in this part of the forest, could we see more than twelve yards round us, and in most places much less. Our unaccustomed eyes reported all impressions at first as I suppose those of the

colour-blind do, in a hundred tones of grey;
though our grey was shot with green. Trunk,
foliage and creeper in that unhealthy light took on a
variety of shades, but one predominant hue which
swallowed all others for a while. Then I saw
suddenly, when we had forced our way for some
distance into this dim, monotonously coloured world,
that the pale-grey mass above me was in reality an
immense cluster of hanging yellow flowers busy
with golden bees. A great tree, rotten at the core,
had fallen in such a way that it would have blocked
the path here, where for a hundred yards or more
the living roof pressed down so that we walked
stooping, and at this point bent double, but the
trunk was partially supported still by the mass of
its attendant creepers intertwined with others:
they had given and sagged but not broken. There
was enough room at one side for us to squeeze,
carefully, for fear of parting the last strand of the
sling, whose strength we could not gauge, under this
barricade of the jungle's ingenious devising. (All
of us but Mrs. Mardick came, in time, to believe
half consciously in a primaeval balefulness, as a
kind of vegetable mind behind the seeming-acci-
dental enmity of matter — Deotlan called it Chivi,
and hung leaf-fulls of rice for it on trees when we
had any.) It would have taken us a long while to
work round the obstacle at this spot.

Going ahead with Deotlan, I drew back my hand
just before it touched the mottled bark of the

tree. A broad dark stripe ran both ways as far as I could see along the crumbling wood. I had taken it to be a natural marking or the effect of leaf-filtered light – the tricks played by light in the jungle are so many that we acquired at first a certain carelessness: but it did not last. The black streak wavered, thinned and then re-formed. Myriads of red ants, in a stream three or four inches wide, marched, endlessly it seemed, up the hollow tree that could obtain no place to lie in death on that encumbered ground, where even strong life had only a precarious hold; so that as it decayed, suspended in the air, covered from crown to roots with parasites in a queer semblance of vitality, the trunk became an aerial roadway for the creatures that had lived among its roots. The colour of the ants was only noticeable at second glance: and while I stood hesitating, because it was almost impossible to pass under the tree without touching it, alive as it was with stinging insects, a thread of pale grey-green, half the length of a finger, reared itself up on end from the leaf of a creeping ground-plant underfoot. It swayed in the air, palping it with a horrible suggestion of intelligence, before setting off towards my foot, moving as a caterpillar does, but at extraordinary speed. Amazingly keen in their sense of smell or their hearing – I do not yet know which – these tree-leeches soon became a misery to us; they are that to any hunter in the jungle in the localities they infest, if he is forced to stand dead still for a while for fear of alarming a quick-eared quarry. At such moments one sees them positively galloping towards one's feet from all sides in their loathsome, purposeful way, and dares not shift as they climb avidly up one's shoes towards the more exposed flesh. At the end of a day's journey we might find three or four of these creatures clinging to the eye-holes of our shoes, or on the ankle, and these leech bites usually festered. For me at least, and I think for the two white men too, the leeches grew eventually to be even more than a physical pest, they were so characteristically a part of the invincible, battening, obscene vitality of the jungle which gradually wore down our spirits. Not till much later, when all squeamishness had been lost, could I bear to pick these slimy things off with my fingers. When I had no leisure or energy to scrape myself free of them with leaves or twigs, I learned not to look down at my feet, for the sight of these limp little bags of blood, swelling as they clung, sickened me more and more.

'No, it's not empty here!' I realised. 'There's life – too much life – to be seen for the looking.' This is, inevitably, the second stage to which everyone comes in progressive acquaintance with the jungle; some fortunate people remain in it after years of knowledge: it is pleasanter than the third stage, which is permanent for those who reach it – 'There is more life here than I can see, and of another quality; it is not hidden, it is invisible.'

Close overhead, but out of sight in the tangle of branches, flew the bird that Deotlan and his people called uneasily 'the Spirit,' because it usually remained unseen while the strange whistling of its wings sounded near at hand.

Mrs. Mardick, who had the soundest nerves in the party, had not long been quelled into speechlessness by a Trenganu jungle, though she still kept her voice lowered in courtesy, I think, to our dumbness, as a well-bred atheist removes his hat in a cathedral. Stewart was doing duty by her at the moment; without verbal agreement we had already begun taking turn and turn about with her in order to gain some sort of respite at intervals. She stopped at this moment, with her head on one side and an upraised forefinger 'Sh! Just *listen* to the stillness! Can't you almost *hear* it?' she said, and she was the sort of woman who by doing that anywhere out of doors appropriates all the neighbouring silence and reduces it for the time being to a background for her personality. The metamorphosis made it appear ludicrous that the rest of us had been walking soft-footed, instinctively, in order not to disturb that appalling quiet. Beyond, the vaster silence that even Mrs. Mardick could not annex still waited for us, retreating at the noise of our passing, and, to our sensibilities, that silence seemed to grow more impregnable and more vindictive because of the defiance of her brave chattering. I think that this was the moment when the idea first came to me that somehow – almost anyhow – we were going to get rid of Mrs. Mardick for our own safety. It was apparently a telepathetic notion, between the original three of us, or at least a coincidence of opinion, I found afterwards. It was also the first step on the path by which this strange country led us, towards a ruthlessness nearly equal to that of the land itself. Malaya with its sunshine and its softening morning mist, its velvet greens of forest and its tender skies, has certainly – though why I cannot tell – as merciless a soul as these insentient things can embody. I cannot imagine that any of us would have thought of jettisoning a fellow-white in a tropical jungle with so little compunction in another part of the world. I suppose we were already growing spiritually afraid, quite apart from our physical sense of oppression – afraid so far merely of a violated stillness that could not intimidate her.

She was alien to us as we were alien to the forest. And as an alien she was infinitely undesirable. Arnold Ainger was the only one who developed a definite technique in dealing with her. He fell into the habit of punctuating her ebullient talk with an occasional 'Good Heavens!' said in a perfectly expressionless far-away voice that would have crushed anyone else. But it had no effect on her animation: she liked him a little better than she did Stewart, who was far kinder and more attentive and lighter-hearted by nature: she never liked me.

There was no wind. Beside me one delicate frond

of a casuarina tree stirred and was still, and then nodded again, though there was no movement of the stem from which it hung to account for this slow, intermittent bowing of the leaves. The way swung sharply to the right at this point. As we opened up the track beyond the corner, I caught sight out of the tail of my eye of a small dark streak that scuttled ahead and then crouched in the path as if waiting, but as we advanced it moved on again a little way, and stopped. Unable to see it clearly, I wondered if it were a squirrel or one of the little mouse-deer of which the jungle was full: but the dark thing on the ground turned out to be only a patch of rich black mould when we came up with it. Then I saw the jungle anew. Wherever one looked intently, there was stillness, or nothing but the explicable movement of foliage disturbed by monkey or bird darting into shelter; but where one's glance settled idly, there something had changed the second before; it was impossible to know what. One saw the end of movements, not their beginning. A leaf tapping in the quiet air, a shadow without substance slipping across ground so dark that there should have been no separate shadows – these brought upon me overwhelmingly the sensation that never afterwards left me in close jungle – the feeling of eyes all about, and more particularly of watchful presences, silent and patient and baleful, from whose guardianship there was no escape.

CHAPTER IV

THREE WHO HAD LOST SOMETHING

Tired out after what seemed hours of struggle and slow progress, I suggested that we should stop for food. Ainger was obviously in need of a rest, though he had not said so, but he agreed thankfully: I imagine that he had made up his mind not to be the first to propose a halt. With the anxiety about infection inevitably in front of my mind I was suspicious of the first signs of exhaustion in any of us, and his appearance worried me. Deotlan, who had seemed increasingly nervous for some while past, had gone on ahead and was now stooping by a tuft of jungle grass, examining it and the earth around it with his long slim fingers as well as with his eyes. He made a motion with one arm that silenced us.

'*Seladang!*' he said when he came back to us, and he and Ainger had a whispered conference, for the tracks were new, and led in the direction in which we wanted to go. We made out first mistake here, if it was a mistake – there seemed nothing else to be done, at the time. Where another over-grown trail crossed ours, a few hundred yards back, we turned west to avoid the chance of an encounter. Only tiger and these savage jungle cattle, when they think themselves pursued, have the cunning to make a half-circle in their tracks, in the form of a capital P with the lower end of the loop incomplete, and to wait there concealed for the passing of the unlucky hunter. Nearly every Malay village in the jungle has a tale of men killed or horribly maimed by *seladang*.

There was no thought of stopping now, nor for a long while afterwards, for we came on other tracks on the new path. Though not as fresh as the first they suggested that there was more than one small herd about.

We made our way even more slowly, and with infinite care to avoid noise as much as possible: but it seemed to me that our passage must be known to everything within a quarter of a mile of us, and at every turn of the path I held my breath in fear of what the next short stretch would show. We found nothing more than animal droppings. Deotlan kicked some of these open with his toe; the inside steamed: they could not have been more than an hour or so old: I did not care to look back at Ainger, close behind me. I knew that his slight store of convalescent strength, always a deceptive thing in a normally healthy man, was on the point of giving out altogether, and that we must go on.

Deotlan admitted in a whisper that he did not

know this part of the jungle; we must try to work back to the original direction later: but the devious track we now followed bent farther and farther westward, we imagined, though without compass or visible sun it was difficult to be sure. Where the impassable undergrowth gave way to high grass and bamboo thicket at last we tried to break through, straight across country, in the hope of striking another path leading in the right direction; but we came on swamp. I accepted the check with some slight satisfaction, we could not go any farther at the moment, apart from the fact that Ainger was not fit to do so in any case: he was stumbling forward as if in a dream, a suffering automaton of a man. We had seen no fresh *seladang* tracks now for over a mile: it was as safe to stop here as anywhere else in the vicinity.

It was then late afternoon, but the damp heat was still so great that it seemed as if the voracious forest growths had sucked away all the air that filtered down through the trees: it was hotter than in the morning. 'Nice,' said Mrs. Mardick with a brave smile, and pointed out again, unnecessarily, her liking for the heat. We found a fairly dry grass patch in the spongy ground and settled there for the night.

Deotlan made a tiny fire shielded by leaves and branches, and cooked rice expertly in a hollow bamboo. It was totally unseasoned stuff: I had reluctantly condemned the dried fish which might

have varied the flavour a little, but all of us save
Ainger ate the whole unpalatable ration that Deotlan
allowed us. He, being used to its semi-putrid
condition, devoured the fish as well, and we took
the brackish swamp-water on chance. Ainger,
lying full length in what was almost a coma of
weariness, ate practically nothing. He opened his
eyes suddenly while I was looking at him, and
smiled at my troubled expression, lazily holding out
an arm towards me. Caught being openly suspicious
I took his wrist and found the pulse, though not
normal, not showing the symptoms I had almost
expected. 'I rather thought I was all right, really,'
he said in answer to my reassuring smile and shake
of the head. 'Only nothing like as fit as I hoped I
was. I oughtn't to have undertaken this trip.'
Handing over his revolver to Stewart he fell asleep
almost immediately with relief, having fully shared
my doubts about his real condition for the last few
hours.

The rest of us revived, with food, into an un-
intelligent cheerfulness, a reaction against the
strain of the day.

> ' "While deep in cushioned lounges,
>   And long, luxurious bars,
>   The rich men eat their oysters
>   And smoke their huge cigars —" '

Stewart quoted enviously, trying to stuff a small
handful of rice into his mouth and dropping some

of the precious grains on to his dirty white piqué coat – the wreck of his one extravagance in tropical wear – from which they were retrieved singly and eagerly eaten. Already, as the green-sifted light turned golden, the jays, monkeys and smaller climbing creatures that were not prisoners of perpetual shadow, were setting up their chattering requiem to the sun, forerunner of the full-throated clamour, appalling and gorgeous in its way, in which the whole jungle would join at dusk. We could talk now, for a little while, without the sense of offending against something immense and venomous.

'Have you noticed how one always spills things on one's best clothes?' Stewart added to me in the grave voice that we always kept for our old game of talking platitudes to one another in public: it was oddly heartening to start it here. (To count, the platitudes must have some bearing on the circumstances, and the aim of both players was to introduce the larger number in the shortest time.)

I countered his first point with 'Yes, but isn't it wonderful how much nicer all food tastes out of doors?'

'Ah, but it isn't the *place*, it's the *people!*' he said weightily, one up again, and bowing, seated, towards Mrs. Mardick, who seemed gratified.

'Of course: and anyway, I always think there's nothing so cheerful as an open fire (or wood fire) is there?' I agreed, drawing even, but looking

round with an involuntary shiver that was not of
cold, as a flame leapt, driving back the encroaching
shadows.

Mrs. Mardick, who did not see that this was a
game, must have felt spiritually at home all of a
sudden, for she took charge of the conversation;
and scored so heavily in the next few minutes
without realising it, that, hopelessly outclassed, we
gave up the game as soon as she had jumped my
best *cliché* while I was still working round to an
opening for it –'Well, the great thing is to see the
bright side: I always say as long as you have a
sense of humour you're all right.'

'Isn't it ridiculous how boyish all men look when
they're asleep?' she observed, incorrectly, of the
unconscious Ainger, to carry on the conversation
that we had unaccountably stopped. '*What* a good
looking – *no, exciting* face, don't you think, Miss
Corder?'

'No, I don't,' I said. When he was awake it was
interesting as the bleakly inexpressive mask of a
distrait mind that I liked, the little I knew of it,
but the gloomy austerity of his appearance, I had
discovered, was almost entirely due to the settled
frown of the very near-sighted, so that for me his
face lacked the absorbing qualities of a chart of an
unknown spirit, as she considered it. She wagged
a playful finger at me all the same, 'Young woman,
you can't deceive me! *I* think you ought to be very
thankful I'm here to prevent this becoming a real

triangle situation!' she said. 'It's so much nicer
as a – well, two pairs.' Triangles seemed to be an
obsession with her; she had a sexually mathematical mind; I could not see how the four of us could
possibly be considered as two pairs. Stewart threw
me a glance full of the frank appraisement of a
privileged relative. 'It takes two to make a triangle!'
he said unkindly. 'Look at Judy's attitude!' and
went on to point out unnecessarily that I had a
talent for looking ungainly, which unfitted me for
the position of apex.

Sitting cross-legged with my skirt hitched above
my knees, I was at the moment ruefully regarding
the garter-like bands of lisle thread still attached to
my suspenders, which was all that the day's journey
had left of a pair of thin stockings, save the parts
covered by my dilapidated shoes. The shoes were
equally unsuited to their present job, but like the
stockings they were the only kind I had had on
board: 'Nice legs, though,' I said absently to
Stewart, regarding them critically as I stuck them
straight out before me, inelegantly.

The shoes did not look as if they would hold out
much longer, either. They were my chief
concern.

'Your best feature,' he admitted. 'But on the
scraggy side.'

'Perhaps a bit,' I said, gingerly removing the
relics of stocking from these scratched and battered
attributes. My looks or the lack of them was not

a subject on which I had any more flattering illusions than he had, and I was not touchy.

The little fire, as it flickered and glowed, had an almost hypnotic effect on tired eyes, and, unable to relax while the vocal accompaniment of sun-down rose and died and wailed through the half darkness, I sat beside it near Stewart, hugging my knees, with Deotlan an immobile pale bronze shadow crouching on the other side of the fire, luxuriously inhaling one of my few precious cigarettes. He had explained to us that as a half-white man he did not care for native tobacco: unable to smoke it myself I watched him yearningly while he consumed pounds of the rank stuff later on, when we had no more of our own to share with him.

Into my mind, unconsciously following up Stewart's last uncomplimentary remarks, light-hearted as they were, there came uncalled the continuation of the train of thought that had started by the stream in the morning, and had been apparently forgotten all day. Grown serious again, I realised detachedly, as if this only affected someone else, that should we reach conditions primitive enough, both men, irrespective of my attractions (if any) would want me as a woman, and I should want one of them very strongly, and not the other. My feeling about Hugh whom I had lost would have nothing to do with it. I looked round, wondering which of these two I should be hungering for soon, if this happened, and thought it would probably be

Arnold Ainger, whose face, in its present over-tired, unshaven, relaxed lines, was not in the least attractive. It was an odd and curiously unpleasant experience, this foreseeing of a situation that one would not be able to prevent. 'It's if we have a period of intense hardship and danger, when sex is naturally dormant,' I thought, 'and then mental relief and some enforced leisure, that there'll be a blaze-up of passion all round. Pity. Because probably we shall all three feel silly about it when we get back to our own world, where the emotion will evaporate. That is, presuming we do get back.' I was not a woman with whom any man was likely to stay physically infatuated if he was not also mentally in love – I had already proved that; it was not humble surmise. Only my figure suited my taste in looks; I had the unfortunate sort of face that is not even memorably plain, all the features being passable by themselves but the assemblage disappointing – the sort of face, in fact, to which well meaning young men say devastatingly on intro-duction 'Oh, haven't we met before?' It took an unusual amount of animation to make it pretty, and then it was not very pretty. Usually I didn't mind much.

I found myself staring fixedly at a patch of intertwined lianas, as though by watching them un-remittingly I could keep rigid the writhen, snake-like stems that seemed to stir with the leap of the flames whenever my eyes wandered apprehensively.

The jungle was becoming increasingly alive on all sides; it was vivid enough by day, that sense or unwanted company, but speaking certainly for myself, and probably for the rest, even Deotlan, we were always on the verge of panic at night because of something – or some things – immediately behind everyone's shoulder, that could never be seen.

Deotlan wove a rough lean-to, open on three sides, out of the living bamboo, helped first by Stewart, who proved again his noted incompetence with his hands, until I took his place irritably, urged on to the effort by the managing woman's stupid inability to sit and watch others doing manual work badly. (In the days when *Young England* had made a feature of '100 Things a Bright Boy Can Do' Stewart had once attempted to mend an electric lamp. Holding the ends of the wires with one hand he had dreamily tried to switch on more light for the job with the other; since when he had never really applied himself to the study of electricity, nor to any of the other ninety-nine things, presumably including the rigging of shelters, to which a bright boy's hands might profitably be turned. Probably no party in any jungle was ever commanded by two more unsuitably intelligent men than ours.)

To stop the competition in unselfishness inaugurated by Mrs. Mardick, I suggested that we should draw lots for the best sleeping place, which was on the thickest patch of grass farthest inside the shelter. No one wanted to turn in yet, but there would be well meant disagreement until this was settled. She won, and immediately said 'But I'd *much* rather you took it, dear. Now, honestly —'

'All right. Thanks, I will,' I said promptly, much to her surprise, to prevent the discussion beginning all over again. I imagine that it was apropos of this that she confided to Stewart the next day that she had always thought a medical training must be somewhat blunting to any woman's natural sensitiveness and sympathy, and though this, of course, did not apply to dear Miss Corder, who was being simply splendid, like Mr. Ainger and Deotlan and Mr. Corder himself — what? No. No, no, not a bit — well it was *sweet* of him to say so but she was afraid she wasn't really — anyway, as she was saying, it was her reason for deciding not to let her daughter become a doctor, in spite of Elaine's fondness for mending dolls.

It took a good five minutes of gathering my determination before I had the courage to get up and make what Stewart and I used to call 'a Shakespearean exit' from the group ('I go to look upon a hedge'). There was a spurious feeling of security in the radius of the firelight and in each other's company. The swift darkness pounced on me as I started back along the path by which we had come. It was not so bad once I had started, and I went some way, thinking that others might

possibly come for the same purpose; some acquired
habits of civilisation still stuck firmly in my mind.
(I lost most of them shortly after this.)

There must have been a brilliant moon somewhere, for when my eyes grew accustomed to the
loss of the fire I could see easily enough. Radiance
seeped down through the trees. I could hear my
heart beating as I had when we approached bends
in the track that might show us *seladang* close
ahead. Small things rustled from under my feet.
Twice I saw in the near-by thicket close-set points
of brightness, that might be the reflection of the
fading light on a damp leaf or twig – might be a
hundred things besides eyes : but they might equally
well be eyes. Without altering my position I saw
these lights fade out, and so passed by holding my
breath. Though all land changes by night and
becomes inimical, the queer transition from passive
to active antagonism, felt among safe trees at
home, gives an utterly inadequate idea of the heightening of malignancy in a jungle when night
releases it.

Big bats had appeared, crossing and re-crossing
overhead and making me duck against my will, by
the time that I started back. In a moment, from
somewhere in the direction of a clump of ipoh
trees, came a small, unplaceable noise that I knew
now that I had heard a little while before, when
I passed the place : there were innumerable little
sounds in the darkness, and my heart leapt to each

one, and straightaway forgot it again in fear of another. But this was continuous. I shrank back into deeper shadow: the clump of ipohs was directly between me and the shelter. Among the many swaying shadows blotching the dark ground crept another shadow, dim in outline, not moving for seconds at a time, and the soft mewing sound continued. My fingers crisped in apprehension against the rough bark of a bough behind me and cracked off a rotten piece. It broke sharply for such soft wood; the whining stopped. A head that I could not recognise swung my way and back, and the creature emerged gradually, terribly slowly, into better light away from the clump of trees, with the sound that was almost like human moaning beginning again. A big, gaunt civet cat, heavy in young, stood in the path about fifteen yards away, turned obliquely towards me. One side of the head had been badly scored in some recent battle, that must have robbed the animal of her mate, or she would not have been out of her lair and hunting so close to her whelping time. Matter and filth had clotted over the ripped jaw and blinded eye, and patched the emaciated, bulging body with daubs of paleness that showed up against the dark fur even in this dimness. The beast must have been desperate with hunger and pain before she ventured out in such condition, but the long, powerful limbs with their tearing claws were still uninjured, and though only in unusual circumstances will civets attack a bigger creature unprovoked, they are magnificent fighters when cornered. Little as I knew of the jungle then, I realised that she would be dangerous through her weakness.

I stood paralysed for a moment as the wounded head lowered to the ground over which I had passed and she started slowly forward, crying at every movement of her stiffened, starving, life-driven body. She could smell that some quarry was near, she could not yet see me because of the blindness of one eye of which she seemed only partially aware; the vicious head swung uncertainly from side to side, but not far enough to compensate for the narrowing of her vision.

Temporarily at least it was possible for me to retreat farther along the path: probably she could not yet follow faster than I could move, even in the encumbered dusk, but her wound-cramp would pass with movement, and I should be separating myself farther from the others. I might shout at once for help, but it could not be instantly forth-coming, and meanwhile there was the guidance of my voice for the beast. Another deterrent from that alternative, a powerful one very difficult to convey, was the feeling – an overwhelming, un-reasoning fear, rather – of bringing the jungle upon me by any violent noise, for the sun had gone some while now, and it was almost quiet again: it was strangely impossible to shout.

Cautiously I moved a few steps, gaining some

seconds in which to decide. The civet heard and advanced more certainly, and from behind me came the stealthy rustle of some other creature's passing. I held my breath again, listening through the civet's whining for any alteration in the whisper of brushed leaves that told of the moving of something of fair size: and I knew that the second thing, hemming me in, was coming closer by the path on which I stood. It was certainly too late now to call to the others: actually it would have been too late from the moment I heard the civet. But there was a slender chance that the unknown thing, being fit and wary, unlike the big cat in her extremity, might be scared by sudden unexpected bluff and advance. I waited endless seconds in cover by the edge of a patch of lighter ground where the path turned, occasionally glancing back at the slow-moving civet, but with my full attention on the bend in the trail.

Wan Nau, the woman whom Deotlan had loved, stopped dead within a few paces of me. The gun she carried was turned towards me, accidentally I think, when she came into view. She held it slackly at waist level on her left side, her sound hand guarding the cocked triggers from the chance touch of twig or creeper. She did not avert the weapon when she recognised me as I stepped forward. Both of us remained still then. I saw her head move slightly as she noticed the civet behind me, crouching back on its haunches now, snarling:

still she did not alter the aim. We were both visible
to the beast. Even with its hopeless courage it
hesitated to tackle two such enemies. It crawled
forward again a little way, gathered for a spring,
and, as the Malay woman twisted her whole body
slightly to cover its advance, it leapt sideways into
the darkness of a bamboo clump and disappeared.

Before she could face me again I had moved too
close for the unobstructed use of the gun, and stood
over her, with no sign of unfriendliness but with a
comforting advantage in height and probably also
in actual strength on my side, though in efficiency
in this situation I should not cheerfully have backed
myself against this slight by-product of a great
Malayan war family. We remained waiting, uncertain of the next move, for a few seconds, searching
each other's half-seen face, and then made our way
to the shelter together, I going first in obedience to
a curt sign from her.

Her meeting with Deotlan was unpleasant, it was
so abject. The change in her demeanour when she
saw him was extraordinary. I had no objection in
general to the subservience of the female to the
male (almost invariably her superior in every matter
in which the two are comparable, in my experience)
but the frightened cringing of one human being
to another is revolting in any circumstances, and she
crawled to him, afraid, I think, of a blow: afraid at
any rate of his anger – this discarded woman who
had tracked us alone all day through the jungle in

order to bring him the gun that somehow — we never knew by what means — she had forced or stolen from his wife. *Sakit hati*, she also, Deotlan told Stewart in explanation of this astounding feat, and did not question her. The dealings of native women, squabbling over the possession of those tokens of his affections to which almost all women were temporarily welcome, were hardly the affair of a half-white man, he conveyed by his air of stolid indifference, as he let her accompany him joyfully to the shelter. Mrs. Mardick was already asleep there, and — marvellous woman — she slept on through the almost unbearably moving and one-sided love-making that must have followed. I am sure she did not wake: I cannot imagine her being tactful enough not to get up tactfully and leave them. Thereafter Deotlan made two shelters at night, when we had protested against his intention of sending Wan Nau back alone the following day, and he had agreed that it was probably safe for them to be together here: moreover, true to the instincts of the greater part of his blood, he preferred to have a woman with him in any circumstances, though this was not the woman he wanted.

All animals mate in privacy by choice, even the usually unabashed Malay: it is, oddly enough, only a high degree of civilisation that can produce the habitual public embraces which are a feature of the parks of European capitals: but Wan Nau was exquisitely shameless in her reunion with Deotlan;

none of us existed for her, save possibly myself, as a slight remaining source of jealousy that never quite wore off – chiefly, I suspect, because Deotlan fed it with boasting to keep up his semi-white prestige. He was an utterly graceless creature but no one with a weakness for mental honesty allied to unscrupulousness could help liking him. The more he let us down, the fonder of him all three of us became. But what Wan Nau saw in him besides his looks I could not imagine: nothing, probably, nor did she need to; he was her chosen God.

Stewart, and the now awakened Ainger, and I sat on by the fire till such time as we might turn in without intruding; and Ainger drew from his pocket by habit, since the fire gave no reading light for a near-sighted man, the Greek testament that he had been studying assiduously on board. In an optimistic attempt to preserve its leather binding from the ants he had wrapped it very thickly in sheets of newspaper pulled from cabin trunks. This, and the bringing of a revolver and a spare pair of glasses, were the only preparations he seemed to have made for the journey: he had already commandeered two of my handkerchiefs.

Throughout the day he had been giving decisions, whenever they were needed, without reference to any of us: he was justified by our greater ignorance of the land, but it must have been slightly galling to Stewart, who said now with some reasonable heat 'Good Lord, Ainger, what the devil did you bring that for? If you were going to carry anything extra, why not food? I suppose we'd all give pounds for something really edible just now.'

Ainger looked across at him for a moment with his glasses on his forehead, before he said with a show, at least, of common-sense: 'What good d'you suppose anything of this bulk would be among five – six now? If we don't get hold of more food somehow it won't make much difference whether we have an extra slab of chocolate or not, you know!' And I thought, 'May things get better or worse, or there'll be open friction in about another twenty-four hours.'

We were three people who had lost something. With Ainger it was health: Stewart, because he disliked his job and had so far failed at the one thing he wanted to do, play-writing, had lost confidence in himself and was growing not resigned but acquiescent towards failure. Both were touchy; they had many pleasant and interesting factors still left in their lives and the hope of regaining the rest. My own loss, being absolute and greater, for the moment at any rate, had given me a certain placidity, I think, because nothing that only concerned my private life retained its old importance.

'By the way, apropos of the Greek testament,' I asked Arnold Ainger, 'what is your occupation in ordinary life?' Now that even Mrs. Mardick's curiosity on this subject had faded away it no longer seemed impertinent to ask. 'Some of us almost got up a sweep-stake about it in our most passionately bored moments in the ship.'

'Good heavens! But I told you, languages. And the Napoleonic Wars. Chiefly languages. I speak seven and read – well, I don't know, a good number altogether if you count ancient and modern separately. About twelve I suppose. My father was an Anglo-Dane who married an Irish woman with Swedish and Greek strains in her. They used to pay each other extravagant compliments and complain bitterly to me in private of their conjugal miseries, in all their available languages: it gave me a good start. But for working by yourself I think it's so appropriate that you can't beat the New Testament as a means of acquiring the gift of tongues that I once sent a subscription to the Society for the Propagation of the Gospel in Foreign Parts – conscience money: I had religion at sixteen. (It's been very handy too – the religious fit, I mean, because now I know the English and Swedish of the New Testament so well.) I sent the money with a suggestion that Malaya, which I've always wanted to visit, needed a good literal translation. But they only took the money.'

'I really meant, what do you do for a living?' I explained. 'That was what everyone guessed at.'

'Oh, that,' he said, as if this were irrelevant. 'Civil servant. Foreign Office.'

'D'you care for it?' I asked, amused and puzzled by his tone. I had never met anyone like Ainger

134

before, except one or two dons and a nerve specialist; but later I came across in his company several distinguished colleagues with the same attitude towards their work, that it was an unfortunate essential which interfered with their hobbies.

'I suppose so,' he said after reflection. 'You see, I get twelve hundred a year. The pay, as you probably know, is shocking in the Civil Service; and I always feel that my gigantic official labours are utterly unrewarded (as well as being practically useless). Still, I doubt if I'd get twelve hundred at anything else.' – From which Stewart and I gathered rightly, though certainly Ainger did not intend us to, that we had with us one of the few comparatively permanent factors in the real government of the British Empire, which is mainly run by obscure officials in the Civil Service, few of them earning more than a thousand, but all of them wielding more influence ,than the majority of Cabinet Ministers.

Incorrigibly a newspaper man in spite of himself, Stewart, who had excellent sight, picked up the wrappings of Ainger's book. The two sheets of different London newspapers dated from before the time when he and I had left England, but scraps of print have a morbid fascination for most writing people away from their work. He bent over them towards the fire.

'Listen!' he said, the late trouble forgotten in the awe with which a mountaineer, benighted among

pure but uncongenial snows, may dizzily regard
the murk of the abyss into which he must descend
as soon as possible. In this random piece of the
Daily Mail (issue of August 5th, 1930, I remember),
appeared the report of an international congress of
biologists for the study of sexual problems, headed
'Experts on Love.' *Reynolds Newspaper* for the
following week (August 13th) featured 'Great
Murder Stories from the Bible.'

'Fair makes one yearn for the refinement of
civilisation, doesn't it?' Stewart said mildly.

'I suppose if you were here professionally, all
this,' Ainger suggested, with a comprehensive wave
of the hand towards us and the jungle, 'would be
described as "The Hazardous Picnic"?'

Stewart was one of those who gain spiritual relief
from rubbing salt into their wounds: ' "Perilous",
not "hazardous"' he corrected, with gloomy pride
in his own low ability. 'And invert for emphasis
when possible –"The Picnic Perilous." At least in
my column.'

Not far off something screamed in sudden
pain or terror, as I have heard rabbits scream at
home in Suffolk. The shrill little throbbing note
was snuffed out abruptly while the whole forest
strained to listen, and it was the listening that was
the more unsettling.

Our thin mesh of talk broke too, and trying to
knit it up again in the resumed silence, I realised
what an effort it all was, and how comprehensible

it became, here, that other men's nerves had given way altogether in these forests, under the sheer living weight of this vegetation and of the things unseen, unheard, and dimly apprehended that it sheltered.

'It must seem odd to you that I am really quite as keen on preserving my life as you are, though I've got the prospect of going back to that sort of thing indefinitely!' Stewart said, giving back the printed sheets.

'Well, it does a bit. If there's really nothing else open to you?' Ainger said. There came again, to make farce of our attempt to fashion comedy in a tragic setting, the foul false octave of a brain-fever bird, that had been calling at intervals for a long time. It is the one creature that even now I could cheerfully strangle, in memory of the angry attention with which, hour after hour sometimes, and always involuntarily, we waited for the repetition of the trill — maddeningly delayed, maddeningly inevitable. It was a well-disguised blessing when it came, two notes short, and not quite in tune.

'Well, I could write plays, and sponge on my people and Judy occasionally, to alleviate semi-starvation. In fact, it's what I would like to do. But I haven't enough self-respect,' Stewart said, 'to give up the certainty of nine pounds a week, which is at present the price of my soul. I sometimes think it's an exorbitant charge I'm making for it, anyway.'

Then Deotlan and the radiant Wan Nau reappeared, to take over the watch that someone must keep all night, and the rest of us lay down in the shelter.

It was more uncomfortable on the uneven, boggy ground than it had been in the river bed. There were no further alarms that night, except when I woke from a few minutes' doze towards dawn to see a dark, moving thing looming over me. It was Stewart, tired, he said apologetically, of merely going through the motions of sleep, and so standing up for a few minutes, with a conscious pathos that must at least have eased his spirit, to get a little rest from his bed of squelchy tussocks.

CHAPTER V

'THE EUNUCH'S-EYE-VIEW'

A FETID gale, surprisingly reminiscent of the London Tube Railway passages after rush hours, was blowing across the swamp when we began trying to work our way across. The smell of stagnant water increased with the heat. Before we could start we had been forced to waste the best early hour of the morning in mending the left hinge of Ainger's glasses. Their breaking adrift was the most inconvenient minor mishap that could have occurred to us: he was helpless without glasses; he always broke them in that place, he said, through the habit of raising them by one side. His spare pair had already been amateurishly mended twice and were too weak at the join to trust for active use, without another pair to fall back on in emergencies. This is the sort of thing that should not happen to harassed people in bad corners of the earth.

From that time onwards Ainger's glasses became an abiding trouble: even the deferential Wan Nau would chatter at him like an excited monkey if his left hand rose towards them in the old way.

Between us, after several failures, she and I put on a split reed serving that held the loose parts insecurely in place. It was done to the accompaniment of a stream of discouraging advice from Mrs. Mardick, who belonged to the glue school of repairers. She reiterated, until I was almost coerced into the credulity of boredom, her belief that her husband – or perhaps it had been someone else, but anyway it was someone who should know – had mentioned a tree common to all Malayan forests from which one could extract without trouble a highly efficacious gum. This, drying in a few minutes, set as hard as cement, and was almost as durable, she said: surely it would be worth our while to look for this obliging jungle product, which she would know when she saw it! We thought it would not, but still lacked the callousness to explain why, beyond suggesting that by this time our biassed minds refused to credit Trenganu with harbouring anything so unnaturally serviceable to man. It was not unlike a cinnamon tree, a distinctive species, she told us persuasively. But the only trees he had seen that were at all like cinnamon trees were all cinnamon trees, Deotlan said, without lessening her kindly enthusiasm.

'There, you see! It's come off *again*. Miss Corder, it's *no good* trying any more that way. If you'd *only* put something really sticky on the hinge and *then* wind the binding round it, it'd stay. Look, there's a camphor tree. That one. Yes, there. That's one. I expect that would do, only I'm afraid it means taking off the bit you've done so far. Camphor sap's as sticky as anything. Just didn't I

140

once get some in my hair! Mr. Ainger, don't you believe in gum?'

'Good heavens,' said Ainger absently, in his most chilling tone.

'But *don't* you?'

'Blast!' I said, officially to a threatening split in the fibres of the reed, and Ainger looked round blindly in concern at the note, almost approaching hysteria, in my voice: he made her repeat the question, which he genuinely had not heard, and then started a counter-irritant monologue of his own. Ponderous scholastic humour, we had found, was one of the few things that could dam the overflow of Mrs. Mardick's volatile spirits for a few minutes: it made her uneasy not to know, in spite of the self-given publicity enjoyed by her sense of humour, exactly where she would be expected to laugh. We rushed to one another's defence with this sort of thing at times – the more pointlessly pedagogic the joke, the better the dam it made – 'The word "believe" has an interesting double significance in English and in no other language,' he said. 'It is used in the sense of "Do you believe in God?" and "Do you believe in fresh air?" meaning in one case to assume existence, and in the other to approve. So that in one sense if I said I "believed" in gum it would be as vague as if I said – as you've probably heard people saying – "I saw a dog in charge of a little girl" Now there's another curious ambiguity for you! Does it mean that she had charge of him, or vice versa? Because one could say "I saw a little girl in charge of a dog," without conveying a different meaning. (Of course, one *should* say "In the charge of –" but brutes like Corder, dead to the higher decencies of philology, have so debased the public ear that not one in a hundred would, nowadays.)'

'Mr. Ainger, do be serious–'

'This is more serious than you realise. Far more. As to believing in gum in the way that I take it you intended – the non-godly, so to speak fresh air sense – How's it getting on, Miss Corder? Oh, fine. Bless you both – well, they seem to be doing it all right without, so it doesn't matter anyway. Ours is a terribly inexact language; I can give you a lot of examples like that.'

Mrs. Mardick had begun to impinge badly on Ainger's consciousness: he heard nearly all her remarks now because he knew that they would probably annoy him, and he did not want to hear them. Until we had finished the job he became dully erudite on verbal derivations, but with an air of rollicking so spiritually among the absurdities of Greek roots that she too evinced amusement at intervals, and probably felt it. Making merry with the Latin contractions used in dispensing I had been equally successful at other times on Stewart's and Ainger's behalf.

Then Ainger retired into himself again, with such an air of having settled this matter finally that the gum question could not easily be re-opened, while he remained peering up blinkingly at an enchanting little sloth that Wan Nau had caught and put on the roof branch of the shelter. The beast hung upside down by all its eight extraordinary toes, almost twisting off its neck in order to peer down blinkingly at him, first from one side and then the other. It made no attempt to escape, and I loathed the killing of it for breakfast.

The hinge of Ainger's glasses came adrift again the next morning. Perhaps Mrs. Mardick's plan was the better one: but we had reached a stage when this contingency could no longer occur to us.

We did not want to retrace our way: *seladang* usually stay in one locality for some while, and we had too little ammunition to waste any of it on game that we could not carry. Having no idea ourselves of the extent of the swamp, we believed Deotlan when he said he thought that it was a narrow belt stretching for some distance in either direction, heading us from the way we wanted to take. Nearly all day we spent in trying to cross by scattered patches of mangroves, making enough progress to keep us at the task of slipping and climbing among the slime-covered roots, lurching sideways desperately to catch at a whippy branch as a foot slid on a tilting patch of grass that had looked firm.

We sank in over the knees, when the boughs to which we clung bent under the sudden weight; and the ooze bubbled up on each side, opening a million tiny stinking mouths as gas bubbles rose with a soft 'plup-plup'-ing from disturbed matter decomposing below. It was not really risky, within reach of the mangroves, but it was horrible, and the insects were merciless. The quickening heat brought new life belching up out of the water into the quivering air, to mingle with the air-borne swarms that dropped new life back into the seething, still-seeming water. Under our feet, the sour earth sweated into such a prodigality of creation that the sun, when it drew away the night mist, drew to replace it by day a haze of winged creatures so thick that it cast a faint shadow on the ground at midday.

We had fought our way so far across the marsh, when the mangroves began to fail us, that we were unwilling to discuss the growing obviousness of failure. Appalled by the prospect of going back by the way we had come, Stewart volunteered to struggle on a little farther, over ground bare of any support, and abandoned the idea after six steps which he spent a long and anxious time trying to retrace. Slowly we waded back to the place from which we had started.

Miles farther west, and towards afternoon, we found the end of the marshy ground. Swamp-shy by this time, we gave it a wide berth in skirting it, and reached the steep edge of a gulley that I demurred from crossing. My shoes were only ragged strips of papery leather now, and the long, cliff-like sides were of sharp shale.

I was too tired to listen to Ainger's protests against making another long detour westward. Let them go down, then; personally I was going round. The sun beat straight down into this bare, airless fissure, so that the stones at the bottom seemed to be dancing like the living cloud over the marsh. My neck and arms and legs were swollen with mosquito stings, and I, having a fair and easily irritated skin, had not resisted the temptation to rub some of the places raw. A few seconds' scorching sunlight on these inflamed patches was like the touch of very hot metal. In common with Ainger I had lost my hat, though in my case this was of comparative unimportance, my starched linen affair having ceased to be of much use as a protection some while before I left it in the swamp. I was as done to the world that day, mentally and physically, as Ainger had been the day before.

He gave in to me, and we clambered along the creeper-bound edge. A second gully, dry as the other had been, opened from the first, running out towards us, so that we were forced farther southwest. A little way along this I sat down to have a long rest at all costs. I had suddenly gone mulish with the misery of cut feet, from one of which I dug a tiki spine with a childish vindictiveness towards all the universe that made me hurt myself more than necessary, and led to a sore on the ball of the foot two days later. The hot wind was still blowing. We wanted water badly, but fortunately this was one of the few staple needs that the jungle supplied freely as a rule. Still, we should have to keep going till we found it, perhaps as much as a mile farther on.

Deotlan told us (redundantly) that he was not altogether familiar with this locality either; but from the look of the land he surmised that there would be a stream at the lower end of the gully.

'Tell the fool to go and find it for certain, and then come back. I'm not moving on the off-chance,' I said. 'I'll do your arm now, Ainger, if you like.' I had got a light touch of the sun in the swamp and my head was splitting. I was producing excuses to myself for keeping the party back; my own thirst was not as bad as the thought of more walking, and I was at the point where other people's thirsts are no longer taken into consideration, without a great effort.

'Without water?'

'Or not at all!' I said querilously.

Stewart bent down and took me under the arm-pits, yanking me to my feet.

'Judy, if you start going all feminine here I shall exercise a semi-elder-brother's privilege and spank you. I've never known you do it before, and you don't get away with it now. We're all feeling about the same.'

'You're not, or you wouldn't be standing up,' I retorted. 'I'm not stopping you going on with Deotlan, am I? I'll come on afterwards.' I knew

146

that I was being idiotic; I was expecting the usual curse of my sex, which came to add another minor trouble to my lot the next day, and (as with most women) the turmoil in the blood beforehand and at the time inclined me to be unreasonable if I was subjected to any strain. My one slight advantage over other women was that I recognised this, but naturally that rarely curbed the tendency at the time. I felt that I should want to cry if made to go any farther.

'The privilege, if anyone's, will be mine as the instigator of the expedition,' Ainger said amiably. 'A sort of local *droit de seigneur*. Remember that light, pleasant exercise was exactly what you yourself recommended for my arm. I'm sorry to put this ungrateful construction on your professional advice. But it really is important that we shouldn't straggle.'

'This is one of those great open spaces where men can afford to be men, not gentlemen, if necessary, Judy!' said Stewart. 'Come on, now; there's a good girl.'

We found no stream where Deotlan had prophesied it, nor in the second place he promised, over the next rise, but we camped after sundown by a trickle that he produced at last, in the third appointed spot, with the lofty air of a conjuror on whose skill aspersions have been cast.

Ainger seemed much fresher than he had been the day before, but Mrs. Mardick was a marvel – indefatigable, as indeed she had been all day, though her shoes if not her skin were in much the same condition as mine: she was amazingly tough physically; much tougher than any of the rest of us. She cooked the four sand-grouse that Deotlan and Stewart had shot, she helped with the shelters, she remarked on her luck — not virtue, just good luck, she insisted — in positively revelling in the heat, and altogether we should have been much less morose if she had not been so genuinely splendid.

We were many miles farther west than we wanted to be, and in actual mileage probably no nearer Kintaling than we had been when Deotlan first saw the marks of *seladang* — a long while ago, it seemed to us that evening.

'The more one sees of Mr. Ainger and gets to know him, the nicer he is, don't you think?' observed Mrs. Mardick when he was out of ear-shot. She heaped coals of fire by proxy on Stewart and me for not showing more of her *bonhomie*. We were too tired to be anything but short with her effusiveness that evening, and Ainger had been the shortest of us.

The more one sees of him the less one seems to know him, I thought. He knew Stewart and me fairly well by now, but still was only an acquaintance of ours. I was incurably like the tactless kind of dog that blunders amiably up to every stranger, expecting a welcome: Stewart, grown more cautious through reverses, would be more likely to approach with a wagging tail but a lip lifted over a fang, to be on the safe side. But Ainger apparently had no need of contacts. It was not that he was secretive or deliberately made mysteries about himself: he remained aloof without effort, as a cat does.

This was the first night in many, I think, that lying awake for a while I did not have to drag my mind, once or often, from the old, unprofitable groove, worn deep by thoughts too tired to break the bitter habit – Hugh and Muriel and myself: Hugh and Muriel: Hugh. When at last my thoughts wandered back to this subject to-night, it was not with an aching unhappiness, too great to be borne without an effort to escape. And first, for some while, with nothing else in my mind, I stared from unfamiliar star to star through the gaps in the leaf thatching, remembering with amusement an anxious compassion of my early childhood for the light that took many years of travelling, I was told, through the dark and cold emptiness of space, in order to reach my earth. Because someone ought certainly to notice it when it arrived at last, after all that steadfast journeying, I used to spend hours trying to keep awake and look out of the window, that it might not be utterly wasted. Physical exhaustion reduces the brain to childishness: I caught myself on the verge of doing this again.

It was always when, growing drowsy, my mind lost some of its conscious hold on itself that the old trouble pushed its way back into the front of my thoughts, and I turned again as always, knowing the uselessness of this appeal, to the defence of reason, on which the weary spirit calls for help against its pain when this grows intolerable – calls not because reason is valiant at such times, but because there is no other defence. Now, because I was too tired to prevent it, my mind skirted round the sleeping sorrow. I turned restlessly on my side on the hard ground, thinking: Made as I am, in another age I should certainly have loved some other man as well as I now love this man. It is not real, then, my love – this focussing of all my desire on that one person. And this hankering in me which seems part of the substance of my being is a disturbance only in my brain and blood because I am young and vitally alive: his personal qualities have not engendered it. Not because my lover is what he is, but because I am what I am, is he so beloved. Then his loss is nothing irreplaceable. It is not real, my love. Born twenty years earlier or later, I might still have met him, but it would have meant nothing to me that there had been a little while ago – or would be soon – a young, fair man with a gay laugh like no-one else's, and a certain way of smiling with a frown when puzzled, having a mind and body something like those I now remember with such strange home-sickness of heart and flesh. It is a trivial accident of time, then, this love of mine – it is not real. A small coincidence not of time only but of my nature, not his: this is not enough to rule me as it has done.

Poor comfort these thoughts were as a rule: to-night they were vaguely consoling, I was so tired.

The odd thing about the next day was that more clearly than things done I remember things said; perhaps because it was the last day for a week or more in which we had any inclination to talk of immaterial things; and being clear, temporarily, of the worst of the forest we could talk almost at ease. Our skins alone, at first, not our nerves, suffered in the more open ground. The going was increasingly painful, badly shod as Mrs. Mardick and I were by now, and the sun was a torment.

We were climbing slightly, walking up a dried watercourse that narrowly parted the leaning jungle, a glaring streak of yellow-white in an over-green world. Between us and the general direction of our course lay a low range of hills, and Ainger had decided to cross them. In my recollection remain, almost inextricably mingled, the scorching of the sun on my inflamed neck and arms and shoulders, hour after hour, the dull pain of blistered feet, and Mrs. Mardick's voice as she toiled after me, telling me as usual of her daughter or panting confidences about her various differences with her husband, and sometimes combining the two subjects. 'You see, he's rather *that* sort of man, if you know what I mean. I don't mean he ever gives way to it; but then men *are* rather more – you know – than we are, aren't they? Anyway, he *is*. And of course I'm not. Rather cold, if anything. But with Elaine, who's really too reserved naturally, I always make a point of being absolutely *frank* about *everything*, however difficult it is sometimes. I feel one simply *has* to nowadays, so there's just *nothing* that we don't discuss.'

I began growing a passionate sympathy for Elaine; up till then we had all regarded her shadowy presence with profound dislike. Mrs. Mardick was one of the women who, when their own under-proof physical ardours have waned, find their main sexual stimulant in forcing themselves to discuss sex freely with their children, to the embarrassment of the latter. This mild and perhaps harmless modern vice is on the increase, among conscientious elderly women whose innate Victorianism is balanced by a resolve not to lose touch with the day at any cost. It must cause them a good deal of discomfort at first; but apparently they have their reward, the practice becomes a relief in the end, and in the instances that I have noticed, it has merely separated the children from their parents earlier than they would in any case have drifted away. But personally I should have found such conversation an intolerable infringement of my precious mental privacy as a child.

With thoughtful graciousness, and a turn of speed that in this heat left us all gasping, Mrs.

Mardick hurried on ahead, panting harder, to have a chat with Deotlan and Wan Nau in their native tongue. How much of her rendering of it they understood it was difficult to make out: they were very polite people. Nods, gestures and disjointed remarks seemed to be the chief means of communication: but she was never happier than when exercising her social talent for persuading incommiscible elements that they were part of a harmonious whole, and we did not discourage her. We felt like balloons whose mooring ropes have been cast off when she left us like this for a few minutes.

As talkers Arnold Ainger and Stewart were nearly as irrepressible as she was, though in a different way. The jungle could make them silent, which was more than it could do to her, but except at moments of extreme stress, it left them as irrelevantly interested in abstract questions as they were habitually, in comfortable surroundings. This was not normal, I thought. Surely no one else would behave so detachedly. It was absurd in these conditions. But their detachment was curiously catching. I found myself taking sides in any argument they started as though the subject were still of great moment. These extraordinary discussions were one of the main features of the whole extraordinary journey.

Launching out into the sort of conversation that could not be enjoyed in Mrs. Mardick's presence, Stewart said that if we, who were now young, grew kinder as we grew older it would be encumbent on us, remembering clearly the distresses and revulsions of the early teens, to be slightly prudish in our reticence with our children. 'We shall be old in their eyes whatever our age. We shall never have been young as they are young. And the dead passions of the old whom one knows are really a little indecent in youth in relation to one's own.'

What on earth does that matter now? I thought. And then memory came to me as a shock and a realisation. I had once felt intensely all that he had just said; but later I had forgotten, as nearly everyone less imaginatively sensitive than Stewart seems to forget. One day, then, children will feel the same about me. I must not forget this. My generation middle aged: it is ridiculously diffi-cult to realise that such a thing is inevitable when it still seems impossible. Soon, then, we shall have no business, pandering to our desire to keep our ebbing youth at flood in our own minds by convincing our successors of its existence, to claim to understand their shining new discoveries of the glory of earth – 'Oh, the apple-tree, the singing and the gold!' – Fortunately the really young will not credit the claim if we make it, but for them there will be tarnish in the suggestion that we, so unfresh and so prosaic, have handled the sacred fire that they approach, know well all that they are learning, and yet these burning wonders have left us only as they will see us, quite vilely unscathed. We, the post-War people, will seem like that soon: I was suddenly surprised by what I had always known, and for a minute I did not hear what the men said. I was absorbed in the uncomfortable conviction that as we grow older we must seem, if we are considerate at all, to remember less and less of the incidents of our youth, the more we remember of its mentality. My wrinkled hands – it is pleasant to arrange these things while I merely know and do not believe that they will be that some day – must not have loved the long fine shoulder muscles and lean thighs of young men's bodies, and their good skins: for this will have become obscene – at last. It is a humiliating revenge that time takes on all our young defiances. There must have been no such defiances it should seem in after years.

Arnold, much tougher-fibred than Stewart, was forcibly disagreeing with Stewart's idea. 'Damned if I knuckle down to my children's repulsive notions of what they would like me to have been! They can make what they please of their own youth, not mine.' I was amused by the contrast between them; I liked Ainger's ruthlessness, but I was with Stewart in insisting that, in particular, gentle-minded parents should not remain lovers in their children's eyes. I know that to many a child it appears that because both parents have been equally and closely related to itself from the apparent beginning of time, they must have been always, equally and closely, related to one another. Show, or even suggestion of physical love between them is infinitely ugly, horrible in

its vaguely resented incestuousness. So much I
have never forgotten of my own early youth.

'I was always fond of your mother,' Stewart
decided should be the gist of his attitude towards
his offspring ('Fond' – when they are discovering
young love! – What blessed poles apart.) 'But I
wrote the love-scenes in my plays from imagination
alone, to comply with the convention of the time
which insisted on realism.' (It will be so easy to
convey the sternness of a sex-starved mind without a
direct appeal for sympathy.) 'And I don't even
believe in them artistically now.'

Both generations – the rising and the passing – I
thought, have a right to their inevitable sense of
superiority in all sex matters only as long as it
remains secret.

The watercourse, which had turned in the right
direction for a stretch of a mile or so, now bent
away in a south-westerly direction again, and we
decided with alacrity to leave it as soon as the jungle,
which leaned down over the banks, became less
of a solid wall on either side; for the heat in this
bare, sun-filled place was appalling, the hot wind
was still blowing.

In return for my dressing of his arm, Arnold
Ainger had daubed my neck and the scorched
patches on my arms and shoulders with mud from
the stream by which we had camped. We were an
odd looking crew: all the whites of the party had
made use of mud as a poor substitute for the oil

that we had not got, but even this sticky stuff was only a temporary protection, drying and flaking off in the sun. The pain where I was badly burned was increasing, and I was afraid that we should get sunstroke. We had torn up Stewart's piqué coat, and made head coverings of it. We trudged on, looking for a gap.

And these extraordinary men talked and talked as though they were sitting round a drawing-room fire at home. First of all it had been the talk that had seemed unreal: soon it became the wretched conditions we were in. This power of being verbally anaesthetised, at least in part, is evidently one of the few advantages of being mouldily intellectual.

'Kindness to the young is overdone nowadays.' Ainger said argumentatively. 'I sometimes wonder whether it isn't our duty to oppress them more than we do. Have you ever considered what will remain for our children of the fight for the latchkey which did our fathers so much good in their day? That's how they worked off the normal adolescent's need of revolting against something, preferably tyranny. But the latchkey or its equivalent in everything is thrust into children's hands now before they ask for it.'

'Certainly they won't have much to fight their elders about, for their soft-hearted elders won't fight,' I said. 'I don't agree that it'll hurt them, but it is rather a depressing prospect for them. Because one longs to cut one's intellectual teeth on something. There should be a jolly destructive period before the mind starts building, if it ever does. And I don't see what they'll find to destroy in this age of scientific child-fancying, when there isn't a complex or an implanted fear or a frustration allowed anywhere near the nursery. I have a mournful vision of Stewart's possible children as would-be crusaders, wandering disconsolately in a world that he and some equally squeamish woman have lovingly denuded of Saracens.'

'Well, you're the product of that sort of thing yourself,' Stewart answered, 'and it doesn't seem to have depressed you. They'd discovered by your day the Awful Importance of the Early Years. Your little ego was cherished like anything: I remember they wouldn't let me bat you over the head when you deliberately broke my model yacht – afraid it would encourage masochism, I expect. Still, I suppose you did have a few preciously unreasonable taboos to cope with: they just lingered on into your childhood?'

I nodded.

'Lots of clean, wholesome fun in combating, in adolescence, overdoses of sex-shame implanted by nurse, and so on?'

'Heaps.'

'To which I hope you attribute your spiritual health and strength,' said Ainger. 'To-day all the children of my friends are brought up unbiassed towards religion, so they'll have nothing to throw overboard with heroic efforts later on, and their minds are sterilised from the beginning by being allowed more knowledge than curiosity. Altogether they're spoonfed with beauty and glutted with intellectual freedom literally from the cradle. Whenever they differ from their parents, instead of being treated as moral lepers, as we were – it gave one a warm glow at heart, and more forcible convictions – they're told humbly that they're clever little things and very likely right. If this doesn't eliminate the pioneering spirit, which has done so much to make the British Empire what, with a little care, it need never have been, then nothing ever will.'

Mrs. Mardick had come back, glowing with her effort of condescension. For a woman who had spent years in the East, it was really a remarkable impulse on her part. We could only wish that it had taken longer to work off. 'Everything depends on how a child is handled in the early years,' she said, having caught the last few words. To avoid her company, Stewart basely dropped back and loitered for a few steps, leaving her to Ainger and me.

My foot, where the thorn had been, was tender and throbbing. Physically we were all in low condition that day, because so far we had been unable to get anything to eat, but this absurd talk with Stewart and Ainger was the sort I had always loved, though I could not have initiated it here: it was like a tonic to get back to the familiar amosphere.

'The only comfort I can offer,' I said, 'is that a few weeks before I left England I read a heavy treatise by a German doctor seriously advocating the gentle slapping of babies as a cure for flatulence. That at least is light on the horizon. If we could return to indiscriminate slapping, for whatever reason, the healthy oppression of the young should once more become possible.'

'Anybody could tell from your talk that none of you have any children,' said Mrs. Mardick with a tincture of genuine sharpness in her indulgent tone, which made it much less aggravating than usual.

'– has,' mouthed Ainger protestingly, and then said aloud, unexpectedly, 'I've got two. And I beat them!'

'You don't!' Mrs. Mardick and I said almost together, one as an accusation and the other as a statement.

'I do. Or rather I have. Once. One child.' He added thoughtfully after a second, 'One slap. Still, I believe that's more than most middle-class parents have done in this effete age. When one remembers that eminent scientists like Bose are trying to extend our Georgian queasiness to the sufferings of plant life, and – '

'Poor little beggar. Was it upset?' enquired Mrs. Mardick, whose conversation often suffered from subject-lag.

'Was what? Oh, that. I really have no idea,' he

said, in a tone that reminded me of his first conversation with her about the historicity of the New Testament. 'It didn't pause in its occupation of trying to push a small puppy – valuable and not ours – through the still smaller mesh of the wire netting round the tennis court. But as the experts say that the psychology of a child of three is infinitely more complicated than it becomes in later life, you can't deduce anything from that. I may have curdled its ego for life. It certainly has become an exceptionally unattractive child. They both have, I fancy,' he added dispassionately. 'But I don't see much of them so they may be quite average for their age, really.'

'I *quite* admit that one *has* to be firm about cruelty to animals, but all the same I don't agree that any good can be done by violence.'

'But it did do all the good that was intended – relieved my feelings,' he said. 'Surely no one who has any common-sense or memory expects slapping to be of benefit except to the slapper. I brought the traditional Victorian phrase up to date for the occasion – "This does me more good than it does you." But the child was unfortunately too young to have any historical appreciation. Pity; I should have loved that in my own childhood. You might try it on Whatsername – Elsie – though. It's a good phrase, and she's older, I gather. Interested in history at all?'

'Elaine,' said her mother, 'was never allowed to

be slapped, even when she was young enough. It is always *quite* sufficient to show an affectionate child that one is deeply grieved to sort of – well, I never like the word "punish," but –'

'To work on its strongest emotions?' I suggested, knowing several well-meaning women who played constantly (and abominably, I thought) on their children's feelings as a convenient means of controlling them.

'Exactly,' she said.

'Then try her with a paraphrase of the Georgian equivalent,' I said helpfully, ' "Mother is not hurt, she is only terribly, terribly angry." That would be a nice change too: I should have liked that, at her age. The original was in vogue in my day. I feel with Ainger that one wants to keep alive all these quaint traditions.'

But Mrs. Mardick had genially dropped back to walk beside Stewart, and it served him right, Ainger and I felt. Soon we heard my cousin's voice sounding as embarrassed as it did only when someone was talking unrestrainedly about beauty or art, showing off their souls.

'Oh, really? So you're fond of Beauty?' we heard him comment in a bright conversational tone as he unfairly tried to quicken and come up with us again. I scrambled on a little faster over the bruising stones. 'Mrs. Mardick is ever so fond of Beauty!' he said confidentially to me, as one reports the remarkable enthusiasm of a friend for mountaineer-

ing or archaeology. He had easily gained on me
because every alternate step of mine had to be taken
gingerly not to be excruciating for my foot. 'Do you
think she would like the poem of overdue reaction
from my play—you know, "Song for the Next
Generation"?' and before I had time to discourage
him he quoted to her:

> I'm terribly keen about Beauty and God,
> Only don't tell my mother.
> The darling would think it so frightfully odd,
> Or some complex or other.
>
> She gets all the kick that is left her, you see
> Out of Freedom, and Truth,
> And discussing her past just as frankly with me
> As they talked in her youth.
>
> My father is still on the blasphemous line —
> (Gets his tickle from that)
> But they want to be friends more than parents
>   of mine,
> It appears from their chat.
>
> So with him I remain sacrilegious enough
> To talk atheist tripe,
> And I'd put up a show of the Œdipus stuff,
> But she isn't my type.
>
> One's got to be kind, and they'd take it to heart
> If they happened to know
> I'm fond of religion, the "pretty" in art,
> And am chaste, as we go.'

No one but myself ever had liked it, but Stewart found a second and unexpected admirer in Ainger, though this sophisticated jingle sounded odd here, where a few yards away three vivid-hued sun-birds were worrying one of the bird-eating spiders that I had wanted to see for years, and now barely noticed. The exquisite little creatures were darting at it and away again, as though the light were stabbing this monstrous insect that had strayed from the darkness of the forest with scraps of brilliance from the spectrum.

Mrs. Mardick did not like his song, except the line about 'friends more than parents,' which started her off happily again on the upbringing of Elaine.

'That heart-rending courtesy and consideration of the young, damn them!' said Ainger. 'I have been called "sir" by a lad of nineteen, the son of a friend, and he didn't contradict me when he knew I was in the wrong, over a new method of lubricating light aeroplane engines, which I afterwards found was his speciality: he just let my elderly dodderings run on. It was one of the most unpleasant shocks I've had. I'm thirty seven.'

'I've had it too,' said Stewart, 'and I'm thirty-two. It is one of those things that somehow one never feared would happen to oneself — "Not you and I; we shall surely die" before being "sirred" by social equals.'

'I only wish young people were politer!' said Mrs. Mardick.

'I think they're devastatingly polite, this coming generation,' Stewart said. 'They can afford to be, too; they have a marvellous chance to do really worth-while things, the lucky devils. Nearly all the generation of writers and artists before us saw things with a suppressed sex bias which affected their work; so we're inclined to give everything they left out an overstressed importance; but the next lot will have inherited mental freedom instead of buying it. They ought to reach something like a eunuch's-eye-view, artistically. I'm all for the eunuch's-eye-view. It's what art badly needs at the moment. I want more of it myself, but I can't get it.'

Deotlan muttered to Stewart, who was carrying his rifle. We 'froze' where we were, I with a tight hold on Mrs. Mardick's wrist because she had started swinging up her arm as if to point. 'Oh, look, deer – l' We were anxiously in need of food; the swaddling vegetation in the jungle and the difficulty of bringing down small game with a rifle, when we dared not waste ammunition, more than offset the plentifulness of quarry. Constantly we heard, but could not see, moving things a few yards away, and this was exasperating, hungry as we often were. Several times already Stewart, the best shot in the party, had fired and missed that day. In any case he could not hope to kill outright, but only to disable. 'Did he hit it?' Mrs. Mardick had asked eagerly on each occasion of Deotlan, who answered 'Yes,' with his habitual politeness as the quarry bounded or flew safely out of sight. Now, as we rounded a spur of the bank, a group of three mouse-deer stood posed on the farther lip of the watercourse a little way ahead. Knowing that they were among the wariest of the jungle creatures, Stewart fired instantly, almost without taking aim, at a lovely little fawn. Wounded, it would have less chance of escaping than the others.

'Got it?'

'Yes,' said Deotlan mournfully as the faun leapt with the other deer along the overhanging edge, where there appeared to be no foothold. The jungle bulged over the side, and here the tangle of creepers was such that even these small animals could not for the moment get through into cover. They were gone in a breath, though, finding a tiny gap a man's height or more from the ground and leaping through, from an almost impossible taking-off place: but Stewart fired again as the young one disappeared.

' — by God!' finished Deotlan, meaning yes at last. The fawn had stumbled and jumped short. It fell back, into our sight, and a few crumbles of earth gave on the bank, sending up a spurt of fine dust and dropping the little beast on to the stones underneath. It rolled over but was up again in an instant as we dashed forward, all our weariness, the pain of hurt feet and the misery of the sun forgotten in excitement. Ainger brought it down with a fortunate throw; the stone caught it on the

loin as it tried to make the bank again, and we
pelted it with stones while it struggled convulsively
to move forward on its forelegs. A fortnight ago
I should not have believed this possible, but now
I stood by with satisfaction while Deotlan half-knelt
on the squirming, silky body and drove into the
creature's throat the knife that he carried in his
head-cloth.

It made us a wonderful feed when we had
cooked it on the spot, though all of us, except Wan
Nau and Deotlan, were suffering from raging
headaches or malaise of some kind, from exposure to
the sun and the persistence of the abominable hot
wind.

Afterwards, when we were climbing again and
more steeply, I became oblivious to the condition
of the others because of the breaking sun-blisters
on my shoulders and neck, the wretchedness of
exacting walking at a time when a woman should
not have to undergo violent exercise, and a foot so
swollen and tender that my eyes smarted with the
sudden pain when we moved on after a rest. They
may all have been in as bad a state as I was; I did
not notice. I plodded forward all the afternoon
thinking of nothing; my throbbing right foot and
one small area on the right shoulder seemed to
divide between them the whole of my personality.
Probably but for the others I should have passed,
unseeing, the break in the jungle that was the object
of our going forward at all.

The ground looked unusually light green in this natural clearing, but from below we could not see clearly against the sun.

A wail came from Stewart, the first to climb the overhanging bank, at the same time as Ainger, his sound arm over the edge feeling for a handhold, cursed bitterly and dropped back, nursing his hand. Stewart was balancing on one leg, like a stork, keeping carefully still among the high surrounding verdure, and gripping his shin hard with both hands. My mind jumped to snake-bite.

'I suppose I'm just "funny that way"' he said in a high-pitched imitation of Miss Hales' voice on the memorable occasion when we had last heard it, 'but I do like an ordinary looking nettle to *be* just a simple stinging nettle, not a squirt of liquid fire.'

Four days in the jungle had completely cured Stewart's mild infatuation: he had already admitted that it was a mercy the girl was not with us.

'Yes, and I'm just the same!' Ainger fluted back in excellent mimicry, pulling his bandaged arm out of the sling to massage his other wrist violently. This was the kind of situation that brought out all the latent gaiety in him: there were times, especially later on, when his laughter made me want to hit him: my own sense of humour does not always rise superior to adverse conditions.

'This is ghastly!' said Stewart, as the inflammation ran on up his leg in spite of his hold. 'And I can't move without getting another dose. What is this bloody plant? It's so hidden in the grass that you don't notice it, for about two seconds!'

Deotlan told him, with dismay. *Jelatang*, the ferocious Malayan nettle, usually covers a wide area wherever it grows. With a set grin of pain Ainger pulled himself up and joined Stewart, surveying the ground ahead from the bank.

'We'll have to go through it all the same, I'm afraid!' he said. 'This confounded ditch turns right off our route again, and I think there's nettle all the way as far as we can see on this side. Isn't there?' Not trusting his own sight he appealed, through Deotlan, to Wan Nau, whom he had pulled up after him on to an innocuous tuft of grass. She agreed.

'But it isn't a very wide patch, and the other side's fairly good going – thinnish jungle,' he said.

'Nonsense. The women can't cross this,' Stewart said, but Ainger had started a discussion with Deotlan in his hesitating Malay, which was rapidly improving. One of Ainger's least endearing traits, in his position of interpreter-leader, was that while the rest of us were waiting for an important decision he was capable of prolonging a talk with Deotlan to pick up the exact use of an interesting collo-quialism which the other had employed. The discussion went on so long that I thought he must be doing this now; Stewart looked as if he thought so too.

'— *Apabila orang chakap bagitu, apa herti-nya?*'
I heard, and the last phrase I was able to translate
by now as 'What does that mean? When do you
say it?' This superb degree of detachment — usually
a quality that I require in all my friends — palled
on me at the moment as it did on Stewart.

'Finding *jelatang*, of all plants, just here, of all
places, and now, of all times, is the sort of thing that
dreadfully inclines a thoughtful person to credit
the existence of a Supreme Being responsible for
everything that we see about us, here and elsewhere,'
Stewart said to me. 'I don't know what we're waiting
for; obviously we'll have to go on up the watercourse
for a bit.'

'Well, no; Deotlan thinks with me that we'd
better plough straight ahead through the nettle,'
Ainger said, at last. 'Two hundred yards or so
won't take long to get across.'

'I am not going to have Judy sent through this
with her shoes in such a state, and no stockings!'
Stewart said firmly. He added, as an afterthought.
'Neither she nor Mrs. Mardick is exactly dressed
for this! Don't be a fool, Ainger.'

'They have about as much protection as we have,'
Ainger pointed out with what for him was remarkable patience. This was true: the men's thin trou-
ser-legs were in fluttering rags up to the knee, and
a good deal torn beyond that.

'Well, I'm not going to have it, you understand!
We'll go on as we are, till we're clear of this lot.

A few miles farther west isn't going to make much difference, we're so far west already.'

'I can manage to get through two hundred yards of this,' I said.

'No, my dear,' said Stewart. The gentleness returning to his voice contrasted sharply with his previous tone to Ainger. 'You don't know what it's like.'

'Judy can decide for herself! She isn't your wife, you know, Corder!' Ainger said shortly, using my christian name for the first time.

'No, and she doesn't happen to be your property, to order about, either!' There was no gentleness about this.

(I imagined it, and it's happening! How ridiculous beyond words, I thought.)

Even intelligent people, when quarrelling, descend to almost unimaginable depths of obviousness and stupidity. Brilliant flashes of repartee occur only when the speaker is not thoroughly angry, and both men were that, by now.

The partially repressed irritation of several days, spent in circumstances that were particularly fertile for ill-humour, was now over-ripe, and every trifling cause of annoyance between the two men was 'remembered with advantages.' The argument that followed, wandering a long way from the original point, was of an intemperance that I had not heard before between naturally controlled people. It would be difficult to guess how much of what was said was due to instinctive antagonism between them, and how much to the nerve-fraying effect of the hot wind, which we had now endured for forty-eight hours. Looking back, from the spiritual vantage-point of a cool climate, I feel that it was almost impossible that such an outburst on both sides should have matured from such small seeds of anger.

Aghast, Mrs. Mardick imprudently tried to pacify them, with interjections of 'Mr. *Ainger!* But really ! You mustn't – *Mr. Corder* – !' Luckily for the chance of speedy peace, they did not hear her. They reached the stage of open insult, when there would have been fighting if Ainger's incapacitated arm had not put that out of the question. As it was, he gave in furiously on the original point. 'Oh, have it your own way, you damn fool. We'll be properly bitched up, going farther into the hill country!'

He raised a sleeve to wipe a hot face (I was no longer to be cajolled or shamed into generosity with my two remaining handkerchiefs), and in doing so he must have joggled his spectacles: our splicing broke. By luck he caught the glasses as they fell, and Wan Nau, who had listened unconcerned to the altercation – a normal form of intercourse between men in her experience – scolded him like a fishwife for a few seconds, before Deotlan silenced her with a scandalised order.

'Dirty native!' he explained apologetically to us and condemnation could go no farther.

Arnold Ainger blinked down at his glasses, and round at us, and did a wholly admirable thing; he laughed. I felt that no apology was needed for Wan Nau's reproaches: I could only catch the drift of half her tirade against his careless clumsiness, and his abominable disregard of all our trouble, but I was in hearty agreement with every word that I understood: it took us almost as long this time to mend the hinge as it had done on the first occasion, and this was the third break in two days due to his forgetfulness. Stewart, owner of the torn-up coat, contributed a rag with bad grace. He was still boiling inwardly, I could see, unlike Ainger. I have never met anyone who recovered his equanimity more rapidly than that impersonal man.

We went on, up the watercourse, and it was a heavy additional burden to our spirits to know that every costly mile we covered took us nearly at right angles to our true direction. But Stewart may have been right and not merely obstinate, as he sometimes was: I had not had a sample of the alternative route through the *jelatang*.

The young deer had not gone far among six, and we were in need of food again by evening. Stewart and Deotlan stalked birds. The bare, twisting watercourse was a good place for this if for nothing else: view and action were less restricted here than in the jungle.

A covey of pelantots rose unexpectedly while Deotlan was working his way towards them under cover of the bank. They flew wildly in all directions. I glanced up into the white glare overhead to see what had alarmed them, for their fear seemed to be directed at something above. I saw nothing for a second or two, and then a growing black wedge, falling headlong from the empty sky, took shape among the dark spots dancing before my eyes because I had looked towards the sun. With the pelantots flying already it was hopeless to try a shot at them, though some of them had come much nearer than they had been before. We watched while the falcon that menaced them chose its prey, checking its dive with a wing's flick, no more, to circle effortlessly over the covey. Lordly in its unhurried assurance, it marked down one of the frenzied pelantots and then flung itself earthwards again, gathering speed with a few eager strokes of its wings before they folded, composedly, and it dropped in a gorgeous stoop that transplanted me, breathless with remembered excitement, to a low cliff at home from which in childhood I had watched just this scene enacted between a tiercel and a plover: other, softer air but the same magnificent mastery of it by attacker and victim: different bird actors but the same swift tragedy.

It was surprising how quickly the other pelantots, noticing which of their number was the quarry, changed their panic to a leisurely withdrawal from the scene of contest. The chosen bird itself, racing for the shelter of the jungle, must have known instantly, too, and realised also that it could not reach cover in the few seconds available, for it stopped its zig-zag flying, designed to put the falcon off its choice while that was still uncertain, and dropping close to the ground, flew steadily along the watercourse in our direction, while the enemy hurtled down from above. There was a fine exhibition of control and judgment on the part of the smaller bird: a swerve one second too soon, and the falcon with its deadly precision in the air would have deflected its fall and followed. The timing of the falcon's approach by the pelantot was superb, for at the end of its stoop a falcon may be travelling at something like eighty miles an hour. A split second before the slim living wedge of feathered muscle and braced talons would have struck it squarely, breaking its back with the impact, the pelantot flung itself upwards at a sharp angle, so that the falcon, missing by perhaps an inch, shot below it with the air whistling in its wake.

The instinct to enjoy someone else's battle seems to be one of the few universal traits in men, however diverse their natures — and we had three very different specimens together here. I was only interested because I was passionately fond of birds and wanted the affair to be over. Mrs. Mardick and Wan Nau were not concerned at all; but each of the three men was watching as if this fight were of the greatest personal importance.

We were only a few yards away, and I saw at this

point why the pelantot had deliberately given up the advantage of height in which to manoeuvre, and kept a few feet off the ground. It was by a sheer miracle of banking and swerving that the falcon was not dashed to pieces on the stones: a trace of sandy dust rose into the air as it turned and soared upwards, so dangerously close to earth it had come. It seemed to climb the sky almost as swiftly as it fell again, an instant later, in another breath-taking dive which the pelantot avoided. The birds passed so close to us, and were so totally regardless of us as intruders in this game of life and death, that we could appreciate the tactics of both. The aim of the falcon was to keep its prey in the open, penned into the watercourse by the overhanging banks and the pelantot's own need of curtailing the freedom of the falcon's dive by fear of the ground. The pelantot's slender chance lay in tiring out the watchfulness of its enemy before it became exhausted itself, and gaining time to dash for the jungle. Time after time it took brilliant momentary advantage of the sheltering bank, of a hollow between stones, of the trunk of a tree that had fallen with its branches in the watercourse and its torn roots still resting on the lip above, making a barrier round which the little bird could dodge. Twice, as the pair flashed by, I, the nearest of the party, could have saved the pelantot by a shout or the wave of an arm between it and the pursuer, as I should have done for the plover – unfairly and sentimentally – if it had come

close enough on the day when I had watched it
fighting as coolly and gallantly and hopelessly in a
wet English wind above a familiar ploughed field.
But by now I had been too anxiously and hungrily
on the side of the hunter myself to be stirred by
facile pity: I did not move. When the pelantot
tired the falcon played with it like a cat with a
mouse, letting it flutter up almost into the safety of
the trees before driving it down again. The pelantot
was killed on the edge of the jungle in the end, and
we killed the falcon at the moment when, grown
unwary with success, it stood motionless for an
instant with outstretched wings over the dying
bird on the bank, a wild symbol of victory.

It was not good food, but we were some way
beyond being particular.

With the birds, Deotlan picked up a short stout
piece of trimmed wood, with a broken cord attached
to it.

'There is a village near here,' he told Ainger.

This was the cross-piece off a spear used in a
tiger drive, not in ordinary hunting, and Malays
would not be likely to drive tiger in such jungle
unless their homes and belongings were menaced:
the risks were too great. The broken end of the cord
had not yet unravelled at all; it must have been
dropped fairly recently. But it was too late to search
for the village that night.

We had an especially long bout of the usual
evening trouble with Mrs Mardick while the

shelter was being rigged, and as it turned out this was the penultimate straw on our endurance of her. Another insignificant irritation from the same source, added to what we already carried vindictively in memory, and three of us felt that our tolerance would give way. She wanted – she demanded and she begged – knowing the pleading vain before she began – to be allowed to take her share in the night watch. The rest of us took turns of what we guessed to be about an hour and a half, sitting in front of the shelter with Deotlan's rifle lying close by or resting across our knees. (The two wrist-watches in the party had been ruined in the swamp, and each person called the next when he or she decided that the time was up. So far there had been no grumbling.)

Knowing Mrs. Mardick's phenomenal powers of sleep and her inability either to concentrate, or to be impressed by the seriousness of any situation, we did not trust her with this job. She was so kind hearted that if any of the rest of us had looked particularly tired she would undoubtedly have prolonged her own spell, and dosed off, for sleep dropped upon her without warning in a few seconds. Even if she remained awake, unless something of considerable size put its head out of the nearest thicket within the first few minutes of her watch, her look-out would have been of the most per-functory nature. She considered that we were unduly nervous. This was tiger country, she knew, but she had never yet seen one of these animals outside a menagerie, so that they did not really exist for her.

Still, she wanted her turn in the exciting game. Fair do's, she said. Until this journey I had always been glad of the tremendous physical courage of unimaginative women: it made my work easier. I have not felt the same about it since knowing her.

Stewart took the first spell. When he crawled back into the shelter under the bank to be relieved by Arnold Ainger, he interrupted a discussion between the two of us about modern poetry, of which we talked in low voices, with one ear to the other's words and one to the disturbing soft noises of the brooding forest above and around us. Curiously, this anxious division of attention lent lustre to the tranquil quotations that we gave one another: a spurious heightening of quality, certainly, but so intense that everything that we referred to in this talk has kept for me some of the sharp new character it gained that night. I was astonished at discovering this liking for poetry, which I shared, in Arnold Ainger; but then I was always being surprised by new and apparently inconsistent sides of his nature; he was emotionally hard, and intellectually impressionable. I thought his literary taste very good (which merely meant, of course, that it more or less coincided with mine!) and I liked particularly his complete lack of self-consciousness when he quoted poetry by heart.

When Stewart stretched out alongside, I put my head on his arm, as I generally did for want of a more comfortable pillow. In a few minutes he rolled over, letting it slip off on to the stones. I protested crossly because I had just fallen asleep for the first time.

'Well, I didn't do it on purpose, stoopid!' he answered in the same tone. 'My arm's numb.'

Sleepily I tried to move back into the former position.

'Here, no, Judy! Why the hell should I have pins and needles all night. You've got a better place than I have, anyway. Can't you find a spot for your head between stones, or scrape up some sand under it, or something?'

Ainger, now sitting out in front, gave his quiet laugh. 'And you were the man who wanted the eunuch's-eye-view!' he said. 'You seem to be well on the way to getting it.'

Later on he roused Deotlan from the other shelter and joined us. Stewart was soon asleep, and I thought that Ainger was too until he moved restlessly. I do not know what told him that I was also awake: he said as though there had been no break in our conversation, 'You know how incomplete lines jolt about in your head like tunes, and you can't get rid of them? – "The sorrows of our proud and angry dust Are from eternity and shall not fail." What comes after that, before "Shoulder the sky . . . and drink your ale"?'

' "Bear them we can, and if we can we must. Shoulder the sky, my lad . . ." ' I said, conjuring up for myself in a line and a half the quickening sting of the whole poem, as all a day's diverse memories leap back to life sometimes with one breath of a familiar smell.

'Yes. Thanks. Of course. "And the flesh grieve on other bones than ours," ' he said contentedly and went to sleep, while I lay awake speculating idly – mainly to fill in the time, because I was always a bad sleeper – whether any happily-loved women knew Housman so well by heart, or as much of other men's work as I did without having learnt any of it intentionally. But as long as I could remember, even at the time of my deepest content, I had been preoccupied with books and theories and the like, though in a rather practical way, and not with the cares and interests that make up the lives of the satisfied wives and mothers I have known. I wondered whether I had been born without much chance of the less intermittent forms of human happiness. There is a spiritual arrogance, it seems, in choosing the great, far off deities to worship: lesser gods of hearth and street and market are offended and take toll of simple things. It is not wise for women to go whoring after beauty and truth: theirs are the jealous little household gods, made to their measure, ready to be kind if given allegiance; and most women chiefly desire kindness in a god. From Wan Nau, with Ainger translating,

I had heard of Fengi, the friendly little thing behind
water-in-the-pot, whom she occasionally propitiated
before she cooked for us. But in the lore of her
people there was also Ahri, I knew; lord of wide,
raging seas; sender of crashing rain and of floods.
He gave nothing to his worshippers, and could not
often be placated when angry. Wan Nau sensibly
shrugged her shoulders and spoke vaguely when I
asked about him; she was concerned only with
Fengi. But I doubt whether those who have once
glimpsed, even from a distance, Ahri and the other
lovely, barren gods of his vast stature can ever
return contentedly to the little deities who have at
their disposal so much more of the gift of human
happiness.

I half woke again, because of the discomfort of
the stones, long before I was due to relieve Wan
Nau, and shifted on to my side, facing Ainger,
unsuccessfully trying to find an easier place for
my head. As I stirred he slipped an arm behind my
neck, pulling me closer so that my head lay comfortably in the hollow of his shoulder.

'You'll get pins and needles,' I said in drowsy
gratitude.

'I daresay. There'll be compensations. I wasn't
brought up with you.'

I slept at ease until Wan Nau touched my arm,
which was then lying across Ainger's chest, with my
hand on his other shoulder. I had turned completely
to him, one bent knee resting over both of his

as he lay on his back. I was surprised and a little amused that my sleeping body should have returned so promptly to an habitual attitude of the past, either not knowing or not caring that this man was physically a stranger.

Shivering from the effects of reluctant waking, though the hot wind still blew, I sat outside by the dying ·fire, while night ebbed invisibly from the jungle, some while before dawn. I tried to keep my mind safely occupied in this eerie hour by puzzling out which of these motives — ignorance or indifference — had prompted the action of that curiously separate entity, my body, for which I am held responsible though the majority of its functions are beyond my conscious control, and only known to me in theory. I hoped that it was ignorance, but suspected that it was not. Myself, I never give anyone the benefit of a doubt of this kind, because people have given it to me throughout my life on all possible occasions, and I have very seldom deserved it.

CHAPTER VI

THE JETTISONING OF
MRS. MARDICK

ALL the next day we looked for the village. It was essential that we should get native foot-coverings to replace our worn-out shoes, and we must get more ammunition or more rice; both if possible. But we did not find it.

Once the muggy breeze brought us, for a few seconds, a stench that was partly of decaying flesh and partly something else that was strange to me. But there were many different smells in the jungle; great stinking fungi of marvellous hue, dead things, and the rich rottenness of wet vegetation, and flower scents, too, which made up together an unforgettable savour that I had almost learnt to disregard while loathing it: I took little notice of this new ingredient at the moment. Later, Deotlan told me that it was tiger; the smell of a kill mingling with the smell of the beast itself, a reek that clings to any place in which it has remained for some time.

We heard the unmistakeable noise of a tiger that night: not the coughing roar with which it charges, but the oddly high-pitched, snarling whine of impatience with which, in its arrogance, the beast tells the jungle that it is out hunting.

Two people instead of one kept guard all night; a practically useless precaution, but the only one that we could take. And even Mrs. Mardick remained awake part of the time, whispering courageously when we wanted silence, speaking half under her breath when we whispered. She was not going to risk sleep-walking to-night, she said with an effort of gaiety. She was occasionally prone to this trouble at home, she told us; and once, the second night after we left the ship, she had certainly crawled as far as the open side of the shelter before I realised that she was not conscious and woke her. But from the way she slept I doubted that she had ever really walked in her sleep; many people can get out of bed, but no farther, without waking; sleep-walking was a supposedly interesting attribute with which she had formerly credited herself for conversational purposes, and now she believed her own myth, I thought. She harped on the subject: wouldn't it be *dreadful* if she woke up to discover that she had gone to meet the tiger? Verbally — regretfully — we agreed that it would.

My foot was too inflamed to let me do more than hobble the next day, practically barefoot as I was by then. I stayed by the shelter, alone, while the others split into two parties, trying to find the village. It was one of the most nerve-racking days I have known.

To the resentment of the possessive Wan Nau, Deotlan suspended from a tree a few yards away, before he left, a big leaf containing the scanty remains of last night's food, as an offering to the spirits for my safety. Most of the time, during the interminable hours that followed, I kept my eyes on this. It was better than staring into the forest, because I was practically defenceless, though the possession of Ainger's revolver was a faint comfort. I saw nothing visit the leaf, but when one party returned at midday with news of failure, Mrs. Mardick looked into it as she always did with these spirit tributes, and found, with her customary expressions of surprise, that it was empty. I had known it would be. These leaf receptacles always were, a few minutes after being offered. Yet we could not stop her looking, nor being astonished afresh each time. Her amused interest made me uneasy; it was an offence against the thing or things in the forest of which all the rest of us avoided speaking plainly.

Her party went back to the search. Hours later Stewart returned by himself, sending my blood racing with acute fear at the sound of something approaching through the crackling undergrowth, until I saw him and could have wept with relief.

'Found it! About two miles off. I said I'd fetch you, and Ainger for once hadn't some almighty better plan of his own.'

He stooped over me as I sat on the ground, and

taking my face between his hands, kissed it un-expectedly. I was so glad to see him that I did not mind.

'How you would hate your hair if you could see it now, darling!' he said, slipping down beside me and still holding me. 'It never looks quite natural when it's untidy, but now it's got a cheaply arti-ficial appearance. The sort of ploughed-field wave that you get a lot of for half a guinea, I believe. Regular as anything. Still, I've never minded its vulgarity as much as you have!' Any approach to love-making between us was bound to be more difficult than between strangers. He was forced by the embarrassment of long familiarity to use a deprecating tone. We both knew that he had always thought my conventionally pretty hair wasted on my uninspiring face.

'I can imagine it,' I said. 'Positively nasty with chocolate-box-lid curls. Let go, and don't be an ass, Nookie.'

He took no notice, his attention being engaged on some tight little strands that he was trying, with his free hand, to unwind and twist in the opposite direction. 'The foulest part of this whole business is having you in it, though in a way there's no one I'd rather have. Judy, dear – !'

'Look here,' I said, pushing him away, 'you know as well as I do that this sudden rush of affection is all due –'

Stewart pulled me into his arms and kissed me

to stop my talking. 'The mistake I've made with you for years,' he said, as one who stumbles on a discovery, 'is listening to what you say instead of noticing things about you. Is there anything you'd like to know about your face, my dear? (Apart from whether it's clean, of course: we're none of us that, by this time.) You haven't been able to look at it for about a week – seems more than that, doesn't it? – and before that I don't think I'd seen it properly for years, if ever. You must have missed it, haven't you? It's a face I shall miss horribly if I ever lose sight of it for as much as a week again!'

'This is not only "so sudden",' I said discouragingly, 'but so silly! I know exactly what my face looks like when it's hot and tired and dirty. Something by Laura Knight – one of her passionately plain women.'

'Well, if it is, I like her work after all.'

'Owing to the abnormal circumstances,' I persisted, harking back to the former protest; but Stewart kissed me again, and made love to me, with a deft light-heartedness oddly at variance with our surroundings, until we came near the village. I put an arm round his shoulders and used him as a crutch in order to get along without too much discomfort.

It was a very small community. All the men were away until evening on a tiger drive, as they had been each day for the past three days. A party of them were starting as soon as possible for Pedagor, to work in the rubber plantation. Before leaving their women they were anxious to rid the locality of the beasts that had made work in the padi clearing too dangerous for weeks. One tiger the villagers had already killed, with the loss of a man. But for the last two days they had been unsuccessful. They had four guns only in the whole village, and the beaters were too few: the quarry broke back through the line, though every boy strong enough to use a spear had been requisitioned by the headman to augment their numbers.

They agreed to give us foot coverings of dressed skin, a very small quantity of rice – practically nothing – and ten rounds of ammunition, not for money but in return for the help of our men the next day.

We were offered accommodation for the night, which Deotlan and Wan Nau accepted at first, in two of the huts: but the four of us from the ship were still plague suspects, though the likelihood of our developing the disease was growing blessedly slight. Ainger declined the offer politely and vaguely, giving it to be understood that we were 'just funny that way,' being Europeans. Deotlan, much less polite and vague with Malays, then said that naturally he preferred to sleep with the other whites, and Wan Nau should come with him. We built shelters close enough to the huts to make it worth while risking a whole night's sleep for everyone, unbroken by watches. Here, in this up-country village,

Deotlan was at last accepted on his own valuation: to us he looked mostly native: to the villagers of an isolated settlement where there had been no half-castes, he seemed mainly white. He talked rapid and incomprehensible English to us while the headman was within earshot, and chucked a chest when addressed (once) as Tuan. It was pathetic, but not in Wan Nau's happy eyes.

From curiosity I looked into the hut in which I was to have slept, with two of the others. The occupants had not proposed to turn out for us; there was enough room for all, in their opinion. It was built on the usual plan of Malay family dwellings, over an open slat floor through which refuse had evidently been thrown for a long while. A small living room, where three men slept, opened on to a tiny compartment at the back, used by the women. There were four of these in the household, one far gone in pregnancy. Above, on a level with the eaves, was a platform or wide shelf, on which three children slept perilously. By comparison the shelter seemed quite spacious that night.

A little before dawn the *pawang*, who was the village wise-man, doctor and priest (of local cults only, though he was nominally a Mohammedan) made a propitiatory chant in which he asked the forest djinns to give us 'these buffalo.' At this point the tired, anxious hunters standing round him in the darkness of the village street murmured in chorus, to call the attention of the ruling spirits to the fact that he did not mean buffalo, without alarming the guardian djinn of the tigers by speaking of them directly. At the time none of this seemed ludicrous; it was extraordinarily impressive.

While they prayed in the growing light, I saw men testing the lashing of the cross-piece on their spears, which was designed to prevent a transfixed tiger from clawing its way up the shaft to reach the bearer. Very slender defence they looked, these long spears that were handed out to the two from our party who were to help the beaters. As our best shot, Stewart took the rifle, and went ahead with four others to the natural clearing made by a stream that ran within a mile of a dense patch of jungle. Here a tiger or tigers were thought to have had a lair, though no one knew if anything were still there.

The weakest points in the human net spread round the thickets were always the ends of the line, where the hunters waited for the beaters to close in. Usually, boys climbed into trees at these corners of the rough capital D formed by the whole manoeuvre, and watched for the beasts' attempt to steal through, shouting a warning of their coming and giving the exact direction if possible. But every boy old enough for the job bore that day, with a nervous swagger, his newly-given status of manhood, and his spear with the additional wooden hilt. As a white man and a reputed shot (Deotlan was a first-class liar and our prestige had become his) Stewart was to be last man on the right of the widely extended line. He would not understand information shouted in Malay, and having been a good climber as a child I offered to act as look-out for him, if I could walk so far – I was still lame though the sore was healing. The offer was accepted at once, though dubiously, by the headman, a little to my surprise. Unasked, the *pawang* stepped forward, squatted down and put out his hand towards my foot. He examined the sole of it perfunctorily, and said with authority that I could certainly walk to the stream.

'So that's that, Judy!' said Ainger, grinning as he translated. 'We're damn-well going to earn everything we get, apparently – and heaven help Stewart if he doesn't live up to the legend Deotlan has started about him.'

With a sombre glance at me, Wan Nau came forward to volunteer as the other look-out. Only jealousy would have made her do it, for the idea of a woman taking even a safe part in a game-drive was improper to her, though she had done a man's job of a really arduous kind for years. The villagers would not let their own women share this work, but we were different.

We moved off silently. I was inaudibly cursing the *pawang*, who had made drawing back impossible for me, long before we reached the appointed spot. Climbing into the tree was not as difficult as walking: it was soon over, and one could choose where one's weight came on the foot.

It was terrific, the tension of waiting, listening for the noise of the beaters in the distance, listening with every muscle, every breath quivering and controlled. I had cramp, sitting in the fork of a cinnamon tree, and could not alter my position enough to relieve it.

The beaters, lightly armed and forcing their way yard by yard into blind jungle, had by far the more dangerous part in the drive. And my mind was with Arnold Ainger. I knew, with the coming of a new, sick sense of physical fear for some-one else, that his risk had suddenly been added to mine – or perhaps not suddenly, but I realised it now for the first time. His safety mattered more than anyone else's; it was the only thing that mattered; and I fought against the realisation of it. I had been afraid on my own account at practi-cally every moment since leaving the ship; it would be misery past bearing to be afraid for two in these circumstances. There is always fear in the shadow of love of any kind, the giving of a hostage to fate. But as we were situated then it would be almost unthinkable, and it would be absurd, I reflected, listening with my heart as well as my ears to the far-off tapping in the forest. There, men were desperately afraid no doubt, as I was afraid here, but luckier than I, each was afraid for himself alone. Surely one could not suffer on behalf of a man almost before one had ceased suffering for another? But that is not true, unfortunately. It is extraordinary how much wretchedness a human heart can ingeniously contrive to hold at any one time. And yet there was a brilliant, excited joy besides unhappiness in the knowledge that I wanted this man, Arnold Ainger. It was like a rainbow in a dark cloud sweeping across my sky, and in a way I was glad that I could not prevent its coming.

Below me the men, spaced out at distances of fifty yards or so, stood like statues, their rifles cocked, but resting slackly in careless hands, one might have imagined from the calm of each pose. Only the quick turn of all heads as one, at the slightest sound from the jungle, made evident the force of the charge of nervous electricity that was firing from brain to brain, making the minutes seem hours as the first of the driven game began at last to trickle through the waiting line, in a thin stream that increased as the sounds of beating came nearer. Monkeys and deer of all sorts, huge jungle rats and civets dashed by. I saw a big snake and a harmless little honey bear close together, taking no notice of one another. The beaters were not far away now. The apparent calm of the hunters broke. Some of them half crouched over their guns. The man next to Stewart was soundlessly muttering what I suppose were incantations. I saw Stewart ceaselessly shifting the grip of his left hand a fraction of an inch up or down the stock. Most unnerving of all was the feeling that, unseen by us, the fierce eyes of creatures slinking desperately, angrily about the narrowing cover, observed us from a few yards away.

Time and again something of fair size moved in the thick undergrowth to my left, sneaking into safety through the diminishing gap, but it would turn out to be wild pig, or, once, a young tapir.

The drive lasted several hours, I thought. There was a moment of gorgeous exaltation, a crisis of tingling excitement, longed for and dreaded, when the head man among the beaters cried out at last on a high, thin note the *Ralawat*, the call to prayer, and fifteen or more young voices took it up full-throatedly. There remained only one dense wall of forest between us and them. The cry was answered from the jungle as it was designed to be – it had no religious significance on this occasion – and answered magnificently, with a roar that quieted the chattering monkeys and squirrels, sending the smaller four-footed beasts belly down to the ground, paralysed with fear, during a silence in which the voices of the beaters came to us, shouting to one another to close in, to wait, to press forward again.

It was impossible to tell from what direction the roar came; it filled the air all round. A tigress bounded into the clearing by the stream, near the other end of the line of hunters. The heavy body scarcely touched the ground, for she was back in cover before the nearest man could fire effectively. A few seconds later came a shrill human scream from the farther side of the thicket, and my blood

stopped, and the scream came again with pande-
monium, but I heard a voice that I thought was
Arnold Ainger's, shouting to Deotlan.

Through the screen of creepers I saw a patch of
tawny movement to my left, and yelled to Stewart.
He fired just clear of the beaters, and the thing,
whatever it was, leapt back into the ground that was
soon enclosed on all sides by men. The tigress,
followed by a half-grown cub, launched herself
from the thicket; swift as a bird she came across the
stream at a point about equidistant from the second
and third man on our side. Another bound and she
would have been hidden in the farther edge of the
jungle, but a bullet caught her in the shoulder. She
stood poised for a second with lashing tail and fangs
bare, raging at the hunters, the most superb embodiment of vitality that the jungle showed me.
She saw her cub fall, and charged along the line,
attacking the third man. But her leap at him was
short; we found afterwards that the first shot had
torn through the shoulder muscle, splintering the
bone. Two of the hunters fired together, and she
sank slowly on her four legs as though bowing with
a ghastly stateliness, and then crumpled up and
died.

Nothing more came out of the jungle, while the
beaters combed it to the last foot. A panther had
broken back through their line, smashing one man's
spear and opening his arm nearly to the bone with
a passing swipe as it leapt by his shoulder; but the

men, bunching together at Ainger's call to Deotlan, had prevented the tigress's attempt to follow.

I remained in the tree longer than necessary, feeling sick, after Ainger appeared unhurt save for many thorn scratches on face and arms. That first moment of seeing him again was full of amazement for me, amazement that I had not seen the familiar face and figure before as I saw them now, not exactly as if for the first time, but as if every trifling thing about him – the way he stood when he was tired, the incurable trick of lifting his glasses by the side – took on a new, lovely importance. His image had not changed in my eyes, but it was lit from within. There were no chance characteristics about him, as about everyone else, it seemed; no insignificant traits and tastes and unconscious habits that could be altered without affecting the man himself. All things pertaining to him, to the minutest detail that perhaps I had not yet noticed, were superbly part of a whole; and nothing must be altered here, for it was almost too excellent, too absurdly painful to bear, that he should look and move and speak exactly in the way that I remembered. And that he was safe. This is love, to my thinking: not the endowing of another person with alien beauty – I never considered Arnold Ainger as good-looking as Stewart, who was himself nothing out of the ordinary – but the flowering into significance of their most ordinary attributes, as wonderful as the putting on of leaves by a bare tree: so that it would be sacrilege to credit them with more loveliness than they possess, for the marvel is that they exist, just as they are.

The panting men that had joined us were leaning on their spears, with eyes half closed. Their twitching limbs were shining with sweat. I could not imagine how these villagers had stood, four days running, this terrible physical and nervous strain. It cured my feeling of nausea to be called by Stewart to see what could be done for the wounded man, but he would not trust me, as a woman and one belonging to neither of his one-true-faiths, to touch his mutilated arm, except to put on a tourniquet well away from the injury. He preferred to wait for the ministrations of the *pawang*, the one man who had remained in the village because a birth was expected, and he was in any case too old to be of much use as a beater. Arnold heard Deotlan tell the sufferer reassuringly that some of the women of his race (that is, the white people) were as skilled in attending injuries as any *pawang*, but the man remained unmoved in his decision.

(Incidentally, in this eulogy I think Deotlan exaggerated, because of what I saw the old man do to the arm in the evening with a strip of skin cut from the same place on the foreleg of the tigress. It should have been from the panther responsible, but he 'charmed' the still bleeding wound that it might not discover the substitution. As a faith healer the *pawang* must have been far ahead of me and most of my colleagues: otherwise he could not have worked any cures at all, as he must have done sometimes for the man to show such confidence in him.)

Mrs. Mardick had had her own excitement in the village; the baby of the woman in whose hut we had been invited to sleep had been born a little while after we left. 'My dear, I *wish* you'd been here!' she said, not interested in the details of our day after hearing that there had been no serious casualties. '*You* could have really helped instead of that dreadful old man. I'm afraid I interfered a little – I really *had* to – and they let me because I was a white woman. Isn't that remarkable – quite different to your case. But of course at a time like that all women do feel rather drawn together. It just shows. I'll tell you what he did and what I did, and you say if it was all right –'

'Yes, if they're both still alive, it was,' I said wearily. 'That's the only test in normal cases.' It is a widespread fallacy that doctors love to ply their trade gratuitously.

'Wouldn't you like to come and see them?'

'No, I wouldn't,' I said, so emphatically that she looked hurt. 'A confinement is less of a novelty to me than a tiger drive,' I explained, 'though I shouldn't mind if I never saw either again. I just want to lie on my back and do nothing until Deotlan's finished cooking.'

I had had enough in one day of big game hunting;

and maternity is a totally ungracious thing, beneath
the sentimentality heaped upon it. Only once have
I seen it made beautiful for an instant, by a chance
grouping of a woman's thick white thigh, statuesque
in its rigidity, and the new-born child lying in the
arch made by her raised knee, with its arm thrown
back above its head, and the strangest expression
of peace that I have ever seen on the face of a living
child. The cord was not yet cut, stretching in an
arc between them. For a second I was staggered
by such unexpected loveliness as they showed
together, and then I bent over them to help her, and
the scene changed back instantly to a normal birth,
which is generally uglier than death, only so much
pleasanter to witness that one rarely realises it.

They were pleased with us in the village. It was
said to be Stewart's second shot that had maimed the
tigress. He thought not, but we did not argue.

At last the hot wind had died: in its place was
an oppressive, sultry calm that made sleep difficult
that night, and our shelters unnecessary as a protection against the usual cold and damp of the early
hours: but as we could not tell that the heat would
last all night we rigged them to be on the safe side,
choosing a spot some way outside the village because
of the noise of the meagre but prolonged farewell
feast to the Pedagor party, which had started as soon
as we returned.

The heavy atmosphere made every movement
tedious as we wove in, without cutting them, the

long bamboo shoots that formed the lean-to side of the shelters. We turned in before the light faded. Mrs. Mardick rallied us on our inability to bear the heat with her equanimity, before dropping off at once into her childlike slumber. 'Nice' was the last word I ever heard from her, as I think it was probably the first, or one of the first.

I woke when it was not quite full dark, and I could just make out Stewart sitting up by me, searching for an ingit that he wanted to expel. From every corner of the shelter in turn came the intermittent shrilling of this creature, which in easier surroundings Europeans call the gin-and-bitters insect, because the first chirp of its evening activity coincides with the customary hour for drinks. It leads both the morning and evening choruses in the jungle. The village was now quiet, but I could not tell whether the faint light outside came from dawn or the after-glow of sunset. Arnold, Wan Nau and Deotlan had the first watches, but I did not remember the order, and I was so chronically worn out in these days that I had no idea how long I had slept. Arnold was sitting out in front now, and beyond him the other two were standing, she with her arm about Deotlan's waist, staring up at the unusual reddish tinge in the sky. It was unbearably stuffy.

I asked Stewart what he thought the time was, and he did not know either. He crawled out with the captured ingit in his hand. 'I've been wondering professionally myself whether this brute should be technically described as a Harbinger, or merely an Aftermath. Better ask the omniscient Ainger!'

Arnold heard that, but remained unruffled. ' "Interesting Facts About Interesting Insects"; it's a harbinger!' he returned. 'Dawn in half an hour or so – and you're due on then, Corder, so you might as well take over from me now. Then we shan't have to disturb Judy again by the change.'

The last few words were said with such an excess of amiability, as well as a hint of amusement, that I wondered what lay behind them.

'You can dam' well take your full time!' Stewart was saying, softly and viciously, when I crawled out too to get some air. But outside it was little fresher than in the shelter.

I did not know till later, when Stewart told me about it with recovered good humour, that some while before Arnold went out to relieve Wan Nau, he had also neatly relieved Stewart of the burden of my weight on his arm and shoulder. Stewart and I were both asleep then, and remained so; I only remembered afterwards that I had thought him very restless. I cannot imagine how Arnold managed to gather me to him affectionately without rousing me altogether, unless, again, it was that part of me knew and did not care. But Stewart woke to find the transfer accomplished, though how long ago it had been managed he could not tell; I was then serenely asleep in Arnold Ainger's arms. I only sighed and stirred and did not wake when he left me. Arnold knew that Stewart must have suspected it was not my doing, and most of the morning, until the matter was eclipsed by more important things, he was slightly more conciliatory than usual to Stewart, who was a little less cordial still in return.

The light grew. We saw one another's faces, drawn and pale and dirty. The two white men, not having shaved for a week, were growing past the villainous early stage of scrubbiness and were approaching bearded respectability. (Deotlan had a very light growth naturally, a native trait which discomforted him.) But there are only two types of young bearded men, to me; those who look ruffianly and those who only achieve quaintness, for the hair somehow remains irrelevant. Stewart was one of the unfortunates who look silly, unshaven; I liked the tough that Arnold had become; but possibly this was not a strictly impartial view; he may have been as unimpressive in this state as Stewart, only that I could not see it.

None of us could sleep any more because of the heat, except of course Mrs. Mardick, who had not awakened. Little was said between the original three of us, but the men's differences were dissolved for the moment at least, by a thought process that affected us all at about the same moment. A long train of cause and effect passed before our inner eyes. There was only need for a few unfinished sentences, a half expressed suggestion, and a question or two. I do not know who took the final decision, but it was some time before we moved, and then action was unanimous. Gently we unwove the standing bamboos from the cross-pieces of broken lianes that bound the shelters: we thrust these lengths of creeper into the surrounding jungle, out of sight. Very cautiously – though there was little need for this care; no ordinary sound would wake Mrs. Mardick – we pulled out of the ground the forked sticks that had supported the roof branches, and with these we went quietly away, starting our day's journey north-eastwards, according to directions given us by the headman. I was limping slightly still and kept one of these sticks as a support. I should like to have it now as a memento: with no tangible evidence that this extraordinary morning's work was ever accomplished it is difficult to credit my own behaviour.

In a few minutes, we knew, the resilient bamboos would stand as though they had never been bent. The grass on which five of us had lain would lose the impression of our bodies. Nothing would show that there had been shelters there. In their wealth of strange tree forms, many parts of the jungle are bewilderingly alike: individual bamboo clumps are unidentifiable, save by the trained observer, and Mrs. Mardick was not observant.

A self-convinced sleep walker, she would wake half way through the day, probably; in a place that would appear to her other than that in which she had gone to sleep, with us. Even she would be able to find the village, after a little search; or probably the well-disposed villagers would find her first. Some of them were going to Pedagor, from where she could get a ship to Bahila in time, no doubt. And by a lucky chance and her own unselfishness, she had carried nearly all our Malayan small change for some days: she should have no difficulty in persuading the party to take her the dreary journey back to the place from which we had come.

It was an appalling thing to have done. In retrospect I can hardly believe that we left her there like that. And still I feel no remorse whatever about it. I never had any. Nor did the others. That is the effect of close contact with the Malayan jungle. I have not heard what happened to her, though I imagine that she came through safely; but somehow I cannot get up enough interest to make widespread enquiries. If I met her by accident I am sure that she, not I, would be apologetic, for she would be thinking of the terrible anxiety and sorrow she must have caused us by disappearing like that from among us; and she would not be reproachful because we had gone on after, presumably, only half a day's search for her. She had a far finer nature than any of us. All the same, I feel fairly sure that in certain parts of Trenganu, and perhaps also in the interior of Pahang and Kelantan, which I visited reluctantly later – though nowhere else, I am certain – I should do the same abominable thing again in similar circumstances.

CHAPTER VII

'*ESPRIT-DE-STY*'

IT was wonderful by contrast, the quiet in which we walked all the morning. After a time our progress, slow as it was for my sake, became painful to me again, in spite of the relief of the new, soft coverings on my feet; but I have never felt so nearly safe, before or since, in the jungle. We were free of the menace of that heroically gay, irrepressible affront of sound flung into the pressing silence of the forest. Yet sometimes, when I glanced at Arnold Ainger, fear came back suffocatingly for a minute, because I had become doubly vulnerable, and the smaller, constant perils of the jungle had grown proportionately, or more than proportionately in my mind, for I also wanted to live, myself, more keenly than before.

We were climbing steeply. The headman had confirmed Ainger's surmise that, having put this range of foothills between us and our destination by our detour inland, we should be wiser to cross them rather than to go back. In a valley on the farther side, we learnt, ran the river that had made it impossible for us to reach Kintaling by way of the coast. (Deotlan had nodded in a bored and impatient manner at the information, making it clear that he had known this all along but not wishing to burden our minds with details of no immediate importance, had refrained from telling us before this garrulous dodderer butted in.) We kept Deotlan with us still solely because he was a good fire-maker, and a nice rogue, and we liked Wan Nau; also – probably the main reason – we should lose his rifle if we dismissed him, and the villagers could not be bribed to part with any of their four guns. He was the only person in the party who still took seriously his official position of guide. Even Wan Nau recognised that we were more or less lost half the time; but this was likely to prolong her association with him and she was glad. She, like Mrs. Mardick, was not afraid, as the four of us were all the time: she had so little to lose.

From a fair distance north and south of the place where we should strike the river, if we followed his directions, the old man told us, the stream flowed sluggishly, gathering itself for its leap through the narrows to a long series of falls. Above these, in all its wider reaches, it was fordable with care at this time of the year. If we followed the river down to its delta, two or three days' journey from the hills, we could skirt the shore for the last half-day's march to Kintaling. Once again it all sounded hearteningly easy, but I was now even less of an optimist than I had been.

The oppressive, stagnant weight of the atmosphere had not lightened by midday, and we had met particularly hard going. It was this, I thought, as well as the discomfort of my foot, which was making me feel more spent than usual by the time that we stopped for a feed of rice. I did not want to eat. My head swam and my legs felt leaden. Deotlan, close beside me, was smoking native tobacco given him in the village. Yearning for civilised smoke myself, I tried it but did not like it. As I was indifferently shrivelling a leech off my wrist with the end of the rank cigarette, while we lounged against a tree trunk, a faint air – a hot breath blowing for a second on the back of my neck, – drifted through the jungle and passed on. It stirred my hair unpleasantly. In a few minutes this strange breeze puffed at us once more, as though the air itself were restless, or it might be that some immense, evil presence brooding over the jungle sighed and waited, holding its breath in the intense stillness, and then sighed gently again.

The sky was hidden from us by the close roof of tree-fern, leaves and creeper, but the green-suffused light about us was subtly different from the luminous pallor that we had learnt to regard as normal forest daylight; it was dimmer, but it glowed, with a faint reddish-purple tinge, as the sky had done at dawn. 'There will be a storm,' Wan Nau said resignedly, and we hurried on in order to reach the top of the hill before the torrential rain, which would

probably accompany it, should have had time to
make cataracts down the slope.

I found with dull surprise that I was moving
drunkenly, and was conscious of blood singing in
my ears, but we stumbled so often on bad ground
that my unsteadiness passed without notice: faces
naturally appeared ghastly in this gloom; no one
paid any attention to mine; if, indeed, it showed
anything. All the spirit seemed to drain slowly out
of my aching body. The top of the hill became the
supreme goal of what was left of my mind; my
wandering thoughts fixed on that with an intensity
of longing, for then we should go down, I supposed,
and suddenly that was all I wanted. Not to rest
but to go down: to keep on descending for a long
time: to go far, far down. I could not have said
why that had grown into an obsession with me.

This last stiff stretch to the top was presumably
the worst climb that we should have to face, for we
had been negotiating little hills and the intervening
valleys for over seven hours, and the northernmost
spine of the low range was reported by the headman
to be the steepest: surely this must be it. We went
on for what I fancied was a considerable while,
though it may not have been so in reality. It seemed
to me that we did not bring the summit appreciably
nearer. I came to believe that it retreated at intervals
into a far off future of space and time, and then I
could have given in to the wretchedness that enveloped brain and body, and lain down where I was,

to find peace of a kind, though what I wanted, as much as I could want anything through the growing nausea that had hold of me, was to go on, at all costs that we might go down. Then after a while, in compensation for having eluded me, the hill-top would rush back towards me, and it did not seem odd that solid ground should be changeful like this. Soon I dared not look up any more to mark our progress, for then not only the hilltop but all my surroundings rushed away for a moment. Yet I was aware in some nightmare way of how near or far off the summit was at any given second.

The counting of my steps had all at once become the essential part of a game that I was determined to play as long as possible, for some unknown prize. The pain in my foot receded and approached with the hilltop. If I counted my steps up to ten several times, while the crest of the hill slid away into the distance, it was forced to swing back and remain only a few hundred yards ahead of me, while reluctantly I took another ten uncomfortable steps. Then it was free again, and I must hurry on through several more sets of ten to retrieve it. Sometimes this took longer than at other times, and needed a greater effort of concentration on my part; and though I was less conscious of pain when it was far away I was harassed by an extraordinary fear that the top of the hill might escape me altogether.

Towards the end of the rise we came on barren ground, where the livid light beat up agonisingly from the stones, and I had to set my teeth and count in fives, not tens, in order to go on.

Arnold was a little way ahead. Dimly I was aware of his turning back to me, and saying with that foreboding laugh, 'Keep firmly in mind that we needs must love the highest when we see it, and look there!' I thought that if he were at hand to keep the summit from spinning out of my grasp altogether, I might safely disregard the new urgency of keeping my eyes on the ground, but I glanced up cunningly, without lifting my head, hoping to deceive the hilltop. It remained stationary and quite close, but over its bare, rounded crest appeared the taller, wooded crown of another hill, hidden from us hitherto by the sharpness of the gradient.

'Oh, don't be so bloody Sard-Harker!' said Stewart, and this was the first conversational exchange we had had for hours.

Under my breath I went on counting, though not steps now, but some arbitrary measurement of time, shorter than a second. 'One – two – three – ,' for at the summit we stood still for a while, looking into the shallow valley that separated us from the next hill we should have to climb. All that remained in the empty shell which was left of me was the feeling of some obscure compulsion of numbers.

There were clouds on a level with us, driving before a squally wind that felt as though somewhere, at shorter intervals now, a door was opened momentarily on to a blast furnace in the bowels of the earth — not that I thought of it in this way at the time: my brain had grown delightfully numb and light, and I felt nothing unpleasant now, except that I was cold for a change, in spite of the hot wind and the blazing sun.

One cloud enveloped us clammily and blew away, and I knew that it was encumbent on me to count as fast as I could before it drifted to the other side of the valley. I reached seventy, I think, watching with unconcerned interest an impressive effect common in these forests: seen from a little distance the jungle presents an unbroken, featureless wall, with the sun abetting the loss of all detail, but now the cloud opened up a valley of sight into the crevices of the riot of grey-green life on the opposite hill. Where the cloud dissolved into the forest, in violent rain, we saw down between the trees, observing innumerable details of bush and vine across two miles of space. It was not a mirage but a prismatic effect of damp and reflection. I noticed a white bird, probably one of the great owls whose cry I hated at night, darting across this narrow cleft in the obscurity of the forest, where the white vapour pushed the foliage gently aside for our eyes while one could count ten.

Then my brain cleared for a second, and all this was blotted out by the mental picture of the moonlit deck of a steamer and the burdens men bore across it, but only for a few seconds of weak, struggling horror before flapping darkness closed in round me, and I sank down, down, a very long way, as I had ardently wished to do. This was strange joy: this was bliss or misery unimaginable, I could not tell which, to go down and down, seemingly without end.

An old habit of mind brought me groping my way back, through strange haunts of the dwindling spirit, up out of this terror-shot pit of blackness into an instable, shrieking world of new fears. I could recognise incongruities: it was absurd, I thought, for Stewart to sail the nailsick *Shellduck* so full that water came over continuously in this solid, battering stream in which I gasped for breath. The wind was twanging the steel standing-rigging and screaming high and fiercely through the cordage, and there was the familiar tumult of fighting air and water about me, but louder than I had ever known it, calling for some memory, some will-to-action in me that the returning layers of darkness in my brain were trying to choke down. I could not see anything yet because of the water drumming on my eyelids; they were too heavy to lift, in spite of the urgent need for action. We must be beating, to go on shipping green like this, but if so the movement was wrong: that was what was chiefly troubling me; there was none of the heave, lift and surge of a properly handled boat tacking in a steep sea, but only this wild rocking of the whole universe. Something at the back of my mind tried to reassure me, but I could not understand what it was telling me; it seemed irrelevant to the present anxiety.

That was the din of flogging canvas! Up in the wind, then! She'll pay off and swamp in a minute, with no way on and this weight of canvas. Get it off her, you fool. It's no use backing the jib and letting the main out: you know the *Shellduck* won't heave-to in a sea. Stewart, lighten her, can't you? And then wear her and run before. That was the Collimer buoy in the Orwell river, that great black thing crashing down by me, with a rending of wood and a screaming of parrots and monkeys. I could open my eyes a little now in spite of the water. No, it was not the Collimer, because Hugh had just stepped out of it, smiling that puzzled smile, and said that I ought not to wear green. And immediately it mattered terribly that I had on an old green dress which I had successfully rebelled against as a child, and burned. It was not fair of them to resurrect it because I was ill. But nothing ever was fair in childhood. Its trivial, hot resentments came back to me. They insisted on listening to my prayers but they would not let me hear theirs, though I was deeply curious to know what they could find to ask, having all the privileges I wanted. And if I lost my temper with them, I paid for it, and if they lost their temper with me, still I was the one who paid. No, I would not be very young again: it seemed to me that there was more unhappiness in it than just these things that I remembered now, but I could not recall what it was; and the boat had gone, and the great trees of the jungle bowed over me in the gale.

That curious part of the mind which works independently of the rest, had got its message through to my consciousness. I lay and giggled hysterically against the uprooted bush into which I had been washed or blown by the storm, between spasms when I could hardly breathe at all, because of the force of the wind. What it had been striving to make me understand was that if I were even partly conscious now, it was a better-than-even chance that this was not bubonic. It might be, but the odds were just a little against it, and the period – seven days from possible infection – was distinctly against it. And though in high fever I had a poor chance of surviving in these conditions, the gale might blow itself out in time: so I clung to the rocking bush and laughed helplessly while this terrible hot wind drove cold water over me in a violent stream. My right arm was numb from a chance blow, and something lay across my feet too heavy to lift. I could not move. It was growing dark; actually dark, I thought, though I could not be sure because of the thickening of the black veils in my head.

'On Wenlock edge the wood's in trouble;
His . . . fleece the Wrekin heaves;
The gale, it plies the saplings double – '

What came before 'fleece'? It was desperately important to remember because of the flickering blackness settling again, and I was going down, and if I were to come back it was essential that I should recall the word now. But I could not, and I slipped away from consciousness fighting in ungovernable terror.

Something living touched me, feeling up my body to my head, bringing me back to the bush and the shrieking wind and rain, and I was now too tired to strike at it. Besides, I knew that I should soon be going away again, down into the blackness deeper than that of this lightning-split night, where it could not get at me whatever it was, and so it did not matter. Arnold Ainger's voice called my name, shouting at full force within a few inches of my ear, between the crashes of thunder that dwarfed the noise of the boughs thrashing together above our heads; I could barely hear him.

Broken branches and whole shrubs and the lighter debris of the storm were whirled over us and about us. I saw them intermittently when the lightning came. The thorn-bush against which I had been flattened had caught on some stronger obstruction to the wind, as a leaf in a flooded gutter catches for a moment on a straw or a twig before it is dragged on. Now the support gave deafeningly, and I was torn from that anchorage and flung into pain-filled, overcrowded space, where invisible things ripped and bruised and tore at me, and all that was tangible

216

gave under my grasp, until, kindlier than before, the smothering gloom waiting in my mind welled up and sucked me down into itself.

Arnold was not there later on, when light returned to beat excruciatingly through my eyelids. No one was there. Except for a feeble squawking and fluttering going on out of sight, behind my head, there was stillness everywhere apart from the familiar, far off whisperings of the forest. A foot or so above my head, as I lay on the ground, was the trunk of a fallen tree, resting on the splintered boughs of another, and together they had made some kind of shelter for me. Many things had eddied into this chance backwater of the storm, leaves and branches were piled up over me against the trunk, and among them were several tattered birds and a small broken-backed monkey, thin with death.

My clothes were drenched and I was shaking with fever. I guessed that it must be very early morning: there seemed to be blue mist between the trees, the little I could see of my surroundings through the space on either side of the overhanging trunk which blocked my view.

I tried to move my head and found that I had not enough strength. For some while after this I was so near the borderland of unconsciousness that I think I slipped over it at times into coma, and when awake, finding myself alone, I was not frightened with any intensity. To have lost touch with the others was merely part of the abounding wretchedness of my state. But that other part of my mind was jubilant, saying 'What did I tell you!' I was likely to die unless help came, perhaps in any case, but it would not be of plague, and this was inexplicably comforting

The squawking thing touched my shoulder, fluttering about it. By slow stages, resting the weight of my arm on my body, I moved a hand up and pushed the thing away, and my hand came back smeared with blood.

In the first day or two of our journey I should have felt unnerved for a second by this. (Illogically, I have always been more easily affected by suffering in animals, and particularly birds, than by human pain, though I consider the second more intrinsically important than the first.) After the first few days in Trenganu I should have been able to kill the thing, out of mercy, without a qualm. Now I did nothing from pity, but I realised that its helplessness, proclaimed by the squawking, might attract the preying animals that would be out reaping a fine harvest from the gale. If my chance of surviving were slight, I did not want it lessened.

I could not get at the creature behind my head, and with infinite labour, resting for long intervals, I began to swivel round on the ground, economising in effort whenever possible by levering myself against the trunk, moving my shoulders a few inches at a time and then lying panting until my head no longer felt as though it would burst. I found new bruises on my body where it pressed unbearably against something hard in each new position. My arm was gradually coming back into use, though I must have damaged the elbow, judging by the pain of every movement. The injured bird turned out to be one of the grand Malayan jays, with a dislocated wing. The flesh had been torn away from under it by a jagged little piece of branch, on which the bird must have been impaled before it broke off. A bit of the wood stuck out above the raw thigh like a pen from a clerk's ear. My hands were too weak to be gentle; I began to despair of this bungled killing before it was done: once I was tempted to give it up, when the bird almost struggled free, but the crying was too dangerous to be tolerated.

Then, having turned round, I fancied I could see Wan Nau many yards away, so hidden by the intervening foliage, bedraggled and thinned though it was, that I could not be sure. If I saw right, she was kneeling in a strange attitude, sitting back on her heels as she often did when cooking, but with her head flung back and resting in a tangle of overturned scrub. Her arms were behind her. I could not call to her; my burning throat would only whisper. Unwilling to face more of the awful exertion of moving, I waited until I saw a slight stir in the bright patch that I took to be her sarong.

On hands and knees, muscular control having returned to some extent through previous efforts,

I began a long slow crawl, interrupted by fits of exhaustion, in one of which I think I slept for a few seconds. I devoted careful thought beforehand to every inch of the ground, planning how to take the best advantage of any help it could give me, plotting a course as carefully as one does when sailing, in order that I might avoid dips and hummocks in the ground, where strength would be wasted. Presently I saw for certain that it was Wan Nau, and she was watching me.

All the suspicion and fear that she had felt of me, the young woman of Deotlan's vaunted race, at whose summons he had left Pedagor, burned in her wide, tormented eyes. Her face was ghastly in its expression, though pallor did not show through her brown skin. Her body was rigid in its strained position; she was gripping one ankle with both her thin, tiny hands.

She did not move at my approach. The little Malay that I had picked up had gone from my confused brain; even when I was close enough to whisper I could not speak to her, but I pulled at her hands. She would not move them, and I was too weak to force them aside. I could not see the leg doubled under her, but where the lashing of the native shoe had given way the foot was swollen and purple, constricted by the soft hide. An almost overmastering desire to sleep came over me, as after some violent and prolonged exertion. It required a constant effort of determination to stay conscious and to work off the shoe, calling on whatever reserves of nervous energy were still left in me. I do not know if the freeing of the foot eased her, for *rigors* had set in. Hopelessly, with the persistence of the semi-conscious, I plucked at her taut fingers at intervals, but when she died without slackening them I dropped thankfully to sleep in a moment.

Stewart and Deotlan, who had just found one another, found me what must have been some hours later, and Arnold Ainger joined them while they were carrying me to a clearing, where they could build a small fire on either side of me. He and Stewart redressed me in what was left of their clothes, which had dried on them. Even in the midday heat I could not keep warm at first: afterwards my temperature must have soared up and remained high, and I could not get cool.

I heard that, clinging to one another and to any shelter offered by the inequalities of the ground on which they crouched, the rest of our party had kept touch until just before dusk. The gale had strengthened then, and we had all been swept and driven off the bare hilltop, where we were safe at least from the danger of falling trees, and in the jungle we were soon scattered. It was impossible to stand upright against the force of the wind, and the torrents of water that swirled down the slope on all sides washed the ground from under their feet as the suck of a receding wave does on a rough day.

All of us were considerably bruised and torn. Arnold had been struck in the small of the back by something ragged and heavy, presumably a flying branch, the moment after he stumbled over me on the windward side of the uprooted bush. It was, fortunately, a glancing blow that only gouged a neat strip of flesh out of his side, above the hip: if it had the force to do that, taken squarely it would probably have broken his back. As it was, he was unaware of the injury for some time after he received it; but the blow flung him away from me, and the gale carried him farther to leeward, into this alternately black and lightning slashed chaos of bending trees, where earth seemed less solid than air. When he fought his way back, against the increasing gusts, to where he imagined that I had been – though the likelihood of his striking the same place again was small – I was not to be found: nor was Wan Nau, who had been near me.

No one knew how the night had gone for her. Deotlan told me, through Arnold, of the four dis-coloured punctures in the skin under the clasped hands. Even in this period of comparative insensi-tiveness, I kept unwillingly at the back of my mind, in the days that followed, a shadow of horror at the visualisation of the long, supple, venomous-headed body on which she must have trampled blindly – a little before dawn, apparently, since I saw her alive by daylight – and of her realisation, as it whipped at her twice out of the darkness, that she could do nothing now but wait, alone, for the sure sequence of pain and coma and death to creep through her blood.

'It will be better for me that she need not go back to Pedagor,' Deotlan said, in Malay. 'It was always a little dangerous for me, her being there. And she will be glad too. She will not have to have Dris again.'

Sick at heart as in body, I hoped that Wan Nau's loyal and steadfast mind had thought of these things while she waited for the daylight, in the meagre hope of seeing him again. To her, if to no one else, they would bring faint consolation. But I was afraid that, at the end in any case, there had been nothing in her thoughts save her jealousy of me, pitiful in the very absurdity that she could not see, because of her deep humility before an indifferent and utterly undeserving lover. 'But I am sorry, just for now, that she has gone,' Deotlan said.

Hurriedly, because we had been long without food and the living must come first, he dug a shallow trench on the farther side of the clearing. A horizontal ledge, wide enough to hold her, was cut in the side of the trench, for earth must not rest on the body, in a Malay burial. I was surprised by the gentle imagination, incongruous with what I had learned of the character of the people, that prompted the holding of a clod of earth to Wan Nau's pinched nostrils before she was moved into the grave, to prepare the spirit a little for what was coming, that it might not be frightened more than need be by the smell of the enclosing earth, and the darkness. Gabbling through the Mohammedan prayers, he loosened her garments lest the body should wish to raise itself a little in reverence to the last, most sacred prayer. Then, holding boughs across the entrance to the ledge in which they had laid her, to keep out the earth, he and Stewart shovelled back the disturbed soil in a mound over the trench, not over the ledge itself. Deotlan picked up his rifle and went off after birds.

I grew very ill again in the evening, through delayed shock. What this particular fever was, I never discovered. I was not often fully conscious for the next two days, and Ainger was also ill, though far less seriously. By the bad luck that seems inevitable with convalescents, his recently unbandaged arm had been scored once more by some of the many semi-poisonous thorns in the jungle. It was hardly a remarkable coincidence; there were few parts of our bodies that had not suffered that night. The place festered alarmingly, threatening general poisoning again, and it was just as well for him that, on my account, we could not move on for some days.

He recovered before I did. The jungle, where the atmosphere and conditions reduce the vitality of almost all whites after a short sojourn, had given him back most of his ordinary health. Some time ago I had stopped worrying because I had no more dressing for his arm; to my astonishment, it had suddenly healed of its own accord. Now, when it badly needed dressing again, I could do nothing, and it healed in spite of this, or perhaps because of it: I am not really bigotted about the value of my services to mankind.

Arnold was even a trifle less lean and ascetic-looking than he had been when I first saw him. Being ill carried with it the advantage of leisure to watch him unobserved, to learn and like the physical defects that were as much part of my love for him as the fineness of his hands and his mouth and the nice shape of his head. I would not have wished away, if I could, the stoop of the tall lanky body, nor its ridiculous boniness, nor any of the lines in his face. These things were all about equally important in the person who could make me happy for the moment merely by looking away, so that I could study them. Till now there had been very little time in which to love, even with the senses alone. Uneasily I knew that when I was fit again I should want more than just this, which contented me now; the opportunity to appreciate. And it was not likely that he would feel for me as I felt for him. Thinking them over fairly, it seemed probable to me that the few more-than-friendly gestures which he had made towards me had been merely responses to the age-old instinct of the combative male in the presence of another – an extraordinarily primitive instinct, apparent at every society function and in every suburban drawing-room. Because I was ill, Stewart had dropped all pretence of affectionate indifference; he was openly solicitous, in the manner of a lover, and the two men not being on good terms, under their patched-up tolerance, that would be enough in such sur-roundings to make Arnold pay me more personal attention than he would have done otherwise. And so I busied myself diligently with watching him, during this short respite from the journey, for now it would satisfy me, and soon it would not.

I was so weak in every way, for a few days after the fever had gone, that I could be content, through-out a whole morning of almost unbroken silence, with Deotlan on guard while the others went in search of food or dead wood, to lie in the shelter and think over a new, trivial discovery about this man for whom I knew my body would clamour unhappily later on, though now it was at peace. It was enough for the moment to have noticed that when he gave the quick, downward twist to his mouth which signified unspoken disagreement, there was a slight pucker on one side of the thin lips that was not on the other.

Physical and mental impulses are too inseparable, at least sexually in women, for me to say that this love was of the flesh alone, but it was mainly physical. I liked immensely his unsparing, concentrated mind, as nearly unprejudiced as any normal person's can be. Unattracted by him as a man, I know I should still have wanted his friendship in any circumstances. But certainly it was not because his brain supplied mine with a good deal that it lacked that I coveted and schemed for and enjoyed the chance touch of his hand, his one really beautiful feature. I strained to miss nothing he said, when he talked to Stewart outside the shelter while I was supposed to be sleeping, for the gratification of the flesh not the spirit. It was about twenty per cent luck that anything he said when they talked of abstract things was worth listening to for itself alone; apart from the pleasantness of his voice. I am fairly sure that otherwise I should not have wanted him, but in honesty one cannot tell oneself that for a fact.

The weather, broken by the storm, turned to rain after the calm of the succeeding day. Torrential downpours every few hours made it impossible to keep a fire alight. In the volume of water that fell with stinging violence, any shelter that we could build was useless, and we were soaked through all day and, worse still, all night, when it became cold. Shivering fits returned to me. This was the beginning of the period of greatest physical wretchedness that we were called on to face.

Stewart and Arnold, because the physical conditions were very severe, were tolerant of one another, except for one minor clash. This was the first time that we had made anything like a permanent camp; Arnold proved to be orderly by nature, and

Stewart had always been in the habit of strewing things about carelessly. He left the fruit shells which we used as drinking cups lying anywhere about the fire, after cleaning them as best he could, and he dumped the firewood he collected in odd heaps, instead of on Arnold's neat pile. He did his full share of work, and occasionally more, but he never finished a job completely and tidily. Arnold was better, but he did things in a laborious way. I lay and nagged at both with sensible advice: I knew it would irritate them and it did, but being practical I could not refrain. They did not take it; I did not expect them to. But my determination not to explain the better and more obvious method broke down, because I was ill, each time I saw them making elaborate preparations for the performance of simple jobs.

'The trouble with you is that you've got no *esprit-de*-sty!' said Arnold, throwing Stewart's native shoe-skins out of the shelter, when he found them among the collection of twigs and leaves that he put under his head at night.

Stewart crawled into the rain to collect these valuable belongings which had fallen perilously near the fire, then just expiring in the rain.

'That was a bloody silly thing to do! If they'd been badly scorched we should all have suffered.'

'It was, really,' Arnold agreed affably. 'But I've a fad about wet, worn shoes on the pillow. I'm just "funny that way".'

The losing of Mrs. Mardick had one unexpected

effect. Now that we were no longer subjected to a rapid fire of personal questions, Arnold Ainger opened out of his own accord, becoming quite expansive, for him. He did not talk much of his private life, and because I wanted to know some things about it more than anything else, I could not ask him what he did not volunteer. He developed a habit of sitting silent and abstracted for a while, when he was on guard by the shelter, and then suddenly throwing back to me over his shoulder, without taking his eyes from the forest, some observation from the middle of his thoughts, without any context. His voice, generally devoid of any expression – the least startling of voices – usually supplied a startling contrast to the things he said. 'All War memorials should be inscribed "To the Memory of Men Whose Lives Were Wasted." Instead of the present legends about "Their Names May Be Unknown to Man, but They are Written in the Book of God. Their Sacrifice was not in Vain." If *that* is believed, it was utterly in vain. For its own security, the world can't afford such comfort to the relatives. Do you know Edinburgh?'

'No.'

'The Scottish Memorial there is the best building of its kind I have ever seen. And the bas-reliefs magnificent. And the wording's sickening. Like that. In fact, I think what I said was a quotation.'

Then nothing else would be volunteered by either of us for many minutes, or we would discuss immediate matters relating to food and shelter, and plan meals to be eaten one day, perhaps, at Simpson's — always Simpson's, because at the moment it represented our ideal of food.

And the next day, without warning, he would break out with: 'Curious that I dislike the majority of people over sixty-five more since the War than I did at about seventeen.' He might have been giving a dissertation on the use of the definite article in Swedish from the lack of emphasis in his tone, which lent much greater weight to his opinions than Stewart's eagerness in conversation. 'I supposed, then, that when I was thoroughly middle-aged myself — thirty-seven or so, good heavens! — I shouldn't mind them so much. Expected to get used to impotent whining tolerance towards things that seemed to me, at seventeen, either too good to be whined about, or too bad to be tolerated. (And in any case not to be fumbled over by hands grown inefficient.) But instead, I get increasingly exasperated with them.'

'I don't remember much of pre-War elderly people,' I said, 'But I do remember their bloody-mindedness during the War. It would have been so funny if it hadn't been so disgusting. White-haired ladies in hydros, and rose-spraying ex-colonels, clamouring for reprisals for every alleged atrocity. They were the only bitter haters then. The fighting services seemed to be notably lacking in their parents' "stick - em - all - up - against - a - wall - and - shoot -

em" patriotism. But you were away at the time; you wouldn't have seen much of it, so that's not your grudge against the old?'

'No – well, yes, it's all part of the same thing. They've remained the only truculent people since the War. That's half the trouble. And the other half is that they still have so much say in things that don't really concern them. Ever since the War I've been growing more and more afraid of the staggering irresponsibility of the old. In my job I hear men, safely past fighting age, talking constantly of maintaining our national prestige at all costs – "ought to take a firm hand with the Italians!" (or the Russians). And I very clearly remember that they could not love us, the dears, so much, loved they not sharing what they called our honour more. Prick their racial vanity, and a good number of the non-combatants I know in England would be ready to herd youth out to avenge it for them again, if they could. And perhaps they could; one can't say. Most of them would hear quite undisturbed, I think, the Bishop of London's unforgettable remark, "War brings out the best in our men".'

There was a long pause here. Something was rustling the bushes a few yards away, so faintly that in civilisation I doubt whether either of us would have heard it. Arnold got up to investigate. Such small things nowadays made my blood stop and then leap forward again. But this disturbance was only due to a bear-cat, an ugly, harmless little beast with a tail longer than its straggly-furred body, one of the jungle's least efficient-looking products. It was a nocturnal hunter as a rule, but, disturbed by some enemy, it had come swinging along the intertwined branches with one eye open for danger and the other looking for any young birds or monkeys or fruit that might be gathered on the way.

'Judy, have you any idea what he meant by that?'

'Meant by what?' My wits were wandering. I had been engrossed for the moment in watching Arnold return, to sit down again in front of the shelter. By now I could foresee, just beforehand, every movement that he would make, to the unconscious feeling for cigarettes in a hip pocket where there had been none for days; and I grew half faint – because I was still very weak – with a sudden desire to touch the back of his neck where the dark hair ended: nothing but that, just then; merely to touch him.

'The bishop. By that remark. Do you think he was referring to their entrails? That's the only interpretation which gives the observation any sense at all.'

'No,' I said, 'if he was, one might have forgiven him. There'd have been at least some truth in the sentence, and a macabre humour in keeping with the time. No, I don't think he meant that. Though it's always hard to be sure, with bishops. You've only to read the reports of any church congress to be uncertain for ever of the limits of what a bishop can mean.'

'But surely even an elderly ecclesiastic can't have thought that the innate kindliness and endurance of men in adversity would be improved – intrinsically improved – by being made public and occasionally rewarded with medals, instead of just existing privately, as it does at other times?'

'No. I admit it would be difficult to believe that. In spite of the reports.'

Delightful, slow, questing voice, hesitating sometimes between words and then pouncing on the most suitable; don't make me talk, I thought. Go on. Whole sentences I should like to hear again, for the unheated, unhurried inflections. (This is maundering; pull yourself together! I told myself.)

'Then there's a temptation to add one wild allegation to another,' he said, staring up unseeingly at the ceiling of leaves, and looking so characteristically Arnold Ainger at the moment that I would have given a great deal to kiss him, 'by saying God knows what the bishop did mean!'

It did not occur to me at the time that this kind of talk was one of the highest tributes of friendship that Arnold could pay to anyone. I still felt that I hardly knew the man.

Stewart came back then to take over from him, laboriously carrying about a fifth of the day's supply of water in the fruit shell cups. The ground, and the trees about us, and everything we had, were so sodden that it was irritating to have to go some distance to get drinking water, but we had nothing in which to catch the rain.

I was seeing a new and rather surprising side of Stewart. One may know someone very intimately for years, and have no idea at all of how they would make love. Stewart was by nature so deficient in self-assurance and so uncomfortably easy to snub that it astonished me to find how accomplished and humorously insistent he was in this line.

'You must have had much more practice in seduction than I imagined!' I said, trying to get back to the old footing of affectionate fooling.

'Oh, much,' he said. 'And so must you, Judy, to be able to parry my best attempts so effortlessly! Really "nice" girls, so I'm told – I've no experience that way – are quite easy game. Hence the dearth.'

We grinned at one another. ' "Interesting Facts, etc." ' I said. 'Somehow, I never suspected you of a deplorable double life!'

'I always suspected you, a little,' he said. 'But not half as much as I do now! As I wasn't in love with you before I didn't care what you did. But this practice of being kind to other men must now cease.'

'It isn't a "practice" of mine. I wish you wouldn't make me sound like the little sweetheart of all the world!' I complained.

'No. I was certain you weren't that. As a matter of fact, I know the one-and-only, don't I?'

'What the hell has that got to do with you, Nookie?' I said, annoyed for once and sitting up so violently that I hit my head, which was still aching, against the roof-branch and fell back again like a jack-in-the-box. I have a knack of looking undignified on occasions when I try to be impressive.

'Yes, I thought I did,' said Stewart, serenely. 'Do lie still, darling. You've got to get well soon because we really must go on. It's over, isn't it, that affair? You might just tell me that!'

'Yes. But do realise that it won't make any difference to you.'

'Gives me some sour satisfaction to know, though. I thought when I met him that he wasn't good enough for you!'

'Tell you the truth, I rather think so myself – now! But to be fair, I expect that's only sour grapes, because I was more in love with him than he was with me. Nookie, will you please leave me alone! For us – you and me of all people – this is a perfectly footling situation – '

'Don't I know it, my dear! You were the last person I wanted to fall in love with. It's horribly awkward, knowing you so well – knowing that you can be relied on to be deadly sensible in all circumstances.'

'Can I!' I said.

'Nearly all, then. If you'd been Juliet's girl-friend, ten to one there wouldn't have been any tragedy. Knowing that is the sort of thing which hopelessly cramps a man's style, on top of twenty years of friendship.'

If people were ever loved for their good qualities alone, or for the possession of a congenial temperament, it would have been Stewart, not Arnold Ainger, that I wanted. Stewart, I knew, would be capable of greater generosity, mentally, and of more unselfishness in practical matters than the other, less easily moved man. Stewart dissipated through many channels of sympathy and impersonal resentment the energy that Arnold Ainger could concentrate upon any subject that interested him. But few things interested him, and in those he would be entirely absorbed at the time; unlike me, and particularly unlike Stewart, who was cut out to be only half-successful at anything he took up, because he did more things than most people a little better than the average, but not much better. I could not imagine Arnold being unsuccessful at anything he really wanted to do. But I felt at home among Stewart's prejudices and enthusiasms, understanding without effort the easily hurt spirit that he covered with a light wit, to hide the perpetual dissatisfaction to which it was condemned: in common with most people with artistic gifts of any kind Stewart wanted the things he could not get, and if he attained something ceased wanting it. I should always remain an explorer in the asceticism of Arnold Ainger's mind; I could not share it. Certainly I could not imagine Arnold not knowing, before he

set out to acquire something, whether it would
have a permanent value for him or not; while,
different from both of them here, I never knew till
I got it – an unlucky weakness. Actually, I think I
preferred Stewart's quick response to all human
stimulus to the fine intellectual impartiality that
I admired in Arnold. But realising this made not
the slightest difference, of course: it was to Arnold's
watch that I looked forward all the time, through
Stewart's spell and Deotlan's.

In spite of the damp and the cold of the nights,
I was much better on the third day, the last we spent
in the clearing; so nearly well that the preoccupation
with my own physical state had gone, leaving me
conscious all the time, whether I looked towards
it or not, of the mound on the other side of the
clearing, where already the avid jungle grass had all
but reclaimed the disturbed ground. Soon, in two
days at the outside, new vegetable life would have
obliterated every trace of it, but only a little quicker
than the continuity and needs of human life would
wipe out her memory from the one mind where she
would have had it remain. We could do nothing for
you, Wan Nau, by remembering. Deotlan, wiser
in his Malay irresponsibility, knew that, and acted
upon it, while the rest of us only knew it. I did not
hear him refer to her again, except once, and it was
not sorrow that kept her out of his conversation.
He mentioned her name doubtfully some time later,
among those of his wives – he had had four – in the

course of a really entertaining story about his matrimonial misadventures.

I wanted to talk, or listen: anything to keep away the pressing awareness of that half-covered mound; but when the others had gone, Arnold pulled out his battered, muddy, soaked, ant-eaten Greek text, and took an occasional few seconds off watch to glance at it. I saw him measure on the wet earth, with a seemingly idle hand, the distance of two thumb-to-fourth-finger spans from the edge of a shadow, even deeper than most of those among which we lived, to a spot where he laid the book down, open, beside him.

He looked round, lifting his glasses, 'Just a fad of mine,' he explained.

Then he forgot me altogether, apparently. I watched one of his delightful hands passing caressingly, while his mind was far off, backwards and forwards over the piece of ground between the book and the shadow, and grew restless with new longing.

Judith, my poor girl, I said inwardly, trying to ridicule myself out of this stupid state, you aren't becoming a nymphomaniac, are you? Surely it isn't natural to want two men so much in so short a time?

— It is natural, in an atmosphere of death and imminent danger, answered another part of me soberly.

— One love affair in twenty years is enough! More than enough, I think.

— It makes no difference what I *think*. No man should have hands that look so strong and are so shapely.

This was the day to which, since we left the ship, I had been looking forward with frightened hope: it was the end of our quarantine period. We were safe from that infection now. One of the party was dead, one had nearly died; we were still very far from our objective, in appalling conditions. And I had thought that it would be a day for rejoicing!

'Ainger, do read a paragraph or so aloud to me, and let me see if I can make out any modern Greek at all,' I said. 'I believe I've forgotten the little classical Greek I knew.' Anything but this silence, with Wan Nau lying within earshot in actual distance, but beyond call.

'I don't want to read to you,' he said, in the level, inexpressive voice I loved, for its nice pitch, or because it was his. 'And don't call me Ainger, as if I were a male nurse.' He followed my eyes to his hand, his fingers barely keeping contact with the ground as they continued to run over it.

'That's quite an unconscious bit of sensuality,' he said, lifting his glasses with his right hand for once, in order to study the left hand better. For a second he was as detachedly observant of it as though it had been some one else's.

'I touch nothing these days,' he said, looking at me but not altering his normal, matter-of-fact tone, 'that isn't your body, Judy.'

I knew that when unemotional people gave any expression to feeling, it was likely to be overwhelmingly, extravagantly emotional: but this, from Arnold Ainger, I could not believe that I had heard, at first. I dared not. I lay still, saying nothing, while a wave of hot blood rushed through me, coming from nowhere it seemed, tingling in every nerve, throbbing in my head, almost suffocating me by its force.

'You have the loveliest figure of any woman I know. And I can't help seeing a good deal of it. These last two days, since you started getting well, you've been tormentingly desirable. But I know – and you realise too, I suppose – that as things are here, if I started kissing you whenever I had a chance, matters wouldn't remain long in that stage. They couldn't, from my point of view, when you're close to me all the time. I'd want so much more than that from you, as soon as you were fit again. I couldn't leave you alone, then. Illness gives you a sort of inviolability, you see: I wonder why. Judy!'

'Yes.'

'Do you mind? My feeling like this, I mean.'

'No. Of course I'm glad. Well, much more than just glad –'

'I've been wondering for days if I could kiss you. But presumably Corder wouldn't have gone off with Deotlan just now, leaving me alone with you and you ill, if he'd had any idea that I might make love to you. He ought to be back before this shadow, *here*,

reaches *here*' (he flipped the edge of the book),
'if he comes straight back from the stream. He said
he was only going for water. Last surviving instincts
of a gentleman: I'm giving him a chance, by doing
nothing till it touches the book. A quibble, of
course, but it satisfies all that is left of my own
*esprit-de-*sty when you're anywhere near me. I'm
backing the odds that no one ever does in the jungle
exactly what they plan to do. He's in love with you,
isn't he?'

'Yes. Only recently. He wasn't when I met you.'

'Are you with him?'

'No.' I added slowly, 'with you, Arnold! At
least, I want you.'

He passed a hand over his face. 'Judy ! I didn't
— didn't even hope that! My dear, I don't know
anyone but you who would have been honest
enough — shameless and darling enough — to have
said that, without being asked! If Corder comes
back in' — he glanced down at the creeping shadow —
'four minutes or less, I'll have missed my only
chance for some time, possibly altogether, and I
shall want to ham-string him. If not, I shall kiss
you; and for me it'll have been worth the waiting.'

'And for me.'

'Don't, Judy! You're making it almost impossible. About three-and-a-half minutes —'

He rested the rifle against his drawn-up knees
and lay back with his hands behind his head, a
hopelessly inefficient sentry, and began to make

conversation, punctuating the irrelevant talk at
short intervals by craning up his neck to mark the
infinitesimal progress of the shadow.

'What shall we talk about? Shall I give you some
of my ideas for reforming the world? Don't you
think that if there has to be some kind of public
trial before divorce – goodness knows why there
should be, except to settle financial difficulties when
one party is destitute – there ought to be one
before marriage?' (Around us the dripping trees
waited in the ominous, hushed expectancy of all
jungle life: and Wan Nau lay near by: and it was
doubtful whether the four of us who still survived
would all come safely to the end of this journey.
And Arnold Ainger talked intelligent nonsense about
marriage and divorce! These are probably the most
amazing minutes through which I shall ever live, I
thought.) 'Perhaps the trial ought to take place
before the engagement is announced. Couples
would be made to produce evidence of compati-
bility of temperament. Witnesses would be called
to swear that both were really devoted to high-brow
music and that the woman was not merely pretending (as I suppose often happens). Parading a taste
that she hadn't got as a bait. Then for six months
before the marriage, some one equivalent to the
King's Proctor would go about trying to worm
admission of collusion and false statement out of
them. Might approach the girl disguised in a
muffler and a stream-lined car as a sporting youth,

full of anti-art snobbishness, ("I mayn't know Epstein but I do play cricket!") and lure her into a confession that she liked dance music better than Bach. Evidence of deception. The engagement would be automatically rescinded.' He sat up and stared into the forest in the direction from which the others would return, but nothing stirred, save stray leaves that tapped against their branches or their fellows, once or twice, in the stillness, disturbed by winds which we knew by now that we could not feel. 'Another minute and a half, I should think. It'd save a marvellous lot of unsatisfactory marriages, that idea of mine. But I'm the sort of unlucky person, myself,' he said gloomily, 'that would have appealed to the discretion of the court, having practically nothing in common with the girl I married, and got it, by sheer malevolence of fortune. About an eighth of an inch more to go. And then there's my plan for organising beauty dumps all over what remains of rural England. At places like Friday Street and Wisley Huts in Surrey, which are spoilt anyway. Famous picturesque spots that could be systematically boosted in newspapers and by placards, and made to drain off most of the cars which are ruining the rest of the country in the week-ends for people like you and me. The key to the scheme is a Boy Scout at every cross-road (doing his daily good turn; so he wouldn't have to be paid for it). That'd be of double benefit; keep the cars on the right roads and the boys from scouting elsewhere. But I won't go into the executive details now, anyway. About half a minute.' He sat up with his head bent, his hands on the ground behind him, watching the shadow eat up to the corner of the book, and a hairbreadth over, for good measure, and then got up. 'I thought it was at least twenty to one they wouldn't get back first, or I shouldn't have been so magnanimous!'

Arnold bent down and scooped me out of the shelter into his arms and kissed me; and when Stewart came back eventually, with edible roots that he and Deotlan had stayed to grub up, I lay with my arm over my face, feigning sleep because I was crying and could not stop, though life had become more valuable to me then it had been for many months.

CHAPTER VIII

TURNED WEST

We went north-west again, instead of north-east, our proper direction. What else could we do?– the river, when we came to it at last, after climbing two more hills, was in spate through the rains, and still rising. Even the wider reaches were unfordable. Below were the falls and rapids, a long series of them, where the force of the current made a crossing impossible at any season. The nearer bank was swamp; we could not follow that down, to cross below the rapids. But if we worked up farther towards the source we had a better chance of finding a shallower stretch, where we might take our chance of the uprooted trees and floating grass islands and all the litter of a gale-swollen river, which made the crossing nerve-shaking in prospect, apart from the possibility of crocodiles (a probability, rather, in any Malayan river). And for another thing, we might come on a riverside village, as we badly needed to do: we were nearly out of ammunition. Luckily, Deotlan's aged firearm was of the type commonest in that part of the world, an old police rifle, probably stolen. If there was ammunition to be had anywhere it was practically certain to be the kind we wanted. One of the innumerable village feuds existed, Deotlan reminded us, between the fishing communities farther down the river and Pedagor, an old quarrel about the fine sheltered fishing grounds in the delta, where the Pedagor fishermen came to poach at the risk of their lives in bad weather. This was the feud that had prevented our going to Kintaling by boat. No help nor tolerance of any kind should we get from a down-stream village, if we arrived with a Pedagor man as guide: but here, above the rapids, where the river folk would not come into contact with the coastal fishermen, we could hope for hospitality and the chance of buying supplies.

Day after day, in vile conditions of rain and mist and intervals of intense heat, we struggled on up the river to find the village that did not materialise.

Then the twisting river bent westward, and we were forced farther into the interior. The lie of the land and every chance misfortune combined to turn us west again. We accepted this, cursing it as an inevitability, in the same way that we accepted the rain and the heat, the impossibility of getting sufficient food while we dared not waste a shot, and the growing depression and weakness and weariness that resulted. It was in this period that I first thoroughly despaired of our getting through. At the worst moments I despaired, now, not of all of us keeping our lives – I had realised before that that was unlikely, we were running serious risks daily and sometimes hourly – but of any of us surviving, unless our luck turned, and it showed no sign of doing that. Still, one can go on struggling and planning for safety a long while after despair sets in, and I think my intense gloominess at that period was largely due to hunger.

Once we made an attempt to get across the river, when the continual westward trend of our progress forced us to realise that we were wasting our time and our little remaining energy. We were covering shorter distances every day, through one thing and another. There was no heart left in any of us, but we went on because we had no option.

We found that floating debris had made a loose dam across a narrow neck of the river, below which the stream broadened again, running turbulently among half-submerged rocks. It was the only feasible spot we had struck, and we were readier to take risks than before, though less able to deal with them. It was hard to reach the actual bank here, protected as it was by swamp, and it took us a long time to wade through to the edge of the dam.

Several heavy tree-trunks, their roots and branches intertwined and holding for the moment, were as far as we could discover the only anchorage of the constantly thickening jam of odd material. (We saw a dead *seladang* calf among the refuse piled against the trunks; it was the only one of these beasts that I saw in Malaya, in spite of the influence their presence had had on our journey. It was in keeping with the whole idiotic affair, I thought, that the swollen calf looked harmless and pathetic.)

Upstream the current ran rapidly through a little gorge. We could not cross by that side; we should be sucked under the dam and inextricably tangled in the mass of roots and branches protruding under water. On the downstream side, where the water spread out round rocky shoals, the current could probably be stemmed with the help of a handhold on the dam; but we had no means of gauging the security of the interlocked flotsam. The whole thing looked appallingly insecure to me, and if it broke up while we were making our way across we had a thin chance of surviving the rocks.

There was a quick, vehement argument as to whether it would be wiser to wait a while, to see how the dam held and to take a chance that pressure and fresh stuff floating down from upstream might wedge it more firmly in place, or to get across at once, while we had the help of this obstruction, before the force of the river broke it up, as it must do sooner or later. All the while other uprooted trees were being borne down from above, end-on, to act as natural battering-rams.

Stewart and Arnold, siding together for once, overbore Deotlan and me, when we tried to put off the attempt, and we did not even wait to investigate the lower reach thoroughly for crocodiles, as Deotlan

wanted to do, with the idea of wounding one badly
before we started across. This would keep the
others busy tearing the hurt beast to pieces, he said,
and was the usual plan in crossing such places.

But we saw no sign of them: we might have had
to wait almost indefinitely to make sure of their
absence, and by now the rest of us were too exhausted
to match Deotlan in passive nerve. If we had not
faced the crossing at once I doubt that we should
have been able to tackle it later. I had no cogent
reason for suggesting a longer wait; I merely wanted
to delay the attempt even for a few minutes – anything to postpone the ordeal.

The water sucked viciously at our legs before we
had waded half a dozen steps through the shallows.
As we lowered ourselves farther into it our bodies
grew light and helpless and stones moved under
our feet as we strove to find some hold in the river
bed, against the rush of the stream. No one could
look for help from the others: it was a full-time job
to get oneself across. Deotlan stowed the little
ammunition we still had in his headcloth, and gave
his rifle to Arnold and Stewart to look after between
them: they were both a good deal taller and had a
slightly better chance of keeping it dry. Arnold's
revolver had been thrown away long ago, when the
ammunition ran out: we should get no more of that
at any rate.

I went third, with Deotlan following, but I had
no knowledge of the progress of the others after

the first minute. With one arm half over a log, I slipped on the instable bottom as I reached out with my other hand for a branch farther along. Instantly, as though the water were a live thing waiting to pounce, a shoot of current swirled round me, sweeping my feet from under me. The soft, terrifying hands of the river tore at my shoulders. I felt the log shift slightly, not giving but rolling over towards me, so that my hold was weakened. I tore with my nails at the smooth bark as it turned, and found a crevice, but now it was only the crook of my fingers that held me against the suction of the river, and I was swinging a little in the changing eddies that formed through the thickening dam, as a rush swings in a half-choked brook. The pressure of water was considerable and I knew I should lose this grip if I put too much strain upon it, so that the log turned over completely. Soon my bent fingers began to tire. Frantically groping round, my free hand came on a submerged stick, caught in the lower side of the dam, but not securely, it felt. Gently I pulled on it, and it gave at once. I let go hopelessly. I tried to shift hands on the log and could not; the crevice was too small. As a last resource I felt below me in the water again, for the loose stick, meaning to free it entirely and make an unlikely attempt to wedge it between the log and whatever was on the other side to act as a lever. The stick came readily for some way, and then held when I thought I had freed it. I could not tell how safely it was caught before I let go of the log as it suddenly turned farther. I drew myself half under water but close against the dam by the stick, and, kicking against the yielding water, made a wild effort to reach a thin root or piece of broken creeper that stuck up out of the dam above my head. My left hand touched it, bent it, and slipped along it, but I managed to hold on, near the end. It gave threateningly under my weight, but did not break. Letting go immediately with the other hand, I was swung round by the water to a position in which I could reach a rough-barked tree, and pull myself head and shoulders clear of the water for a breather.

From this vantage point I had one look down-stream, at the whorls in the water boiling over hidden obstacles, and then no more: it was too discouraging to further efforts. I remembered that one should never look over one's shoulder when running before a steep sea in a small boat, because the water always looks far more vindictive than it is.

Over and over again I tried to get bottom with my feet, but the water carried them away. Knowing that I was possibly out of my depth altogether I gave up trying and relied only upon my hands.

As I worked my way out into midstream, the tug of the water increased beyond my expectation: but it may have been that I was losing courage and it merely seemed to strengthen unduly fast. I was becoming panicked by the relentlessness of the

current, as one is almost unnerved sometimes when
sailing by the merciless persistence of a high wind.
If it would let up for the space of a breath, vouch-
safing even a second's rest, it would not be so
terrible; but it goes on without a second's inter-
mission. Now, at each shift of my hands, water
tried to slip between them and their objective, water
cushioned every outward swing, deadened my
efforts, so that, gasping and afraid, I reached short
of my aim, and at each small error in judgment,
water poured chuckling over my shoulders, sometimes over my face.

Always uncertain of the strength of my hold,
I progressed only a foot or less at each anxious
move, and occasionally not at all for long seconds
at a time, when everything I touched felt too yielding
to trust. Eventually I would be forced to depend
on it, for want of better support, and by luck it
always held. There was one particularly bad patch,
where a sapling was caught only by its branches;
the slender trunk, floated away from the dam by
the stream, was very nasty to work round: it cost
me a struggle to let go of the dam and rely entirely
upon its flimsy hold, yet it was impossible, for me
at least, to duck under the trunk in this fierce
current: I tried twice and failed. Long parasitic
creepers clung to the young tree, and I felt the
water gently folding these still living streamers
about my head and shoulders and arms, as I tried
to force myself down under water. I had no idea

how the two who went in front had negotiated this
bit. Deotlan nearly caught up with me while I was
trying to collect sufficient heart to go hand-over-
hand out to the sapling's roots and back.

There was a constant gentle creaking, thudding
and shuddering of the dam, as the material in it
'worked' under pressure of the current and of the
stuff bearing down on it from upstream. Above that
and the noise of the water, I heard Stewart yell an
urgent warning, but the words were indistinguish-
able. Then Arnold's voice took it up and shouted
the same thing twice, but whatever had happened
I could not move at the moment: a handful of
brushwood and small vines had loosened in my hand,
and, swung out at full length of my other arm, I was
fighting to keep hold on a slippery, tapering root
and to drag myself back against the current. I was
in another rotten place, a kind of bay in the dam,
where there was nothing substantial within reach.
Every fresh grasp, when I could touch anything at
all, brought away handfuls of the small stuff – the
friable material of floating islands – which acted as
binding to the bigger logs. I heard Arnold shout
again, with fear in his voice (no new thing in any of
our voices) 'Judy! Get on to the dam. Out of the
water, Judy!' But a little thornbush, towards which
I had been striving, had just disentangled itself
from the dam. Inexorably, purposefully, turning in
the current in a leisurely way as a deliberate-man-
nered woman turns to disengage her dress, it

floated off downstream, leaving nothing less precarious than matted grass to which I could hold.

I tried to shout back, but the long-drawn-out effort had made me breathless, and my answering call sounded feeble in my own ears. Arnold shouted again, and then he and Stewart did what would have been impossible in cold blood, and impossible I think even in a lesser emergency. Having somehow climbed out on to the dam itself, at imminent risk of breaking it, they ran back along it for twenty yards or so.

Even had time allowed, they could not have crawled over it so far: hardly anywhere in this loose wedge of floating rubbish was there sufficient support for a man's weight, out of the water. Trunks turned under their feet, small branches broke, and they jumped wildly for another patch of tangled rushes and creepers and grass, and leapt on before that had time to give way entirely. One of them – I did not see which – straddled two logs and leant out perilously to reach me, while the other lay full length on a light mesh of rubbish, that should not have held for a second. I was hauled up regardless of the ripping edges of broken branches and saw-like grass: I did not realise till later, when I began wondering where all the gore in my vicinity was coming from, how much they hurt me between them while getting me out.

Stewart, well past midstream, had been making his way along a difficult stretch towards the goal of a fair sized log, a few yards ahead, when the log stirred, curved lazily in a half-circle, and sank. Some drowned and partially eaten babirusa were caught in that side of the dam, nearer the bank. He saw several spiny tails, that he had taken for boughs, flip up gently and disappear as he yelled and scrambled unavailingly among the breaking, yielding debris, threshing water with his feet as he tried to find a solid hold. It took him what he described as a long while to climb out: but it could not have been more than a few seconds of mental agony.

All this, naturally, he and Arnold did not tell me at the time, but one Malay word 'Buaya!' shouted by Arnold to Deotlan was enough to make me understand. It was enough for him too. A fisherman, he was more agile in these surroundings than we were; he was half out of the crumbling dam before Arnold yelled to him again.

We were lucky that the beasts were gorged: but a crocodile kills wantonly, for the sake of killing: it would be as easy for them as for us to get from the water on to the dam. We could not stay where we were, and the strained, haphazard structure on which we crouched would not bear us if we tried to crawl along it. But we were relieved of the need to make a decision on which everything depended: for once Malaya played on us a more or less kindly practical joke – detestable, like all practical jokes, but ranking as kindly because it was not the worst that might have happened; and in this land, which I loathe, something a little less than the ultimate horror seems to me all that one can reasonably ask of Providence. But probably I am a bit biassed about this; the country has its ardent lovers, before whom I am always speechless.

The dam gave, near the other end. That was a ghastly sample of eternity, the endless stretch of time in which we felt the thing buckle and slip, jerking itself free as the stream tore, one after another, the last strands that anchored it. At the bank from which we had come it held for a few instants longer, and those instants saved us. Like a gate opening, the remains of the dam swung round downstream, disintegrating as it did so. The part where we clung reached the shallows before it broke up altogether, depositing us within easy swimming distance of the bank from which we had started. We even recovered the rifle, which dropped in the water and took much labour to free from grit and damp: but Arnold lost his only reliable pair of glasses, the calamity that we had been anxiously staving off since we left the ship. He still had the emergency pair, now cracked in one lens, but they, although horn-rimmed, had thin gold sidepieces, 'tired' on the left side by his incorrigible trick with that hand. In his mind this loss loomed much larger than our failure to get across the river. He now had nothing to fall back on in an emergency.

So we went on upstream, looking for a ford or a

village, all the rest of that day, when we had re-covered sufficiently to move at all; and I think all the next day as well, and half the morning of the next day after: but time telescopes in recollection of arduous days. I can remember clearly nothing but the walking, sometimes at dawn, sometimes at dusk, sometimes in the dreadful heat at midday. The weather changed back to fine sultriness, and the character of the country was altering too, as we climbed. For many miles we were clear of the jungle, and walked in stony places among scrub that gave little shade. That was appalling. Our clothes could not yet fairly be described as rags (they still had some sound areas) but they were approaching that condition. We arranged them carefully over the sun-sores that the heat brought out again, and the wind blew them aside, and then the sun was like a knife on neck and shoulders.

We hardly spoke at all: we only laughed once in several days, I think — on the occasion when Deotlan brought back to the shelter (one did for us all, now) a very small and mouldy durian fruit that he had found while absent for his own purposes. It was growing dark and the three of us had turned in, but he insisted on rousing us and making Arnold share the thing with me, giving none to Stewart, nor to himself, though all natives dote upon this repulsive fruit. It has a rank flavour, and a still more violent smell, which most Europeans take years to learn to tolerate. He was so earnest about it that I ate some from courtesy, disliking it very much.

'Did you come from Pahang, originally?' Arnold asked him, surprised.

Deotlan, squatting by the fire, nodded in a confidential, man-to-man way, with a warning glance in my direction, and Arnold laughed.

'This – ah – gift of kindly and versatile Nature is credited thereabouts with – er – distinct aphrodisiac properties, Judy!' he said, relying on Deotlan's limitations as an interpreter. 'He evidently entertains benevolent feelings towards me, if not you, and deplores my neglect of opportunities. I'm touched. I hope you are!'

We all laughed, and Deotlan looked puzzled. Surely the Tuan could not have been so foolish as to tell the woman and perhaps spoil his chance? '*Sakit hati, mem Corder*!' Stewart explained, lifting his hands, and looking up to the deep blue velvet sky, to convey how exceptionally hard my liver was; and then Deotlan laughed with us.

'It's no use trying to make a Malay understand that there's no better chaperon than being dam' tired,' Arnold said, crawling back into the shelter and lying down with his head on my knees, because in this locality there was nothing handy to arrange as a pillow. 'He can't get as tired as all that. I am where I never hoped to be during my active years – beyond temptation!'

Stewart on my other side grunted a friendly and

amused agreement and went to sleep. I was not so
far gone in weariness; I still wanted Arnold, and
kept my feet stiller than my burning shoulders,
which only disturbed Stewart when I moved them
wretchedly. But then compared with an intelligent
man I, like any other normal woman, consisted of
remarkably little but instinct at such times. Or,
indeed, I thought in a moment of modest depression,
at any time.

My thoughts, rushing here and there, active and
alarmed all day, were taken up with so many pressing
things of the moment that this desire was not yet
the incessant dissatisfaction of mind and body that
I had known once, and was reluctant to know again.
But at the back of my mind remained a feeling, not
a thought, that did not vary with the rest, but
waited, and it was turned always towards him. And
the new fear – fear for him and, through him, fear
of greater intensity for myself – was never long out
of my mind. We had not kissed one another since
that last day spent in the clearing where Wan Nau
was buried. We might never have an opportunity
to do so again: but that would make no difference
to this feeling, half frightened, half serene. It
existed independently of my busy thoughts, which
flew to and fro in the light, as bees do in the service
of a queen that stays in the dark and need not work
to live. And like bees, my thoughts came back to
this feeling, this queen-motive, this desire, quietly,
at night.

I do not think the durian fruit had its intended effect. Something – propinquity – nature – the urge of complementary genes – whatever it was, had thoroughly forestalled it.

Unexpectedly we ran into a hunting party of five Malays the next morning as we skirted a thicket. We all stopped dead within a few paces of one another. They were armed with *parangs*, but no rifles.

There must always be an instant of tension at the meeting of armed strangers in wild country; the time between the first quickened heart-beat and the next, when men's hands move, not openly towards weapons, but in nervous preparation for anything that may happen. Deotlan spoke to them, and then Arnold, and the foremost man answered courteously. They were from a village perhaps a mile and a half farther up river, they said ('to be walked in twice the time in which a woman cooks a rice-pot'– the common denominator of Malay time. I recognised the phrase from Deotlan's frequent use of it). Yes, there was a little ammunition to be bought, the *pawang* had an old rifle, rarely used. And they would ferry the Tuans over the river, though the water was angry and they would need compensation for risking a challenge to the disturbed spirit, which should be left in peace until it grew calmer. Venturing upon it might mean a continuation of its wrath, which had already robbed them of fish for many days, so that they were forced to hunt, as we saw.

A man who had been staring intently at Deotlan interrupted the speaker with a few words, said aside to his own party. He came forward and scrutinised Deotlan aggressively. I heard the word 'Pedagor' mentioned, though neither Deotlan nor Arnold had told them where we had come from, as far as I could make out.

While Deotlan argued, denying something without success apparently, Arnold turned to Stewart and me. He spoke cheerfully but rapidly, smiling as though nothing were wrong and he merely translated what had gone before. 'Fisherman from a village below the rapids, where they're at feud with the Pedagor fish-poachers! For filthy luck, this is unbeatable! And he's married and settled into the village near by. Seems to be some sort of personage, the *pawang's* son-in-law, I gather.'

Deotlan claimed Arnold's attention, to back up some of his lies, and there was further argument. The man from downstream was growing more and more surly, and the attitude of the others had changed: they were not yet hostile, but they were suspicious. They had heard many times, one-sidedly, of the unparalleled iniquity of the Pedagor fisherfolk.

'This confounded fellow will go straight back to the village when we part, and set everyone there against us. They won't actually molest us here, I gather, but that's all. We shan't get a thing.– *Tida, Kintaling, Deotlan ta'pernah* – Look bored

Judy, and start collecting firewood as if we were due for a meal. Dump it just out of sight round the corner of the wood and come back for more. Drift in and out of sight as if you don't understand what's going on and aren't interested.'

In a few seconds he called, 'Bring me some piece of wood that looks too hard for you to break.' He put his hands carelessly into his pockets, and turned back to the other men. I did what he asked and he gave me unobtrusively our few remaining Malayan coins, while handing back the broken bits of wood. 'Make a dash for the village while we keep them talking. They won't bother about the woman of the party being out of sight, at first – think you're cooking. Buy ammunition. I daren't tell you in their hearing the Malay for it, but you can make the villagers understand. Try the women: they're quickest. It's the *pawang* who has it, remember. Go straight on upsteam afterwards, about three miles, and wait for us. The village can't be more than two miles from here, probably a good deal less. By the river. These men know the paths and you don't, but we ought to be able to give you at least a quarter of an hour's start. Don't worry, even if they do catch you up, by bad luck, these men aren't likely to attack a white. They might go for Deotlan if they caught him alone. And in the village, if you get there first, the people are certain to be friendly. Only be careful on the way – my dear – and *race*. Good luck.'

He threw himself again into the fierce argument.
Deotlan had by now given up trying to bluff the
other man out of his recognition, and the age-old
dispute about the right to the delta channels was
being threshed out bitterly and inconclusively once
more. Men are generally ready to share one
another's quarrels in this land, and the fisherman's
fellow-villagers sided with him. Like two dogs on
the verge of a fight that each is unwilling to begin,
both parties seemed equally unready to be the first
to turn tail and walk away. I wandered off, stooping
occasionally for sticks, and when a thickness of trees
was between me and the men I dropped the collection and began half running, half walking, at a pace
I thought I could maintain; it would be useless to
risk losing my wind at the beginning by a spurt of
speed. The angry raised voices floated down-wind
to me for some while.

The country was open, but undulating, and I was
not in fit condition, I realised at the end of a few
minutes, for a sustained effort like this, demanding
stamina. Without great strain I could not keep up
anything like the pace at which I started, moderate
as it was, and I dared not slacken very much.

I made a small detour round a hillock, to keep out
of sight, worked back to the river bank, and was
lucky in striking a faint trail that I took on trust as
having been made by the feet of the villagers; and
it led me right. I ran sometimes, when fear overtook me; the pain of the sun, scorching my shoulders

and neck, almost forgotten in the suffocation and distress of bursting heart and lungs. At other times I dropped to a walk, looking back over my shoulder.

To move at all through the open in this heat was a torment: bushes, stones and the gleaming water swam about me, and sweat lay heavily in the creases of my eyelids, pouring down my face. Every sound from the thickets beside the path held so great a menace, now that I was completely defenceless, that I tried not to listen, and listened more intently because of it. The loudness of the blood hammering in my ears was a blessing; it dimmed my acute hearing. I had no choice but to come unarmed. Throughout the argument between the men the rifle rested, ready loaded and cocked by accident as it might be, under Stewart's arm; and pointing, again accidentally it seemed, towards the feet of the other party. While they stood a couple of yards or so apart, warily, it would be quicker to bring into action than a kris, even in Malay hands. It was the best argument on Deotlan's side.

I lost all sense of time and distance. I began to wonder if I could have passed the village blindly in avoiding some hollow or wood. I made desperate bets with myself, for no stake but the checking of panic, that I would not look back again until I had passed that clump of trees – reached the top of this knoll. I was not as sure as Arnold had seemed that in an unfederated state the villagers would on no account risk violence against white people, particularly if we were caught trying to circumvent them by cunning. I doubted that Arnold himself was as convinced as he sounded. But this was our one chance of getting what we must have at almost any price, and if he were wrong about our security I should have been no safer had I remained with my own party – four exhausted people with one rifle, one knife between them, against five who were fresh, and all armed.

The track ran round a bluff, and with relief, as I came in sight of the river again, I stopped and looked round, before reaching the place I had appointed for myself; for there in the hollow ahead of me lay the village. Behind me the country was visible for about half a mile. Nothing human moved in it.

I wiped my face on the remains of my skirt, and forced myself to walk slowly, now that I was in sight of the first huts. My knees were trembling violently from the strain. I ought not to appear at the point of dropping from weariness and recent exertion when I arrived, but I must take the chance of the villagers thinking my appearance too strange to pass without investigation, on top of my coming alone, a white woman in dilapidated clothes, presumably from some party travelling by without stopping. I am one of the naturally pale people who when overheated grow paler, and I hoped that unused to whites, having seen at most half a dozen of them in their lives, the natives would think it not abnormal for any of this peculiar race to appear distressed by the full heat of the day. Apparently it was so: children clustered round me in wonder at the outskirts of the village, and women came out on to the platforms of their huts to stare as I went by, using all my control to prevent myself hurrying, but when I got to the *pawang* at last, by the expedient of repeating the word to everyone in sight, he was more interested to know where my party was, I think, than in the state I was in.

I waved an arm vaguely in the opposite direction to the river, and embarked on a series of gestures, drawing a rifle in the dust of the main street as well as I could. He and the growing crowd of onlookers laughed heartily at my attempt, and made no effort to understand it: certainly it was not very good. There followed quite five minutes, I should think, of nerve-racking anxiety: the old man was slow of comprehension; and in any case he was in no hurry; this conversation entertained him and (by the time it was over) most of the village. Someone brought me coconut milk in a gourd, and I had to drink it moderately, though I was unbearably thirsty: it would not do to show undue haste. Above all there must be no suggestion of anxiety. At every approaching footfall I scarcely dared look up in dread.

The women standing round out of curiosity showed themselves, as Arnold had predicted, sharper in the uptake than the men. Prompted by a girl, one of the latter went leisurely into the *pawang's* hut at length and brought me a cartridge questioningly. The sight of it put me off my guard; my eagerness in seizing it and demanding more surprised everyone: I saw men look at one another, puzzled, and some of the women laughed. If they turned suspicious now, they would prolong the transaction indefinitely, while they decided what to do. The situation must certainly have seemed odd enough; what should a ragged white girl, unable to speak Malay, want so urgently with ammunition? To act down my slip, I asked for more milk. Nothing was done till it was brought. Then came bargaining. In a village like this they would have little everyday use for money, but occasionally Chinese traders worked their way up or down the river, as they do all over the peninsula, and during their visits it would be an invaluable commodity: the women were more anxious to have it than the men.

I was willing to pay all that I had in my hands for as much as they would give me: but the old man and the bystanders were not to be baulked of the native joy of haggling. Seeing what I had to offer, they showed me all the ammunition they had in the village – too little for that money, only about thirty rounds, and of this they could not spare more than half. They offered about fifteen rounds for so much of the money. One man then took away two of the cartridges, and, grumbling, another returned some of the money – too much, thought a third, subtracting another cartridge, and then the whole bargain was discussed again vehemently: and the moments crept on; and second after second I waited in a kind of numb expectancy for the fisherman and his friends to arrive and discover me.

Hearing those about me chattering amiably, between their shrill disagreements over quantity and price, I found it strange to know how quickly they would change in manner, these gay, fascinating, heartless people, if my expectancy were fulfilled before this interminable purchase ended.

Rapid footsteps, heavy enough to be men's, approached from the other end of the street, and I kept my eyes stupidly on the little pile of cartridges, fearing to look up, listening without breathing. They were running. Someone spoke to me and I made no answering sign, being paralysed by a horrible certainty. My terrified stillness impressed the little crowd; no doubt the *mem* did not think the cartridges enough, and would not pay. A man put back those he had subtracted, in spite of protests. I cowered for a second longer, and saw out of the tail of my eye men's feet advancing, as the owners pushed through the crowd, shouting to someone behind. They stood round me, closer than the others, and, hopelessly, I looked up. Three youths had come in from the padi-fields, judging from the mud on them, and, hearing what was going on, had come running lest they should lose all the excitement. They grinned at me. I could not smile back, even with relief.

I tumbled the cartridges into the gourd, added another dollar to the price, and sprang up, making my way determinedly towards the other end of the village, despite the babel of half-hearted argument that started instantly.

I thought the children would never leave me. They and one or two of the more curious elders, hoping to see the rest of my party, escorted me garrulously for some distance, so that I was forced to go out of my way, away from the river, in order that on their return they might give the angry hunters a wrong impression of my direction. All the time that they were with me I was conscious of how easy it would be for men to follow this noisy group. I gave no reply or recognition to the children's advances, walking as fast as shakiness allowed, and in twos and threes at last they dropped behind, when we came to the outskirts of the land tamed by the village.

When the last of them was out of sight I ran for some way, returning again towards the water, so that my route after leaving the village completed a triangle with the river as one side; and then I crawled into the thick undergrowth about a group of nipah palms, and hid there for an hour or so, to see whether I were being followed or not. No one came by, and I went on up the river, wondering whether I were going too far and would miss my party that way, or if I were still too close to the village – and wondering, too, whether this particular anxiety

were unnecessary and the affair had gone badly with them after I left.

About three miles upstream, Arnold had said. Not having come straight from the village it was even harder to guess the distance than it would have been in any case. I went on, far more than three miles, I thought, and then turned back a little way to a rise, from which I could see for a mile or so towards the village. No one was in sight. Then I hurried on again for what seemed to me an unduly long time, and, convinced suddenly that I had overshot the distance, I returned cautiously almost to within sight of the village. I was not now as much afraid of the dark thickets as I had been: fear of what they might bring forth lurked side by side with the other panic, barely held in leash in my mind, but it was dwarfed by this growing terror of being alone, not knowing what had happened to the others. While I lay in the bushes, watching the way I had come, they might have looked for me by the river, and, not finding me, have decided that something serious must have happened in the village. In that case it was possible that they had gone in desperately to find out: this was the kind of rash courage on the spur of the moment of which I knew Stewart to be capable. With the villagers aware, by now, of being if not exactly tricked at least manipulated deliberately, there would certainly be fighting, and the three of them would have no chance at all. Any one of half a dozen mishaps might have occurred to account for their absence. There were all the ordinary perils of the way. They ran through my brain, each suggesting another. But the most likely explanation was a fight forced on by the fisherman and his four friends soon after I left. It must have been four or five hours since I had sauntered away with firewood in my arms.

When I turned away from the village again I had reached the stage of hopeless despondency in which time ceases to count as a factor in anxiety, although it has hitherto been the main one. As the minutes went past and still there was no sign of them, it did not seem to me that the likelihood of my finding them diminished any more; it made no difference now; I still looked for them, but not with expectancy. I kept on upriver, stumbling from sick weariness, and the reaction from physical effort, and a painful hunger that I did not recognise till later. I was not keeping a look-out, and walked on only because I was impelled to move in some direction and this was as good as another. I had no idea of the ground over which I passed, except that it was cut into small valleys and hills. I think I must have gone about six miles, but it may have been much less, when I heard someone shout. All three of the men, though separated at the time, saw me long before I saw them. Stewart told me that with the gourd held carefully in both hands in front of me, I was walking with small steps and bent head like a child carrying a jug of milk, not looking right or left.

They – or I – had badly misjudged the distance: it was very easy to do that in this country. In our relief we did not argue as to which of us had made the mistake; probably there was some error on both sides. After I had got away they had managed to keep the hunters in increasingly angry discussion for longer than they had dared to hope, breaking off the talk only when the menace of a hopelessly unequal fight became really imminent: none of the Malays seemed to attach any importance to my absence: what had a woman to do with men's affairs? The two parties had separated stiffly, each of the villagers being still unwilling to make the first aggressive movement, because of the rifle in Stewart's hands – though, to give Malays their due, none of them would have held back for a second once the decisive step had been taken by a friend. But the crisis, seeming inevitable at times, was postponed again and again, and at last skilfully avoided altogether, by Arnold and Deotlan. The two parties had distrustfully watched each other nearly out of sight – long enough for Stewart and Deotlan to be sure that Arnold had been right, and the vindictive fisherman and two of his companions were making their way as fast as possible back to the village, to ensure an unfriendly reception for us if we were foolhardy enough to try our luck there.

After that the three of them had given the village a wide miss, rejoining the river at a point that they imagined to be roughly three miles above it. When I did not appear, hour after hour, they had separated to search the country round for me. In the network of roughly parallel valleys and hills we may have passed close to one another unseen.

Arnold, who reached me first, put out a hand to steady me as I stopped, and I know I stared at him unbelievingly. Without intention I moved forward into his arms and kissed him, not caring that it was before the others. I did not notice Stewart's face at the time, I was too tired to care. I went to sleep sitting up with my head propped against someone's shoulder while one of the others produced food of some kind which I woke to eat mechanically. It was found so hard to wake me afterwards that we encamped there for the night, dangerously close to the village.

CHAPTER IX

'KERPN'

BEFORE the fisherman's party turned threatening, Deotlan and Arnold had learnt from them that there was another ford two or three days' journey up the river. It was in bad country, they said vaguely, and further than this they were not inclined to help us. Later, they would not have given us even this information.

We pushed on towards it, across partially open country which gradually robbed us of all awareness save that of the torturing sun. I suffered most, being fair to insipidity, but even Deotlan felt the forced marching in this heat, though he was free from our greatest misery, sun-sores. They made day and night alike a wretchedness beyond description. In spite of the precautions we took, with ingeniously concocted spine-pads, I do not know how we escaped sun-stroke, nor blood-poisoning from the assortment of germ-laden stuff — tree gum with mud over it, animal fat mixed with anything that would hold — with which we tried to protect these skinless mattering patches. But as before, do what we would, a malicious tepid wind fluttered apart our rags, dried our messy preparations and made a way for the sun to stab through with a merciless golden probe.

Arnold's defective eyesight stood him in good stead. He escaped, with Deotlan, the opthalmic trouble caused by constant glare; his importunate glasses could be smoked. Every time the brittle grass lashing broke (and even in my unfairly favourable view he seemed to break it far more often than anyone else would) the carbon got rubbed off the lenses while we were renewing it, and then the long anxious process of smoking them had to be gone through again. Stewart and I had aching, bloodshot eyes all the time. With the curious obstinacy of the human spirit we kept on at the best pace of which we were capable, climbing farther and farther into the hills, though we hurried now not with any definite feeling of urgency to return to such far-off things as jobs – they were more or less forgotten. We had left the ship over ten days ago: presumably we should still be many days on the way, if we ever made Kintaling at all. Indeed, we recognised with grim amusement by now that we should undoubtedly have saved time by remaining in the ship, and taking everything into consideration, that would also have been the less dangerous course. But we had endured so much to come so far: we were going on with a vague impulse to race time because privation, fear, and hatred of this country had reduced us to unthinking

creatures, determined to carry on with a pre-
conceived plan that no longer mattered very much.

To force myself to stand the pain and weariness,
I made my idle mind aware of time as I have done
before as a means of getting through bad hours.
There – that's a second gone – gone for ever – its
misery cannot come back. There's another to join
it. This wretchedness cannot go on for ever. The
seconds will see it through, at last. Another's gone –
by so much I am nearer to release from it, however
release comes.

It is interesting to me to find that, looking back,
the periods in which one exists numbly, living only
to get through time, seem to be those in which one
has lived most intensely. This phase of the journey
is vivid still in my mind. I can recall at will birds
and animals seen, and our scanty meals, and trivial
incidents to which at the time I paid little attention.
And it has been the same in the *Shellduck* which
Stewart and I shared, and in the cranky boat I ran
before that entirely on my own. Stretches of time
in which I have been very much afraid, and have
struggled to keep my mind blank save for practical
matters, for fear of fear, can be resurrected in startling detail a long while later, and I know that then
I was alive to the bounds of my nature. There
was a moment in this stage of the journey when,
careless through a long hope's realisation, we were
standing round the body of a wild sow we had shot,
and a boar charged out of a thicket while Deotlan

was re-loading at leisure. Arnold, the nearest man, leapt aside in time, though one of the tusks gave him a passing blow on the thigh, ripping it slightly. Deotlan shot the beast as it checked to turn and charge again, and, wounded, it disappeared into cover. I hope never to be again so tinglingly aware of life in every nerve as I was in the few seconds of its rush.

I was not in a fit state in those days to be concerned over Stewart's feelings. I did notice that after he had seen me kiss Arnold he withdrew from me into himself – keep away from me physically he could not, in the circumstances, whatever his feelings were, for we slept in the same shelter – but I could not greatly care, then, if I had hurt him, though actually I suppose I was fonder of Stewart than of the man I loved.

By this time the country had changed again. Higher on the hillside, down which the river thundered, we came to more patches of jungle, as dense and evil as the forest about Pedagor. I should not have thought it possible that I could welcome it as I did: the sun was a more intolerable enemy, though a less nerve-shaking one perhaps, than the menacing, brooding silence – a real presence of silence it had become in our minds – lurking among foliage that stirred at times for no ascertainable reason. The sense of watchful eyes about us returned to us horribly as soon as we began to work our way through the undergrowth.

Soon the thickets became more or less continuous, and we whispered instinctively again, because here was the real jungle. Deotlan seemed more attentive to every sound, more ill at ease than usual. He was evasive when questioned as to his reason for moving camp hurriedly to the edge of a thicket the second evening (the ford, as usual with everything in this land, proved to be farther away than we had been given to understand). We did not press him for an answer, knowing that, in his faith, to name the thing you fear from the jungle in the hearing of the jungle is to call it to you. But when he tried to return to open ground, after we had penetrated deeper, we declined resolutely. Any time now, as we scrambled and pushed through the heavy vegetation on the river bank, we might come on the wide reach which was said to be fordable: (certainly it should be that by this time, for the river had been abating for two or three days). We were not going to give up the idea of reaching it now.

Deotlan gave in sulkily, without arguing, as he had done at our first meeting, when we insisted that if he acted as our guide at all, it must be to Kintaling. Being more of a fisherman than a hunter, he had never had more than the vaguest idea of the overland way, we now knew. Professing one religion and observing the rites of another, like all his native kinsman, he was also a fatalist and yet intensely superstitious at the same time. He would dispute endlessly over small matters – whether we should cook the last of our rice or be content with small birds: if a shelter should face this way or that — but on no subject which might have a life or death significance would he say all that was in his mind, for that would be 'unchancy.' The disposal of all important things was out of men's hands, he thought, and if we, who were unbelievers, grew obstinate on some point like this we were still no more than instruments in the hands of a controlling spirit; of what use could it be to explain to the helpless instruments the malevolence of the djinn? He thought that in deciding as we did, we decided our own destruction, but he did not tell us this. If we were to be lost, it would happen one way or another. It was best to give in, and mollify the spirit who had taken control. Yet I know that at heart he was as much afraid as we were.

His increased alertness brought more forcibly into my consciousness than before, the series of scarcely perceptible sounds and movements in the forest for which we could not account, and the wisdom of looking only to one's steps, lest one saw at every moment some disquietening sign of the unseen life that observed and waited balefully. I could have sworn several times that we were being followed. It was likely enough. It may have happened to us before, without our suspecting it. There were many patient, voracious beasts in these parts.

All day we had been working our way through close jungle as fast as possible, with Deotlan now forcing the pace. But on the following morning we were immobilised temporarily by the loss of my native shoes, the only ones I had. Damp, and liable to go stiff if not dried properly, they had been left on the edge of the circle of firelight, to leeward of the fire, where the smoke would dry them slowly. The person on guard naturally sat to windward, so that the obscuring flicker of the flames had been between the watcher and these small objects, which had both disappeared. Even so, it was amazing that anything living could have come as close as that without being seen. It was also disturbing, apart from the difficulty of finding a substitute for the shoes.

This delayed us considerably. My feet were so much harder now than they had been at the beginning of the trip, that I could safely stand the chafe of roughly dressed skins, which would have been dangerous before. After half a day's fruitless hunting, Deotlan managed to kill a small barking-deer, and we dried the skin over the fire and contrived coverings that did fairly well, though I was always having to stop and tighten the slippery fastening. Having wasted a day in this manner, we slept in the same shelter as on the previous night. I lay awake during Deotlan's watch, as I often did for the greater part of the night. Arnold was lying by me. Stewart, holding aloof, had tacitly accepted that order of lying, and was on the other side of Arnold. If he happened to be awake too, Arnold sometimes put

out a hand and touched my arm or shoulder
friendlily; once, he claimed, he had kissed me without my knowing it.

Deotlan was walking about restlessly with his
rifle under his arm. Stewart, judging by his breathing, was certainly asleep; I did not think Arnold
was. I heard him turn over towards me, I thought,
though it was too dark to see. I did not move when
a hand passed gently down my arm: the reassurance
of a caress, shutting out my awareness of the forest
for a second, was what I longed for just then: it
was my guard next and I disliked the prospect, as
always. I lay still for a second after the hand withdrew, ridiculously moved by this warm human
contact: it had been so light that if I had not been
awake I think it would not have roused me. When
I put out an answering hand to Arnold, my fingers
touched the back of his shoulder. In that position
he could not have reached out to me like that, and
in any case he was asleep. I woke the two of them
with hysterical, terrified laughter, laughing because
I had been deeply stirred by the contact.

We found a little gap at the back of the shelter,
about six inches from the ground, where the yielding
bamboo had been pressed aside: nothing else,
though Deotlan fired both barrels after a fleeting
shadow in the thicket. This was the only time that
I knew Deotlan's nerve give way in the pressure of a
moment. It was only one of many half-shadows,
shifting with the wind, and I did not think it moved

unaccountably, or more unaccountably than any of the writhing shadows of roots and creepers on which the firelight flickered. The shots sounded appallingly loud in the stillness. After the reverberations had died the jungle crept closer by a pace or two, to listen again.

'Sakei!' (one of the negrito hill tribes) said Deotlan with resignation. He began twining a loose tendril of vine on a nearby tree into a cross within a circle, to ward off evil, taking care while bending the spray not to break any part of the stem; but he showed less confidence than usual in the efficacy of this rite. Sakei were a more material form of menace than djinns and less amenable to this kind of treatment. But at least it could do no harm, while it might do good: one never knew, in the jungle.

By the light of a burning stick from the fire we examined the shelter. The Sakei had got nothing, unless it was then that I lost a piece of the sleeve of Stewart's ex-shirt, which, soaked in deer-fat, I had been using to ease my worst burns. Demolishing the shelter, which offered too good cover for others besides ourselves, we huddled round the fire for the rest of the night. But nothing disturbed us until the ingits shrilled before dawn. We might have been utterly alone, for all we heard or saw, in this great emptiness of trees, save that our awareness of eyes had increased tormentingly.

For some time Deotlan had suspected that we

were in Sakei country, he said, from several signs that would have been meaningless to us – an old sap-cut in an ipoh tree – a dead monkey with a puffy poisoned face. I knew that these people of the interior, with the Semang and Jahun, were the original inhabitants of the land into which the Malays had overflowed from Sumatra and Java, many hundreds of years ago. The newcomers had traded with them, cheated them, driven them back farther and farther into the hill jungles, and died at their hands when the Sakei caught them alone. So much dead knowledge remained from the far-off period in which I 'did' anthropology with bored inattention – days when, as far as I was concerned, natives in general, like religion, were somehow true but not real.

Now, as we crouched by the fire with our eyes constantly over our shoulders, I heard the living facts about them.

Almost anywhere that a squirrel can pass, a Sakei can go, among the highest branches; they slip effortlessly through thick jungle in which a Malay could not cut a path. Shivering – the night was clammily cold – I thought that probably we could discount much of this, but afterwards I discovered that for once Deotlan was speaking the exact truth. They are as timid as the rusa-deer to whom they can creep unseen, cutting the animal's throat while it sleeps. (Actually, this feat was boasted of to me by one of the Jahuns later on, and I believe it; they are not often intelligent enough to be able to lie.) I acquired a fantastic feeling from Deotlan's talk that night that they were part trees and part animals, hardly men at all, and I never quite lost it.

Through accredited channels, in company with Malays whom the Sakei knew, many white people have come in contact with these remnants of a dying race, have won as much of their confidence as the wild can give to the civilised, and have written about them. But without warning we had come armed into their territory. They would be afraid of us, and dangerous because they were afraid. Deotlan was oddly contemptuous in his fear of them. A descendant of two less primitive races, he stressed, like a suburban lady deploring the provincialism of acquaintances, the shocking fact that they had only four numerals in their twittering tongue. He referred to this several times – *ne*, *na-nu*, *nar* (one, two, three) and after that only *kerpn*, meaning many – as though this seemed to him the most notable thing about them. But I remembered the soft touch of that hand, preceded by no sound of approach whatever, and I listened eagerly for the first of the ingits.

There must be *kerpn* of these hill men about us now, we knew, though we could not see them and did not see any of them for days. Many as they were, they would not dare to attack us yet, while we were comparatively strong, though as thieves their extraordinary dexterity made them bold. In spite of precautions, we lost the rifle the next day. In full daylight, or as much light as the green roof allowed, it was laid on the ground for a few seconds that Stewart might use both hands to break through a thin screen of creeper across our path, and when he looked down it had gone.

This shook us all so badly that we did not even discuss the loss, nor the hopelessness of the future.

Afterwards there was something inevitable in the way in which trivial things disappeared from among us by no apparent means: but once the rifle had gone, nothing else mattered.

They waited for some while to see whether we were weaponless, and finding that we had only a knife, which Deotlan with useless tenacity kept in his hand day and night, they began to harry us, hunting us away from the river, farther into the hills.

Barring our way if we turned back for any distance, a shower of little darts would fly rattling among the leaves ahead of us. Unarmed, and growing weak with want of food, we were driven like game. Twice at night we saw the glimmer of a fire, but when we made our way to it, desperately, hoping to establish contact with these shy people, there was nothing there save the tiny heap of smouldering wet wood. They could have killed us at any time, but apparently they did not want to; at any rate not yet.

Like kites, they waited for the enfeeblement of the prey. The only food we could get without a

gun was fruit, which produced violent diarrhoea,
as weakening as the continual hunger. It was the
strangest hunting, this: the quarry striving only
to meet the hunters who eluded it time after time.

I think it went on for two or three days. Being
strung up to the highest pitch of fear of which one is
capable, for a considerable period like this, blurs all
memory of time. I remember incidents clearly,
not their duration. I know that we tried once to
escape their vigilance at night. But many of the
Sakei never see broad daylight throughout their
queer, leaf-shrouded lives: our eyes were blind beside
theirs in the darkness. We had a proof of their
presence before long; darts that sounded like hail
hit the bushes all round us, it seemed, and we
stopped. It was in any case a forlorn hope: as
trackers they are equal to the Gonds of India, and
they could move many times faster than we could
on this ground.

We four were back now at the beginning of
human time, when man, the thinking worm, not
fleet of foot, neither armed nor strong as compared
with his enemies, was hunted through the forest
with only his slow, groping mind, agonised by new
effort, with which to fight for his safety. Men died
fearfully in thousands then, that Man might live:
but our deaths here would be useless.

Reasonably, I should have been more afraid in
those days than at any other time in my life, but one
can only fear extinction to a certain degree. The

bounds of terror are set wide, differing with individuals, but there is a limit beyond which fear cannot increase, and I had reached it before on this journey. The torture of extreme dread could go on until something gave way, but it could not be augmented. This is small satisfaction however: the saturation point of fear is very close to the border of insanity for everyone, and beyond it for some. Such terror is, in itself, suffering beyond description, unless the mind gets numb with it, and probably in every case it is more terrible to bear than the thing feared. – But this is a still smaller source of satisfaction.

Deotlan knew one or two words of several of the negrito dialects. The boldest of these people occasionally come down from their fastnesses to trade gum and skins with the Malays, at an exploitation rate, for the rice they seem unable to grow satisfactorily for themselves, and the thin long-jointed bamboos used for blow-pipes which are rare in many parts of the interior.

When we were at the end of our tether, Deotlan shouted to them over and over again, his voice breaking with weariness. We knew that they were on all sides of us: we heard the forest pause in its quiet, multifarious activities to listen to his cry with an intolerable sense of straining for an answer, as we were straining; and then the far-off whooping of baboons, and bird and insect noises, crept back over the trembling stillness. There was no reply.

They were bestial in their shyness and we were weakening: it was worth their while to wait.

But we could not wait. Arnold expressed the decision to which he had come some time ago. Since then he had fought against it in his own mind. 'We'd better separate,' he said. 'They'll starve us to death before they'll attack four people. Deotlan says they've done that to parties of Malays before now. Not through calculated animosity, probably, sheer timidity.' He laughed with a dry sound that brought tears – tears of weakness more than anything else – into my eyes. 'I always have disliked shy people! If each of us is alone, and they know we've no weapons, it's just possible that none of us will be killed. Even two people together they won't approach. Chuck your knife away, Deotlan, anywhere; they'll find it all right. They might – it's a very small chance, but what else is there? – they might show themselves at last to each of us separately and we could come to some sort of terms with them – unless they cut our throats first, from shyness!'

I caught hold of his hands and cried over them. 'I can't . . . I can't.' I had been alone in the jungle for a short time before, but then it had been with some prospect of rejoining the others, and it had been almost more than my reason could stand. Death together was, by a little, preferable to death alone in the forest, and I saw no hope: I knew Arnold saw practically none either.

We were lying by a stream that ran through a

small clearing; we were too exhausted to move further. He put his arm round me, pressing my head against his shoulder with one hand. 'There isn't anything else, Judy,' he repeated.

'I don't care. I can't face it,' I cried.

It is not possible to convey the horror of the next hour or hours during which we talked it over, coming back inevitably, time after time, to the conclusion that Arnold was right.

'Dirty natives!' observed Deotlan dispassionately, and stood up to search for wood with which to start the task of fire-making, though he was almost too weak to complete it. A very brave man on occasion, he called something into the unanswering forest when the first flame licked among the punk wood and twigs, and stuck his knife ostentatiously into an anthill that towered up above our heads. Leaving it there, he sauntered away – tottered, rather – tightening the fastening of his sarong with a trace of the ineradicable swagger of the Pahang Malay.

The Sakei killed him, I think; presumably because he was a Malay, pure Malay in their eyes. They may not have troubled to do even that, but at any rate we did not see him again, and for anyone left weak and unarmed in such jungle there is no hope of survival.

Stewart left the party next, and Arnold wrenched his hands free suddenly and went too. I did not see their going. I lay face downwards on the ground, trying to shut out the sight of the surrounding forest. Soon I either fainted or slept. The midday hush, deeper than that of other hours, hung over the jungle when I came back to full consciousness, jerked from the comfortable borderland of dreams by the realisation of being alone. I crawled over to the stream, being almost as weak as I had been in fever. It was at least four days since we had had anything approaching a fair sized meal, and about two days since we had had any food at all.

Something small shrank back into the bushes as I moved. I did not look closely at it. Soon there would be other things. After I had drunk, and piled brushwood on the fire that Deotlan had made me, I lay by the stream with my eyes closed, waiting. The thing lurking in the bushes did not approach, and dusk fell.

Then came to me a realisation of the jungle, as it is at night, deeper than I had yet known. In civilisation the night is an alien thing, almost unknown in its power, an intruder shut out of its old kingdom by light and the sounds of day prolonged; we have raised a hundred barriers between it and our profoundest consciousness. And forests, too, remain strangers to us, though we loiter in their silences by day. They are not part of us, who are products of tamed land, and we do not belong to them: neither to them nor to the night are we native to-day. We remain only visitors when we go out into either of them. Four walls between us and the night, or the knowledge of four walls to which we shall return from the forest – these secure more than protection of body and peace of spirit: they shut out the essential night and the essential forest from our minds, even when they are close about us. But sleeping or lying awake through the darkness without shelters, as the four of us had done these past few nights, we had come into some sort of fresh contact with the jungle and the night. Yet it was nothing to this new knowledge of both which I now gained unwillingly.

From childhood I had been nervously aware of the change which takes place in trees and earth a little while after dusk, and of how familiar things recede and grow antagonistic then, like a lover when passion dies. In the jungle it was inescapably strong, this sense of a new charge of life flowing through the inanimate forms. Before that night I should have said that I already knew intimately that panic-edged, writhing darkness of the forest. But lying out now by the banked fire, I learnt something that I have since partly forgotten: it would not be possible to remain sane and hold it intact in one's mind. In any case it was incommunicable in its entirety – partly a feeling, as nearly as I can recall or express it, of close and unbreakable communion with every part of this savage, suffering earth, though this was but a fraction of the sudden extension suffered by my understanding. I fought against my realisation of being bound up in it all, helplessly and for ever. One grows light-headed in extreme hunger, and my enormously enlarged consciousness of every blade of grass and every grain of soil, here and elsewhere, may have been only that. Against this appalling sense of oneness with the night, and the forest, and with everlasting things whose images were these straining trees and this pointless wealth of air and water and ground, I could put only my wan faith in personal annihilation, clinging to the cold, comely pride of the spirit in accepting no trumped-up mitigation of its hopelessness in the face of death. And soon the life in me seemed to flow away into the ground and leave me empty and unexpectant, more or less passive. The horror ebbed too, and I was unconscious for a blessedly long time, I think.

CHAPTER X

THE FLITTINGS

THE Sakei were round me when the daylight returned: little men, mean-featured, emaciated: the certain extinction of the race within a few hundred years will be a loss only to biologists: they were the worst physical specimens of mankind that I have ever seen. Ten to fifteen of them stood in a wide semi-circle, chattering. I knew that they had been there some time, but I knew very little else for a day or so. Some low fever, inevitable I suppose in the condition I was in, got me down thoroughly. I can remember nothing of being moved, by slow stages, from there to a place farther up in the hills; nor when I first saw Arnold again.

As a child before it can speak grows into some knowledge of its surroundings, unaware of how this knowledge is acquired, I became gradually conscious that someone — recognisable later as Arnold — was doing things for me. There was some burden on my mind that I could not understand, but it seemed that it was not of immediate importance, since I could not clearly define it yet, and my brain went to sleep again for a while, at peace because Arnold was there.

We were in a small kampong, a collection of rough, beehive shaped wind-breaks, which the Sakei used for shelter at night. Arnold took up his quarters in an old one so dilapidated that he had it to himself. I was put into a slightly bigger one, in better repair, which I shared with an old man and woman who came in at dusk. There seemed to be no watch kept on us, and no check on Arnold's coming and going.

At irregular intervals the Sakei gave us a little unappetising and unsatisfying food – roots grubbed up by the women, and the roasted pith of plants.

It was some time before I realised that I had not seen Stewart nor Deotlan in the camp. Arnold was not with me at the moment when I woke up, knowing this suddenly. I crawled out of the shelter and stood up giddily. A crowd of miserable looking Sakei children gathered round me, at an awed distance, as I went round the kampong – only about twenty-five huts – calling the two men alternately in a desperate way, not fully sensible of what I was doing but very much afraid.

Arnold came hurriedly out of one of the big family shelters and tried to persuade me to go back and lie down. I looked ill enough to frighten him badly, he told me afterwards, but I heard a weak voice calling 'Judy! Judy, is that you?' and I made Arnold help me into the shelter where Stewart was lying. Some Sakei children, too young to be frightened of us, lay about the earth floor too, and there were evidences of family occupation all round.

He had been brought in a day later than we had, after a forced march that must have nearly killed him: he was suffering from a poisoned heel, though whether he had been grazed by a Sakei dart or, stumbling blindly in the night, had ripped the skin on the spines of some venomous plant, it was now too late to say: the poison had spread up to the knee by the time I saw it. He was dangerously ill, though to Arnold's eyes he did not appear to be in such a critical state as I did, though I was merely exhausted after two bouts of fever and a period of malnutrition. Two or three days would probably see me fairly fit again: two or three days might very well see Stewart out.

'He said you weren't fit to come, my dear,' Stewart said, smiling thin-lipped with his eyes closed. The leg was horribly swollen, and the pain at this stage must have been intense. 'I thought you'd turn up. Eager as a Florence Nightingale at the smell of blood! That's Judy.'

This was not literally true at the moment. When I am out of sorts myself I am as squeamish as a probationer (and when I am fit I am so overburdened with vitality that I should give myself, as an invalid, a headache in ten minutes – I cannot imagine anyone employing me professionally for choice). But a gust of anger with Arnold, for not telling me of Stewart's condition as soon as I was conscious, whatever his reason had been for keeping this from me, helped me to clear my brain of the lingering mistiness. I examined the prematurely healed-over scratch, and explained to Arnold what to do, but was beyond giving any assistance myself when he lanced the foot, hurting Stewart appallingly. We had no antiseptic, nothing that could remotely be called clean, and no sharp instruments: but somehow Arnold got hold of a makeshift knife belonging to one of the women who used the shelter. To the Sakei, the thunder is the voice of their chief god Karei or Kareid raised in anger; and when it sounds the women gash themselves with sharpened pieces of bamboo, presumably to placate him with a blood offering. Arnold charred one of these bamboo blades in the fire before using it, and then for several days we could only wait and see what would happen. With rather bad grace (while Stewart grumbled at everything the other man did for him) Arnold heated damp earth in the ashes of a fire and encased the unlacerated part of the foot and leg with this primitive form of poultice, and either it worked well or Stewart's natural health prevailed, for at the end of about five days the worst of the danger was over, though there could be no thought of our moving on yet – even supposing, of course, that the Sakei would let us go; and this we had no means of discovering at the moment.

He could just crawl out of his shelter to sit near the fire at night by the time that, as near as we could

reckon, some of the other passengers off the ship
we had left would be catching their connections at
Colombo for England. Arnold was my lover by then.

In this period of enforced leisure and recuperation
had come the blaze-up of emotion which the conditions of our life together had almost ensured, though
they had also delayed it for a while. After fear and
long sustained effort, we had come into comparative
safety and peace of a kind. Wanting Arnold as I
had done for what seemed a very long time, I was
still slightly incredulous – dismayed and amused
at the same time – to find this new, fierce access of
passion lighting in my own blood. It was a little
absurd to have seen this situation coming, to have
weighed the probabilities with the utmost detachment, and then, when it came, to be absorbed in it
heart and mind as I was now. I no longer desired
Arnold as something to be added to me: there
seemed to be nothing left of me except this crying
need of him. I had known exactly, from unhappy
experience, what he meant when he said 'I touch
nothing that is not your body.' But at this time I
could have said truly: I see nothing, hear nothing,
breathe nothing that is not an extension of you:
all the world is narrowed down to the size of one
person and glorified by that in my eyes. So much
of me has reached out to you that I am empty
except for this fire running in my veins.

In spite of this, when the two men quarrelled
openly as they did, inevitably, and more angrily

than they had done before, I joined with Stewart against him. For the first part of our stay in the camp, Stewart was too ill to be seriously annoyed by anything: the real outburst came when he had developed the normal convalescent's irritability. I still think he was justified in resenting what Arnold had done – taken it upon himself to decide that I was not well enough to be told of Stewart's condition, because, in the circumstances, telling me was synonymous with calling on me to exert myself on his behalf. Arnold thought I was dangerously ill: I was not, and Stewart was, and might easily have died, though Arnold did not know it. I was fairly sure – and so, of course was Stewart, which did not soothe his feelings – that if Stewart's position and mine had been reversed, Arnold would not have hesitated to call on him for any effort necessary to help me.

'I have a right to use my own discretion,' Arnold said sharply to Stewart.

'You'd no business whatever to back your own judgment in a case like this,' I said, and suppressed a smile because it was curious, in a Sakei wind-break, to hear my official voice sounding precisely as I had heard it in Whitechapel when dealing with mothers who would not bring their children to be vaccinated.

Arnold turned on me suddenly, with an expression in his eyes that startled me. The other, latent turmoil in all our nerves made grateful any violent expression of feeling, and added vehemence to anger.

'This is not your affair, Judy! Will you please go away and leave this to Corder and me?'

Stewart stretched out a weak hand and caught my arm.

'This is Judy's affair. We all see that it would have been to your advantage if I'd gone under, and been out of the way – you aren't the only person who wants her – '

Here was roughly the same situation as the one that had led to their first altercation; only that this was many times more serious. Again there would have been fighting but that one man was incapacitated. I had a second's hysterical feeling that this business would recur at intervals for ever.

Arnold, getting control of himself, laughed suddenly, the soft impersonal laughter that I listened for all day.

'No, but I'm the only one who's going to have her – get out, Judy, will you? ' And I went, and wandered about aimlessly, waiting for I did not know what, until I came to the edge of the camp. Not afraid for once of the heavy stillness of the jungle, I went on into it and sat down. Nothing happened for a long time: there might have been perfect peace in the kampong from the silence brooding over it. These round wind-breaks muffled the sound of furious voices. Listen as I would, I could hear only the forest murmurs intensifying the stillness.

There were very few of the Sakei about the place, only some of the children and very old women – old, that is, for negritos: I do not suppose that many of them live beyond forty. They were rotten with tropical diseases of all kinds – yaws and spleen troubles mostly. If I had still wanted it, I now had a marvellous opportunity to study *kurap* at close quarters. The children, who collected in a gang to stare at us unblinkingly for hours, were nearly all crawling with it, like many of their elders. I kept them at an even greater distance than their shyness dictated, and looked elsewhere. It was not difficult to avoid contact with them: we saw extra-ordinarily little of the Sakei considering that we were living on them and among them. Except as trackers and stalkers they were almost unbelievably stupid, remaining very timid, even when we were helpless. They were not hostile: I think that they had never been really hostile, though we should certainly have died through their harrying and stealing and unpredictable, frightened fits of aggression if we had kept together. But whether they would ever be willing to return to us the rifle, without which we could not leave them with any hope of safety, was a matter on which it was quite useless to speculate. Naturally, we did little else but speculate about it.

Turning round suddenly, for no reason of which I was aware, I glimpsed a Sakei woman, slinking like a ghost of grey-brown earth or grey-brown forest dusk, through the jungle close behind me. I am sure that I had not heard her pass, though she was within ten yards of me, in thick undergrowth. I watched her fascinated: she was a hideous travesty of a woman, but she moved as all her people did, as if they had some special lubrication of the skin, as fish have undoubtedly to minimise the friction of the water, so that the clutching arms of the forest could not hold her in the way that they held us.

When I turned back, Arnold was walking rapidly in my direction, looking for me, I knew: I could not easily be seen from where he was. But though I wanted to, for some reason I could not go to meet him. He called and I did not answer. I knew that something definite had happened or would happen now, and I was apprehensive. The constant fear of those days comes back sharply at times, and realising that it is now only the thin shadow of the substance I knew then, I am glad of the invincible barrier of time, shutting it away from me; it is so overpowering, even in memory. The jungle had crept into my mind in these last few weeks: it waited there, in a strange hushed agony, as it seemed to wait in the outside world for some immense and long-desired consummation which should destroy it. We had been in danger for too many days to remain quite sane. And danger's power of spiritual oppression had been augmented for me (and for the others too, I suppose) by the insecurity of the beloved person. I had grown easily fanciful in these surroundings. It seemed to me obscurely that Arnold and I would pass from danger to a certainty of disaster, and give the last fatal hostage to ill-fortune, by snatching from life at this moment the precarious satisfaction that our bodies and our hearts and minds demanded.

It was a painful joy to watch Arnold, unseen myself for a moment. There was little in common between the self-absorbed sick man I had met in the ship and this swift-moving person in rags: every tall, ill-held inch of his figure I knew well by sight, and loved. He was eager and angry now, very much awakened, but when he saw me in the end he came over and sat down on the ground by me, without touching me, saying nothing for a while. Soon we were attacked by red ants, which forced us to move. (*Sic transit* practically every tense moment of my life – red ants or hiccoughs or some other devilish indignity.) We cursed, and shifted on to a fallen trunk.

'Well, if these are the circumstances necessary before two men can be in love with me at the same time,' I said, in a mournful attempt to sound light-hearted, because the silence was growing impossible again, 'I'd almost rather languish in unrelieved continence.'

'That is not one of the alternatives we were discussing, my dear!' Arnold pulled himself out of a frowning day-dream to answer with the utmost gravity.

302

He did not volunteer any more about his row with Stewart. Reassured by the knowledge that, as one party was a crock, it could not have ended in violence, hopelessly antagonistic though both men were by now, I did not ask anything more about it. Arnold did not want to talk of it until his temper had cooled, and so started – at this moment of all moments! – a discussion of synthetic magic, which the Sakei practise, drumming on the ground for rain, and imitating the cries of the most skilful hunting animals in order to imbue themselves with the beasts' cunning. He had studied the subject, and dealt with it thoroughly. He seemed to expect me to take an intelligent interest. After a time I did find myself joining in, with the same sense of unreality which had pervaded, for me at least, all our talks on irrelevant subjects in the jungle: it was as if these conversations went on in some different sphere altogether, and I was listening to them from a long way off. Part of me was even enthralled by the discussion.

I knew that Arnold was deliberately putting off saying something of importance: this did not make the waiting easier for me. To keep my attention on the moment I made bets with myself where the talk would turn next. Conversation with Arnold had a jolly habit of ranging through an amazing variety of subjects. Now it led on to religion through his remark, made so irritatedly that I guessed it must bear on his personal affairs, that some religious women, who look upon children as the gift of God, seem to regard the act of physical love as a form of synthetic magic, though apparently not as entertaining as ground-drumming or animal imitations.

'"Only believe and thou shalt see That Christ is all in all to thee!"' quoted Arnold. '*Only*!'

I nodded agreement with his gesture of incomprehension. That staggering line has always been of interest to me, because it embodies so well an attitude of mind at which my imagination has boggled since early childhood. How fundamentally it divides mind from mind, this incomprehensible power, manifested by half the world, to believe what it is comfortable to believe, because it is comfortable. Among those who are congenitally inefficient at this sleight-of-reason are all my friends, and the strangers who are potential friends.

I said something like this, in phrases which I knew even at the time to be badly chosen: it is curiously more difficult to be in earnest and choose the effective word than to do it with one's tongue in one's cheek. I added that I had always been bewildered, too, by the aggrieved attitude of the religious-minded towards the unbeliever – the unspoken suggestion that the latter 'only does it to annoy, because he knows it teases.' Can even those for whom the will-to-believe and self-conviction are almost the same thing imagine that there is anyone, faced as we all are with inevitable dissolution, who would not passionately welcome faith if it were

compatible with mental integrity? Or that sometimes, in weak hours, the bravest among us have not
wavered towards blind belief, cowed beyond thought
for a moment by the advancing darkness into which,
at other times, we stare with unflinching hopelessness, because there is no choice, for us?

Arnold did not speak for a moment, and when he
did, I knew that he had understood my groping
sentences, and his answer was not wholly irrelevant.
'Judy, about the bitterest thing in my life is finding
you now – like this – instead of some years ago.
Even though I am going to have as much as I can of
you. What do I take from any other man by making
love to you? I don't mean Stewart, he's had the
same chance with you as I have, or better. Is there
anyone else?'

I shook my head.

He said, 'I've been feeling up till now that if you
said there was, it wouldn't make any difference!
Now, I want to know. I shan't be breaking up
everything for you if I have you for a short time?
Because it can only be a short time, Judy. You
know I'm tied.'

The unseen things that were always behind our
shoulders in the jungle crowded in, I thought,
because the time of waiting was over.

'You take only what someone else didn't want for
long.'

I think that anyone who heard us talking, but
did not understand the words we used, would have

said that both of us were quite calm. It was as if we were discussing the details of something that had really been settled a long time ago.

'What shall I be taking from your wife?' I asked.

'Very difficult to say, without being entirely loathsome. At a guess I should say, nothing for which she has the slightest personal value: but then you can never tell exactly where attachment stops and vanity – the pride of public possession – takes over. You see – ' he looked away, and suddenly it was hard to attend to what he said, every muscle in the turned throat, the set of the arm in the loose shoulder next me, the lines of mouth and chin outlined against the grey-green forest background, took on an enormous, inexpressible significance for me. All the desire of the flesh, knowing its own transience, was in these things, and the unending pain and joy of human longing wore for a moment the garment of our tried, weary bodies, burning them into a new semblance, as doomed vessels of immortality. It seemed to me in that instant that there was little left of me that was not already his, and whatever I should be taking I had already taken, in all but fact.

' – You see, I married at twenty-two (why do they let children do these things? But I suppose I'd have had a sporting shot at breaking the head of anyone who tried to stop me, then). And the girl I married has become the mother of my children, and nothing more. Her choice, not mine. No, that's not fair; just her nature and certainly not mine. You must have met some of the young women – no particular brains, just average – who marry and have children and then – well, goodness knows what happens to every intelligent interest and opinion they ever had. Just swamped, apparently, in a rush of maternity to the head. – Women in comfortable circumstances, I mean, who have no need to be permanently immersed in little Johnnie's bath, and what he said in it, to the exclusion of everything they've ever had in common with a man. Except as the lover of one of her children, I don't think you can rob the really maternal woman of anything that greatly matters to her, besides her dignity. My wife does care very much about appearances. If we get through I shall go back to my family, Judy. I'll have to. She and I have never had what she would call a serious disagreement. Being unable to talk to each other on anything but trivial matters doesn't count as a disagreement. Sorry this all sounds so rotten, but you wanted to know. I suppose I had no business to try to cut Corder out with you. Because I've nothing to offer – '

'Except what I want, now. Even if we only have each other for a little while. And we mayn't get back to England.'

'Judy!' He turned and we looked at one another, and then this calm that had held us both dissolved. It was as though the intangible things in the forest said that our time was short, and vigorous flesh and blood cried back their age-old defiance, 'We shall remain; we shall be always the same!' — lying consciously, proudly, in the immediate glory of the flesh. The mind could not bear the stress of such moments of overwhelming happiness for long, even if they could be prolonged: soon they must dissipate themselves by their own exhausting strength, with which we are over-charged. But sometimes they can leave behind an after-glow in the heart, not too great for it to bear and hold indefinitely. So a Sakei, climbing above the dim levels of his grey-green world, may come suddenly into full sight of the sun, and shrink back shielding his eyes from such intolerable brightness; and yet never wholly forget again, among the perpetual shadows to which he gladly returns, that somewhere outside his ken the splendour remains — visible even at the moment, perhaps, to other men like himself.

Arnold kissed me. 'There are probably Sakei about!' I said when I could.

'Doesn't matter — teach them something — they don't kiss,' he answered, and in a moment added a remark that coming from Arnold, in his unsentimental voice, made me laugh aloud in spite of the listening forest (though chiefly, I think, I laughed from happiness) 'The poor mutts!' he said idiotically.

Arnold became suddenly alarmingly practical: I do not know why this shook my ragged nerves as much as it did.

'Judy, will you come across to my shelter to-night? Here the jungle's too alive with men by day, even though I don't regard the Sakei as entirely human. We'll have to wait till to-night. I can't come to you; there are the two terrible old people who sleep in your shelter.'

'Arnold I – can't.' I could have borne the idea of waiting for him to come to me: the thought of going to him, with the myriad eyes of the jungle night watching me, was somehow appalling.

He caught hold of my shoulders with the instinctive anger of the lover turned possessive. 'You can, and you will. Because you want to. And I must have you, my dear. Will you come?'

'Yes.'

He put his hand up to his face in a gesture I had seen him use before in a moment of excitement, and now I looked for it eagerly because it was something familiarly his – something he did habit-ually – something to quicken my blood because Arnold was Arnold and the day would not last for ever.

'If I sit and talk to you, to make time go by, I think I shall go mad,' he said. 'I can't talk to Stewart; that's finished – besides if I did I'd sound vilely triumphant, I couldn't help it. I'm going to have a shot at talking to the old women by the fire. Even if they don't scuttle away, as I expect they will, we probably shan't be able to make each other understand anything. But I may pick up a few words of their language.'

Getting through time for myself, I went to see Stewart. Turned away from the light, and unable to move without pain, he called 'Who's that?' sharply while I was still only in the opening.

'Oh, for God's sake leave me alone!' he said when I answered, and because of my own preoccupation with the dragging hours of this day, I was barely touched by the angry wretchedness of his voice. I never knew exactly what had passed between the two men in this shelter, but whatever it was, some definite arrangement seemed to have been reached. Stewart recognised that I belonged, temporarily at least, to Arnold.

'Hadn't you better let me look at your heel, though, Nookie? It hasn't been touched since yesterday morning –'

'I'm all right. Leave me alone.'

'I seem to be spending a considerable part of to-day being told to get out of here,' I said, and mooned about the jungle in the vicinity of the kampong, sometimes catching a glimpse, between the trees, of Arnold's shoulder or head as he pounded roots with two of the women. I was too restless to stay long in any place.

Ah, but what a fool you are, I told myself. You're going into this with your eyes open, knowing it's only for a little while, and knowing what it costs in pain, afterwards. – Arnold has light, loose shoulders and narrow hips, memory reminded me as an irrefutable argument on the other side. – A man's skin where it is protected and soft over firm sinew can be lovely to touch – more wonderful, that way, than anything else. But it has been dead matter to me for what seems a long time. I can hardly believe that it has come alive again. My nerves if not my mind have almost forgotten already that the lean hard bodies of men can be anything of closer concern to me than moving forms of beauty, or fine machines gone wrong and interesting for their weakness not their strength.

There was a moment when, looking up into the great tree among whose roots my wind-break stood, I could not see the fork of the trunk, just visible in full daylight high up in the sea of leaves and small branches. Then I knew that in only a few minutes it would be night, and after so much waiting, my heart sank. When the darkness came I delayed for a long while, feeling the jungle change round me ominously once more, and belicving – as one can believe any fantastic thing in a Trenganu night – that I should give it a new power over us by my action.

I was stiff with sitting native-fashion, with my arms round my knees, in the shelter, waiting for nothing, when I got up desperately at last and went out into the stillness, stepping over the two old people. They were awake (I never saw a Sakei sleeping:) but they did not move as I passed. Some of the hunters, carefully hollowing out bamboos for

blowpipes, were still squatting over the tiny fire
in the centre of the clearing. They watched me
with their dull, patient eyes, and one spoke briefly
to his fellows, but not to me. These people did
not interfere with us at all, once we were in the
camp. I suspect that physically we were as repulsive
to them as they were to us, and it was more than
timidity that kept them away from us: only the old
could bear our proximity.

Arnold did not move when I crept in. For one
curious second I hoped wildly that he was asleep,
and then I could go back at once, having kept my
word. It was too dark to see anything, even in this
half-ruined shelter. I felt across the earth floor to
him and his hand closed round my arm, and pulled
me down to him. Neither of us spoke because of the
presences crowding in with us from the night
outside, gathering where the leaves whispered
through the rents in the woven reeds. We lay in
one another's arms as with ghosts: to each of us,
the other person might have been anyone else,
except that the measure of our feeling was in our
silence and swiftness and a kind of gentle brutality
of gesture. Possession was more satisfying than I
remembered. Afterwards we made love to each
other with words and the caresses and endearments
for which there had seemed no time.

Then came to me a conviction, gorgeous and
unexpected, that the jungle had waited too long
to strike: this knowledge was sudden and

overwhelming in the relief it brought. The hidden malevolence might spring now, or soon, or at any moment: we might indeed have unleashed some malignant force by our trivial defiance: but we were newly armed too, for this shared delight was irrevocable. Even our deaths would not mean full victory to the forest; for to the end beyond which we should not need it, the memory of what we had already filched from the jungle would remain. I could have laughed in triumph.

Gaily I taught Arnold anatomy, mixing cold science embalmed in worn Latin with more essential lore, for the pleasure of being deliberately irreverent towards one or both of the things which I most respected. It would be hard, though, for me to tell in which process the irreverence lies, in love dropped into science or science added to love, but I do know that this is excellent sacrilege, to follow by mouth over the warm shoulder the pectoralis major muscle – the beautiful long muscle that lifts the breast slightly when the arm is raised – and to translate the fine sinew and blood and bone under one's lips into dry-as-dust technicalities. 'Here – iust here, where it's pleasant to kiss – the deltoid muscle spreads fanwise to cover the top of the humerus, and the juncture of clavicle and scapula – and runs deviously – so – to *there* – equally good to kiss. What main artery passes under it? I've told you before.' And to have the beloved person forget, in laughter that desire ends.

We had a week or ten days of such love-making – one of the best periods of my life, in some ways. (Though for sentimental or moral reasons this is not often recognised, a second love affair is usually far more satisfying to a woman than the first. The memory of its beginning is not marred by an impression of severe physical pain, which scars the mind at such a time more than is generally understood; and the woman is more sure of herself as a lover, far less nervous and easily distressed.)

Finding that with practice we could accommodate ourselves to its exigencies, I moved over altogether into Arnold's wretched little wind-break, though it was too small and too dilapidated to be shared with even a semblance of comfort. Stewart recovered in this period, well enough to hobble about a little with a stick.

For want of any other help, he let me attend to his heel when the pain grew bad again; but we were silent and awkward together. This seemed odd, after twenty years of close companionship.

At the end of about a fortnight in the camp we were ready to try our luck for Kintaling again, by very slow stages, if the Sakei would give us back the gun. We knew that they had hidden it somewhere, being unable to use it themselves. But either we could not make them understand, though Arnold had acquired about twenty words of their two to three hundred word language, or – more likely, I thought – they did not want to understand. Like avaricious children, they were loth to give up even things which had no value for them. Unarmed, we could not feed ourselves and were only a burden to them. Now that they had satisfied their frightened curiosity – the same kind of curiosity that brings the rusa-deer within killing distance of a hunter who waves a rag on his rifle barrel – they were willing that we should go, as far as we could make out, but they would not help us in any way, and without weapons we dared not leave the camp, where at least there was food of a kind, though very little of it. All the negritos I saw were pitiably under-nourished.

Patiently I set out, at Arnold's instigation, to try to get into some kind of sympathetic contact with the old man and woman who slept in the wind-break where the Sakei had first put me. I was not good at languages, but he suggested that it would be easier for me to get their confidence than for him; they were likely to be less besotted with timidity before a woman, and these particular people were already used to my approach. But I discovered with surprise (all old negritos looked alike to me) that they were not always the same people who came in at night, or not both the same. Occasionally one only would be there. I was constantly starting again the disheartening job of battering at a blank wall of vacancy. There was one old man who seemed a little – a very little – more intelligent than the others. This was a Jahun from the Pwe valley: I could not make out why he had settled among the

Sakei, nor why they supported him, for he was past hunting age: but these communities, like those of the ants, are tolerant of any parasite once its presence is accepted as a familiar thing. He was the man who conveyed to me, mainly by pantomime, that he had cut a deer's throat while it slept. He seemed sometimes to understand my few words, and taught me others (the names for various tangible things. I never discovered any verbs in his talk). But at other times his mind clouded over, and he sidled away nervously as most of the others did when we tried to approach them. The most maddening barrier to our efforts to get in touch with them was their inability, like that of very small children, to keep their minds for many seconds together on any one subject. Even when I seemed to be making some progress with the Jahun, I could not press enquiries about the rifle nor about the fate of Deotlan. I never discovered anything definite on either of these points, though I returned to them as often as I dared, since they were the only reasons for the pursuance of this laborious enquiry, in which half my days were spent. After a time he grew still vaguer, and more troubled in manner, whenever I mentioned them, and started to sidle away. I realised then that these efforts were useless.

A new-born baby died. There were only about forty or fifty people in the kampong, counting the children, but there must have been more than that in the vicinity. From the size of the throng which took part in the hurried exodus following the burial I imagine that there was another camp not far away, with a free coming and going between the two: these people had no settled homes.

According to the Jahun, the spirit of the Sakei dead, lingering by the grave, seeks to take with it for company those who are nearest to it: running water must pass between a new grave and a camp as soon as possible.

An old man suffering from yaws died in this hasty journeying, with which we, especially Stewart, found it difficult to keep up even on the first day. I was not surprised to gather from the Jahun's talk that at times of drought, famine or sickness, more of the weak die from starvation and exhaustion on the march than from the original affliction.

Presumably other deaths followed quickly on these two, for we began a series of wanderings, going sometimes more than half a day's journey at a stretch to cross a stream that had no grave of recent date on the other side. After an indefinite period, I gathered, the spirit loses its power: or else the Sakei forget the whereabouts of the burial place, for all this part of the jungle must be full of old graves, and so unfit for human habitation.

There may have been an epidemic raging to account for this terrible bout of restlessness: I do not know. It was amazing how we lived, in the camp but not of it, knowing nothing that was going on. After a while I realised that I had not seen the Jahun for some time, and we did not see him again. But we had more pressing troubles to bear than his disappearance or death.

It became obvious that Stewart, though he put up a fine show of endurance, could not maintain much longer this nightmare journeying, day after day. It taxed Arnold and me.

It was more than I could bear to watch Stewart, greeny white of face and silent with pain, hobbling along on sticks, or with a hand on one of our shoulders; or making a gallant effort, unsupported, to mend his pace when we were all getting left behind, as happened inevitably towards the end of each journey.

It was like our first day in the jungle, when I thought Arnold was going to crock up, or like my own experience of forced marching with an injured foot, save that this prolonged ordeal of his was many times worse than anything either of us had suffered. In these conditions the healing process of the foot was naturally arrested. If that is all, I'll be thankful! I thought. But the next day the flesh round the lance-wound was unwholesomely congested: and I could do nothing to help him. We were walking nearly all day.

'This can't go on!' I said to Arnold.

'I know; but what can we do?'

The Sakei, like a swarm of bees hovering where they will not settle, had stopped for the night at last. The main body of them had crossed the stream by which we now lay – the friendly, running water which bounded the activities of the dead – some hours previously; but we had only just reached it, with the stragglers and the sick and the carriers of food. All round me were hurt and ailing and yaw-ridden children and old people, whom I suppose I ought to have helped when I could, but Stewart's critical state prevented my taking any interest in other people, and in any case I had come to loathe these hill folk, though they gave us food when they had enough.

They did so now, but Stewart was too exhausted to eat it. He lay where he had dropped when we realised with relief that we had at last caught up with the others, and I could not tell whether he was asleep or not, his eyes were closed, but the lids quivered. I have rarely seen any face so wasted after a short illness.

I honestly do not think that the Sakei were intelligent enough to realise that three more people carried on the commissariat of a tribe meant a little less food for everyone. It was an amazing position we were in – being kept by them, being even forced to make gigantic efforts to remain in touch with them, while our movements were entirely unwatched and we longed above everything to get away. It was also an appalling situation now. We could only hope that the negritos would not move again. In any case Stewart could not do another whole day's march. The epidemic, if some illness were really the cause of their shifting, might have worked itself out now; there might be no stream-bound areas hereabouts without memorably fresh graves in them, so that they would have to brave the menace of the lonely, relentless spirits of the newly dead, and remain where they were: many things might happen, I told myself that night with a forlorn effort of cheerfulness.

No windbreaks were made: we huddled together for warmth in the early hours. Stewart was in pain all night, and in the morning looked ghastly.

There had been, for the last two or three days, a bad period round about dawn, when the camp slowly came alive, in which we could not tell from the activity of the Sakei we saw whether they would start again that day on this heartbreaking wandering. Those we asked did not know, or, knowing, would not say. Who made the decision as to where they went it was impossible to find out: I thought no one person was responsible: they seemed to have no recognised chief: as in migrating flocks of birds, first one led and then another. Now we watched narrowly, anxiously, for the first sign of another flitting — a gradually increasing movement of men in one direction setting up an apparently aimless human current, into which the rest of the tribe would eventually be sucked, so that the ordeal began again for everyone.

No one stirred that day, however, while the light grew. Sprawling by one of the cheerless little banked fires, which hardly kept me from shivering in the cold blue mist, I dozed a little at last, having been awake most of the night.

I woke with Arnold shaking me. 'Come on,' he said wearily, and I saw Stewart walking away with a deliberate, slow step that wrung my heart because of its determination and the impression of suffering it conveyed. Ahead of him, the negritos were streaming out into the jungle, along a beast-track that we could barely follow. An old man, lying on the other side of the fire, watched us go with uncomplaining animal eyes, but did not move.

Stewart was amazingly game. He stood about three hours of it, and they were terrible hours, packed with so much pain for him that by degrees the ever-present fear which was driving us on, grew, if not more bearable, at least less dreadful than the continuation of this torture. All the time there was the added uncertainty of the track: we three were anything but forest people by instinct, though we had improved enormously in physical observation in these few weeks, and often we were out of sight of all but the weakest of the stragglers, who were almost as likely to be left behind as we were. Even so, ill or incapacitated by age, or in extreme childhood, all of them made me envious by the way in which they passed through dense thickets, as though in some occult way they melted the impeding foliage by their touch. Only those burdened in some way were obstructed as much as we were by the natural barriers that the forest set against us. By noon no able-bodied person was behind us, as far as we could see, except a man carrying a heavy load of the roots upon which these ill-fed creatures fell back when the hunters were unsuccessful. Yet I was not appreciably slowing my best pace for Stewart's sake; the jungle rate of progress was of necessity so slow that it required little more effort for him to keep up with us (though not with the Sakei) than to move at all. But this was growing more and more difficult, I knew, though for my own comfort I tried not to look at him. There was a low murmuring in my ears to which I paid no attention, beyond wondering if I were going sick again: it did not look as though it would make much difference to the final issue whether I did or not.

Stewart stopped, leaning against a tree. I stopped, too, half thankfully, thinking, or trying to think; well, if we give up now or later, it makes no odds.

'The river,' Stewart muttered, and I realised that the sound in my ears was external. 'Afraid I can't do much more,' he apologised.

'This is our best bit of luck so far. There's a ford here, then,' said Arnold, in such a dead, expressionless tone that even if I had not known the whole situation I should have realised the thinness of our luck. 'We'll get that man behind us just before the crossing. Get the food, at least. And stay this side.

For a bit anyway. Then later we'll take a chance of working down the river, on the other side. We may do it, with some food.'

'I see. In fact, "The infantry will occupy the objective; serious" ("serious" – oh my stars!) "resistance is not anticipated",' quoted Stewart, with a flash of his old gallows-humour. It made me realise, thinking of the incident afterwards, that his friendship meant almost as much to me as Arnold's love would do if I could be sure of it.

'Can you go on at all, Stewart?' Arnold asked.

The man, bent under the the load of food, was passing us.

Stewart nodded, and walked on, with tiny steps. 'I shan't be much use, though, in a scrap.'

'Arnold, what are you going to do?'

'Get hold of that food, somehow. Go on ahead, Judy. If it's humanly possible, catch up the next bunch of Sakei and keep with them till you get to the ford. If you hear anything, talk to them, shout – sing – anything. And when they're across, come back.'

I did what he wanted, by an effort of will of which I should not have thought myself capable in this half-starved condition. Looking back just before I lost sight of the three men, I saw Stewart and Arnold walking one in front, one behind the carrier of food, apparently ignoring him as he ignored them.

I poured out a jumble of Sakei and Malay and

English words to the people, two men and a woman and child, whom I joined near the river. They were apathetic with weariness and did not answer: but I went on babbling while my thoughts remained with the other two, wondering how far they would have to go to do what they intended, and whether they would succeed in any case. And if not, whether we should all be killed. I had no feeling for the defenceless Sakei. I supposed Stewart and Arnold would not kill if they could help it: physically, they were both superior to him: it should not be difficult: but every second stretched into an eternity as I struggled on, listening through my own disregarded babble.

No alarming sound came. Not far off, baboons were making their fiendish din, which for once was welcome.

At the river's edge I sat down, as if to wait for the others, while the remaining Sakei waded across. I was shaking so violently that I could hardly have gone on.

The river was much broader and calmer here than it had been where we had seen it previously, if it was the same stream, as we believed. At the ford it was only waist-deep for the taller Sakei. Part of me picked out, and carefully memorised, shore marks on either side, so that I should know the exact place at which to cross, if our turn ever came.

Three children, sprung from nowhere, appeared beside me, whimpering and calling shrilly to the rest of the tribe, who had almost all disappeared into the jungle on the farther bank.

One of the last men across heard them by chance, and waded back to help them: it was a strange, haphazard migration.

What had they seen? Unknown to us, they must have been behind Stewart and Arnold when they attacked the other man. What had happened by now? What might not have happened? I thought.

It was possible that the children had seen nothing, being on a parallel track. I did not wait for the man to reach them and hear whatever they might have to tell.

Terrified of what I might see at any moment, I pushed and tore my way back in the direction from which I had come. In a hundred yards or so I had lost my way, and defying the softly crackling silence, that made shouting an offence against one's own instincts if nothing else, I called and called as I went on frantically.

Arnold answered eventually. I found him holding the Sakei face downwards on the ground, by a grip that must have nearly dislocated the man's shoulder. He and Arnold were both badly bruised, and that was all. We were all glad that there had been no need for killing: though even now I cannot quite regard Sakei as human beings.

Stewart, slowing his pace till the man was at his heels, had swung round at a word from Arnold and knocked the man backwards almost into

Arnold's arms, but the Sakei was surprisingly lissom and tough considering his poor physique. He slipped under Arnold's grasp. If he started to run they knew that there would be no chance of catching him, here on his own ground. Stewart flung the stick with which he had been walking, between the man's legs. He stumbled, and before he recovered Arnold, from behind, got an arm round his neck and a knee in his back. Arnold flung himself on to the man as the Sakei went down, but the frail, ribby body seemed to turn fluid in his hands: it had the supple strength of water, and was almost as difficult to hold. The man was expecting to be killed. He cried out once, and Stewart, with no time for the niceties of single-handed combat, kicked him effectively on the head.

He was conscious again now, and looked from one to another of us with a desperate calm that reminded me of the old man we had left by the fire.

'He's a lovely fighter,' said Stewart. 'I'd like to give him back his blow-pipe. Only that we can't have him tracking us, waiting for revenge.'

'The odds are, he won't stay longer than he can help on this side of running water, even for the sake of doing you in!' Arnold said. 'We can't let him go for a bit, till the others are some way ahead, and when we do, if we make him go unarmed and he can't catch up the tribe –'

'Break the inner bamboo of the tube in one or

two places,' I said. 'He can mend it eventually, but it'll take time, and they're very rare, those long thin-bored pieces.'

We did this in the end, and gave him back two only of his darts. He would not be inclined to waste them: his companions had over three hours start. He melted like a shadow into the jungle when Arnold let him go.

Arnold's glasses, knocked off during the scrap, were a trampled mess of glass and tortoiseshell splinters when we found them; only one of the gold side pieces, which had previously cost us so much trouble, had survived at all. We left it there.

CHAPTER XI

SAIGON

WE spent four days on this side of the river, wondering whether the Sakei would return to attack us; but their dead were friendly to us.

We could not move much because of Stewart. We were unarmed, and the roots on which we lived were almost uneatable, raw: none of us could make fire, though we had watched Deotlan do it many times. We did not even keep up a pretence of hope in this period.

Then, when Stewart had recovered a little, we crossed at the ford. We supposed that the Sakei would have been forced to move on again by now, across another stream: in any case we had so little food left that it would probably make no difference whether they were there or not. Occasionally we found shell-fish on the shore. We lived on them and fruit and, when we were lucky, nuts. We knew the river was teeming with fish: it was maddening to be so inept in native ways that we had no idea how to catch them. Rigging a shelter – at which we were not too bad by now: it was our one useful accomplishment – suggested to us an attempt to bind together, with the same strong creeper used for

328

securing the thatching, the dead branches and odd drift-wood that lay about the shore.

Stewart could not walk without pain so that a raft seemed to be our only possible means of getting down river; but we had no success. Everything we fashioned collapsed when we tested it with our weight in the shallows. All three of us became so bedaubed with mud that we were almost unrecognisable. When our last essay in this line tipped up, depositing one of the men in the water again, I, having been looking away at the moment of the accident, could not tell for a second which of the two men was this filthy, dripping, bearded figure who tried gingerly to climb on board again.

'What I always say,' it remarked in excellent imitation of my uncle's voice — not unlike Stewart's but with a vintage quality — 'is that yachting is one of our few really clean sports.' And then I knew who it was and pointed up-river, to where something moved, I thought.

'What's that?'

It would have been of no use to ask Arnold, even if he had had his glasses, for the speck on the dazzling water which I was watching was over two miles away: without his glasses he lived wretchedly in a visible world that extended no farther than his arm.

There was a blinding sunset to hamper us. Evening after evening we had these gorgeous, unappreciated displays. Blood red river and sky, streaked with royal purple and gold, seemed close together, firing one another with their brilliance. We were shut into a steamy tunnel of light with deep green sides.

Stewart did not answer. Neither of us said anything: we were afraid of speaking our wild, growing belief where the things in the jungle might overhear. Hidden first by one bank and then the other, as it zig-zagged down to avoid the shoals, there seemed to be a boat.

It was unmistakably a boat when we shouted in cracked, breaking voices to Arnold, who had returned to the bank. Malayan waterways (in the less developed states) are the main highroads of the country. We had been hoping for this, day after day, saying nothing to each other because for so long, on another occasion, we had walked up the river and nothing had passed.

We began screaming and waving too early, from hysteria. We were hoarse long before the boat was abreast and we were all three very weak by now. We waded out from the shore as far as we could, regardless of possible crocodiles, but we could not get out of the shadow of the bank, and the sunset was straight in the faces of the people on board if they looked our way. We had wandered some way downstream from the ford; the river widened here into a bay on our side. The broader deep-water channels were near the other bank, and the boat slanted over towards it. The breeze, deflected downstream by the trees, was blowing slightly towards us, and the three men we could make out on board the boat were rigging a mat sail with much clatter. It rose between us and them, tinted shell-pink by this wonderful, devilish light. If they heard us they attributed the noise to baboons or shrieking parrots, and they passed on.

We were too stunned to do anything for a minute when we realised that they had not seen us. I turned to wade back: I did not want to watch our salvation diminishing downstream. Stewart suddenly hit me a violent blow between the shoulders. The boat, now about a quarter of a mile below us, was swinging round into the wind, and the men were getting out paddles. We were no longer obscured for them by the glow on the water, and someone had happened to look astern. But even after two Dyak boys had landed and were hailing us, I could not believe for a while in their reality, nor in that of the waiting boat.

There was a Chinese trader on board. What a man! He took us into the boat without question, knowing practically no English: Arnold's Malay as well as ours had temporarily disappeared, and for some time we could say nothing. He fed us, and I made myself very ill with overeating. I told the others to be careful not to do this, as it would be risky in our condition, and then gorged myself: it would make little difference in my case; at the release of any long-continued nervous tension —

after every examination for instance – my digestion always gave way completely. For the next three days I was in a state bordering on collapse. Then the Chinaman, in a mixture of English and Malay and gestures, drove an outrageous bargain with us for carrying us as far as the rapids, and finding a means for us to continue our way by boat below them. It was ludicrously extortionate, but payment was not to be made until we reached England: he understood that we could not pay now. Why he expected to get the money eventually I cannot think. We could hardly have looked impressive: we had no means of identifying ourselves. He made Arnold sign a paper in Chinese, of which he gave us a copy. We had no idea what was on it, but at Saigon we found that the terms were exactly those to which we had agreed. There was no discussion of what would happen if Arnold declined to sign what he could not read: but I am fairly sure that having heard our story, Li Mei would have been capable of dumping us in the riverside hamlet where I had bought ammunition, and leaving us to the care of the villagers. What a man! I have never been so implicitly trusted. Having signed his document, we were given everything we wanted that was on board. This was the river that we had struck before, and for our sakes he did not stop at the village which I had visited two months ago, though he had intended to trade there. We sailed past: it was a strange feeling, to lie at ease on the bottom boards of the boat, smoking his cigarettes (two I wasted through being sick, but he courteously gave me others) and to watch the weary distance that we had trudged slipping easily past us, backwards.

At the delta there was a French survey-ship. Mei had told two native boys, who worked for him occasionally in a village below the rapids, to take us down to the river-mouth and he would pay them later: he had given us all his ready money, so that we might not arrive penniless at whatever port we could make from the delta.

The skipper of the French ship kindly took us all the way to Saigon.

The mind adapts itself so rapidly to new conditions, particularly when they are better than the old, that by the time we were there I was no longer actively glad of safety: I was already taking it for granted again, and Saigon meant the beginning of my losing Arnold.

Arnold made no pretence that it was not so. We had a wonderful week in the boat, where it was assumed that I was his wife. And now we both recognised that it was nearly over, our association.

'Write out a cable to my wife for me! Will you, Judy?' he said, coming on deck to where I was sitting under an awning, while the port authorities gave the ship *pratique*. He could not comfortably write himself without glasses; all the same, I thought he might have asked some one else. But Arnold was capable of choosing me deliberately for this. I understood, myself, that instinct to hurt anything dear to one when one is suffering oneself:

'— and then put "Love, Arnold" ' he said tonelessly. 'Thanks. I wonder if she thinks I'm dead?' He gave a short laugh. 'She wouldn't go into mourning till she was sure — that might be considered *outré*, and it's so important, what other people say — but I am willing to bet she's in a new grey or mauve dress at the moment. That would be correct: a little uncertain, you see.'

I moved wretchedly. The voice went on hurting me as it hurt the speaker.

'And in a month or so I'll be back in the atmosphere where it's a ten-minutes' battle every time I want us to do a theatre or a dinner out or a dance — things we both used to like. (Our main shared interests were amusements.) I'll go on arguing down one flimsy excuse after another, till we get to the real reason. Even when they're asleep, she doesn't like to be out of call of the children, though we have a competent nurse. If we do go to a show — am I boring you?'

'Yes!'

'No, I'm not! Anyhow, you shall have this slightly overcoloured picture of my life as a present. I am asked in the interval "Do you know what the charwoman said to-day of Vivienne?" (that's the younger and more affected of the two). I say, "No, and do you know, I passionately don't care?" But I'm told all the same. I think it's rather a funny situation, really. Give it to Corder and see whether he can make anything of it! Unfortunately I can't live my own life separately because she'd be hurt, being in her own way fond of me –'

'Arnold, don't!'

'My dear, I'm sorry,' he said, softening. 'This business is so damnable: I'm feeling I want to hit out at the whole world, you included. But there's no way out of it. Come on. They're lowering the boat. Let's get ashore, and see the British Consul about our passages to our happy home land.'

The funeral of some local notability was going on in Saigon when we landed. Stewart, a tattered figure still hobbling on two sticks, was stopped by a gendarme as he tried to cross the square which held the British consulate: the cortege was expected in ten minutes and the streets were being cleared.

He told Stewart to wait a moment: they were still allowing people to cross in parties; but not to wander at will. When Stewart, understanding practically no French, became peremptory about his need for reaching the British consulate immediately, the gendarme decided fiercely that he should now wait until after the passing of the cortege. It was a funeral with full military honours.

Stewart, who had been on ahead, turned back to us fuming. 'Confounded fellow all hung about with medals won't let us across! And you know the hours these slow-motion funerals take!'

'Great War medals?' asked Arnold.

335

'I think so. Why?'

'Where is he?'

Stewart pointed him out.

'*Dis donc, le copain! Sommes des camarades, quoi!*' Arnold said in his most persuasive tone. '*Mon ami*'— he waved an arm at Stewart '*a deux fois verser son sang pour la France. Aviateur. Blessé au visage: ça se voit. Et moi*'— he drew himself up and joined his heels with what would have been a click if he had not been wearing sand-shoes —'*j'ai eu l'honneur de la defendre par terre. On nous attend au consultat* —'

'Dangerously militaristic nation,' he observed after the gendarme had motioned us on. 'Ever since the occupation of the Ruhr I've considered that France is far more unsuitable than Turkey to be at large in Europe.'

CHAPTER XII

'THE CURIOUSLY TOUGH THING'

'I HEAR from your sister that you're a journalist!' said an effusive woman writer, settling herself by Stewart on deck the day after we sailed from Saigon, bound via Singapore for England.

(Bovril brought round at eleven o'clock. Baths and regular meals again. I must remember that this is luxury, and compare it constantly with the last three months. I must remember that it is paradise to be here, safely. I must not think that when we reach Southampton I shall lose Arnold.)

'I was,' said Stewart cheerfully. 'I'm hoping that I'm not now. It all depends on whether my job has been kept open for me by mistaken kindness.'

Stewart's recovered self-confidence was one of the good things on which I must try to keep my mind. Whether he went back to that particular treadmill or not he was going, he said, to start the play that he had been carrying in his mind for months before he left home, too discouraged to write. '— and I don't care if it doesn't even get produced this time. (That, though a lie of course, isn't quite such a lie as it would have been three months ago.)'

337

He seemed to have decided that, having remarkably survived this business on top of a European war
nothing else was going to depress him overmuch.
I had an idea that Stewart's intense feeling for me
would evaporate sooner or later when we got back
to the old conditions, leaving behind only the
excellent sediment of our former friendship, with
a little wistfulness thrown in – which would not be
altogether unwelcome to his nature. (Already, as
I had foreseen, we both felt awkward when the
subject of his infatuation cropped up in our conversation.)

'I – er – write a little myself – just novels you
know,' said the lean and avid red-haired lady with
that air of terrific modesty now in vogue among
professional women, who boast to one another of
their cooking and their ability to renovate evening
dresses and their visits to Ideal Home Exhibitions –
being carefully non-peculiar. 'But I *don't* expect you
to know my name! Do you know Malaya well?'

Stewart pressed the courteous question and was
told her writing name.

'Of course!' he said, 'I remember reading one of
your books when I was at death's door with pleurisy
– Judy, here, will confirm my touch-and-go condition – and I skipped towards the end in case I
should die before I finished it.'

'Wretched man!' she said, and asked us the most
searchingly intelligent questions about Malaya,
practically none of which we could answer satis-

338

factorily. She had spent three weeks in Singapore on the way to China, but she knew much more about the country and the natives than we did. We were amazed at our all-embracing ignorance, and so, I gathered, was she. We did not know the names of most of the things we had seen, so that from her point of view we might just as well not have seen them: and various things that we remembered by name were jumbled together in our minds. The Sakei could not have been Sakei but Jahai, she told us, and the Jahun, judging from my description, was almost certainly a Semang. I should not be surprised if she were right: she was, quite genuinely, far more of an authority on most of the things that we had seen than we were. As first-hand observers we had missed so much of their significance: and we avoided her carefully for the rest of the voyage. Her forthcoming book will not suffer for that.

Arnold, like Stewart, had got back in these three months, unlikely as it seemed at first, the thing that he had lost: he was perfectly fit again. I was not so lucky.

Now, as day after day we left the wanton land and all that kindred part of the world farther and farther behind, and its influence thinned out in the intervening space and time, I began to feel acutely our responsibility for the deaths of Wan Nau and Deotlan. This had not occurred to me when we were close to the events, but the idea, once it had taken root in my mind, grew almost into an obsession.

Returning sensitiveness turned morbid. If we had
not left the ship – If, on the day of the storm, I had
not gone on through pride when the fever first took
me – But as a doctor I knew where that train of
reasoning was likely to lead the brain which
followed it too far. I tried to think of Mrs. Mardick,
knowing that on this point at least my mind was
and is obstinately sane: whether in that case we were
directly responsible for her fate or not, it remained
of no importance to us. (This is psychologically
unsound: by now we should have been more concerned over her than over the others, but it has
always been a sombre satisfaction to my practical
nature to notice how much of one's own experience
runs contrary to the best theories about life.) Constantly, though, my thoughts went back to Wan
Nau as she crouched on her heels, gripping her ankle,
her eyes fixed implacably on my face; and to
Deotlan's figure swaggering weakly into the silent,
peopled forest. I was lucky in that period in having
another and more personal preoccupation which as
we neared England shut everything else out of my
mind.

Arnold and I spent our time together looking back,
not forward if we could help it, save occasionally.

'How much of all this are you going to tell your
wife?' I asked.

'Oh, everything she cares to know. Except the
details. She is, in some ways, a sensible woman.'

We were silent for a minute, watching the wake.

340

Water, you slip astern too easily: time, you will begin to creep slowly, very slowly for me again one day soon, why are you hurrying now?

'There's nothing I can say — Judy —'

'Oh, no, my dear. I've always known that our affair would be over when or if we got through. That's all right.'

I was thinking of an observation made several years before, by a man who was dissecting with me: a stolid person, who meant it literally, I think. 'Curiously tough thing, a human heart.' The words had struck me at the time: I would bear them in mind now. It *is* a curiously tough thing.

Arnold and I fell in love with each other on this voyage: we had time to talk, time to get to know one another's minds, time to do more than make love; and losing him physically no longer seemed the worst thing that would happen when we reached home.

At Southampton none of us was met. It had not been certain up till the last minute what connection we should catch at Singapore, and after our first cables we had sent no others. But there were piles of correspondence. We did not mean to travel up in the train together, but at the last minute I had a sudden weak, childish desire to be with Arnold while I still could; and Stewart's correspondence was mixed with mine. We were constrained now, the three of us together. For want of anything to say we read letters.

341

'Now, isn't that wonderful, I have lost my job!'
said Stewart. 'Lend me half a crown, Judy; and I'd
like five shillings from you, Ainger; I don't need the
money yet but I want to break in as many people as
possible to the job of supporting me.'

My job had only been filled temporarily. I could
take it up as soon as I arrived.

Arnold, characteristically, had not let his depart-
ment know where he was from the time he started
his sick leave. Cables and wireless messages had
been flying about the East for him for months.

'Heavens,' he said, suddenly going off into fits of
laughter, having just opened another letter. 'They've
given me – Oh how frightful –' It took some time
to make out through his laughter what he had been
given 'O.B.E.!' he gasped, 'Oh, how awful! The
O.B.E.! Civil servants can't refuse these things when
they are actually offered, but they can pull strings
to prevent such horrors descending on them. They
did it on me in my absence. Serve this Government
right if I went straight back to Sarawak.'

Minute after minute went by. We had nothing
more to say to each other. Why had we nothing to
say, even though Stewart was with us, I wondered
helplessly? In a few days, I knew, my mind would
begin to turn over avariciously every moment
we had had together, and I should remember that
these were wasted. But still they slid by, unused.

*   *   *   *

342

I met Hugh about a week after we landed. By habit, something in my throat seemed to tighten with excitement when I recognised him, and then I smiled inwardly, knowing that it was only habit. We ran into one another in Oxford Street, where I was intending to buy either pale-gold or pale-grey velvet for an evening dress; and we talked awkwardly. He suggested that I had been away. I said yes. I asked if Muriel were all right. He said yes. And then we had nothing more to say, though not for the reason for which Arnold and I had been silent, sometimes, during the voyage home. Because I had nothing to tell him I showed him the two patterns, and asked which colour he would get, in my place. He chose the grey. I looked up suddenly and laughed: 'You'll be delighted to know, Hugh, that you look superbly unattractive to me to-day! Your ears are too small. Stupid-looking on a man.'

'Ooray,' he said, laughing too. 'I'm so glad, my dear!' and we shook hands warmly and parted. It is a curiously tough thing – I went on and bought the gold velvet.

I had had a letter from both Arnold and Stewart that morning. I opened Stewart's first, because I did not know the precise little writing on the other envelope, and it looked uninteresting. Stewart wrote, from our home at Chelmondiston, that for my amusement he was concocting a brief account of our main doings during the past three months, to run parallel with an account of exactly what had happened in the Great World at the same time. 'The dog has cheerfully returned to its vomit, or rather to what has vomited it, and I have been reading relays of old newspapers. This, you may like to know, is what Mr. J. L. Garvin wrote in *The Observer* on October 12th – the day we were trying to get across the river by the dam –"Every child knows that reciprocal preference for Dominion staples in the Mother Country and for British manufacture overseas would be the fundamental proposition in the Conference." It is lovely not to have to be any longer as intelligent as a Fleet Street child.'

Arnold's was a half-sheet of notepaper with, on one side, nothing but cold facts, enclosed in abrupt sentences.– He was very busy. His wife was in Switzerland with the children still, coming back the next day. (And all these days and nights I had been unwillingly picturing them together.) He had enjoyed his first week-end in the English country; the woods were just now at their autumn best. He had even been walking for pleasure, which he had never expected to do again. He would be at Simpson's at one the day after to-morrow for our farewell lunch. Anyone could have read that letter. There were no endearments beyond the inevitable 'Dear Judy' at the beginning, and it was signed only with his initials. Overleaf were lines so badly written that it took me some time to make out that here was a sonnet, and then I realised, with a sudden flood of

longing, that the hard and impersonal Arnold was
the only man I knew who would be unselfconscious
enough to send poetry, to-day, to a woman he loved
if he felt like doing so. It was so conventional and
so old-fashioned that, coming from him, I knew it
sprang from a full heart —

> 'It does not hurt me yet that you have gone.
> I still grow rich at heart when lordly trees
> Throw golden largesse for the beggar, breeze:
> Still earth, once shared, is good to walk upon.
> I shall have learned your absence later on.
> Now I have private joy in woods – my mind
> Waits numb, in almost peace, for pain to find.
> But that will come before Spring's benison.
> I must make anxious haste to love the earth,
> Missing no hue, no cobweb, not a thing;
> For I remember sorrows I have known,
> And how they robbed all loveliness of worth.
> I must foretaste, too, woods re-gilt with spring,
> Before I grow aware I am alone.'

A nurse knocked at my door (I was resident at
the Croydon clinic.) Someone wanted me in the
ward; and I was glad. Anything was better than
leisure to re-read that letter indefinitely.

In Trenganu we had promised ourselves this
lunch at Simpson's. In the ship coming home we
had promised ourselves one more meeting. But I
was sorry, when the time came.

My friend among the waiters hurried forward as I arrived. Stewart and I had been going to Simpson's, whenever we were temporarily in funds, for the past seven years, and we always sat at the same table.

'Good morning to *you*, Madam! I was only thinking the other day, we hadn't seen you or the gentleman for too long! Been away, if I may surmise, Madam? I don't think we had redecorated the last time you were here?'

'Yes, been away. No, I don't think you had – at least – I don't know.'

Everyone said to me carelessly 'Oh, have you been away? I thought I hadn't seen you for ages,' and then went on with an account of their own affairs of the week. It was natural enough; it only seemed to me that I had been away a lifetime or so.

I wanted to go on, into the farther room where our usual table was, not hoping to see Arnold yet but longing to be quiet for a few minutes before he came. I was a quarter of an hour early. I had a raging headache, not having slept much for two nights. I was a fool not to have done what I had thought of doing in a panic yesterday – written to put off the lunch. It was a senseless idea, this torturing ourselves with a brief glimpse of each other after we had really said goodbye. Yet I knew that if I had been told where Arnold was lunching, even with someone else, I could not have stopped myself going there, just to see him.

But I could not get away from the dear old waiter: his voice followed me, whispering deferentially in my ear, 'If I might suggest, Madam, not the usual side. There's a gentleman behaving very funny —'

'Oh, then I expect that's the person I'm lunching with.'

If a gentleman had the nerve to 'behave funny' in Simpson's, and Arnold were lunching there on the same day, the law of probability made it nearly certain that Arnold was the offender.

'I beg your pardon, Madam! Of course, as it wasn't the usual gentleman —'

It will soon be finished now. Say goodbye again, and the worst's over. You can stand more than this. It is a curiously tough thing —

I went on and saw him behaving in the way that is considered most peculiar in England; he was sitting by himself and laughing; laughing with his head between his hands. For one second I thought he must be drunk. Then it crossed my mind to wonder fantastically if he had just been given a knighthood: this silent laughter was so much more convulsive and sustained than the burst that had greeted his unexpected minor decoration. Then I had a passing sense of irritation that he could find anything amusing at the moment when I was feeling as I was just then. Then came hope.

He staggered to his feet when I appeared, seized my hands and sat down, forgetting for a second to let go.

'I told her and – *sakit hati*, my wife also! – And I always thought she was a sensible woman about some things –'

'Arnold!'

'It's so funny'– he waved a weak hand in the air –'to find that I'm much less lovable than I was afraid I was!'

'– Do you mean – do you mean – you can leave her?'

' "Leave her?" she's divorcing me! Not hurt, just raging angry! How *dare* I lend her private property – ? So I'm to be punished by being deprived of the custody of the children!'

I began to laugh too, I did not know why. The waiter hovered near us, faintly pained and faintly regretful, every inch a Simpson's waiter.

'Pull yourself together for a moment,' I said. Now there was so much to discuss and so much time before us to discuss it in, that it would all wait until we had ordered lunch. 'My old friend thinks you're behaving "very funny." He said so to me as I came in.'

'The devil he did.– Waiter, have you any English meat? Because if so we'll have roast saddle of mutton.– That'll "learn" him!'

The man went away without a word, an embodiment of magnificent impassivity, towards the kitchens.

'He's gone to repeat that to the *chef*. The shock will kill him if the cook doesn't. You've sent that man to his doom,' I said. 'And you will go down to history as "The Man Who Specified English Meat in Simpson's."' Everything was so wildly funny,—even in the stolid atmosphere of Simpson's, —intrinsically so funny, somehow, that I could not keep my mind on important matters. There was only one salient fact, and I knew that now.

'Can you support yourself, Judy? Because I shall never be able to keep both of you.'

'Not if I'm mentioned as co-respondent. Struck off the register.'

'My dear! Will you mind?'

'Terribly, I expect, some day. Not in the least now,' and we both relapsed into the weak, overwhelming, objectless laughter that, coming over us at intervals ever since, has made it so difficult to attend to the footling legal business connected with Arnold's re-marriage.

Other *VIRAGO MODERN CLASSICS*

EMILY EDEN
The Semi-Attached House &
  The Semi-Detached Couple

MILES FRANKLIN
My Brilliant Career
My Career Goes Bung

GEORGE GISSING
The Odd Women

ELLEN GLASGOW
The Sheltered Life
Virginia

SARAH GRAND
The Beth Book

RADCLYFFE HALL
The Well of Loneliness
The Unlit Lamp

WINIFRED HOLTBY
Anderby Wold
The Crowded Street

MARGARET KENNEDY
The Ladies of Lyndon
Together and Apart

F. M. MAYOR
The Third Miss Symons

GEORGE MEREDITH
Diana of the Crossways

EDITH OLIVIER
The Love Child

**CHARLOTTE PERKINS
GILMAN**
The Yellow Wallpaper

DOROTHY RICHARDSON
Pilgrimage (4 volumes)

**HENRY HANDEL
RICHARDSON**
The Getting of Wisdom
Maurice Guest

BERNARD SHAW
An Unsocial Socialist

MAY SINCLAIR
Life & Death of Harriett Frean
Mary Olivier
The Three Sisters

F. TENNYSON JESSE
A Pin to See The Peepshow
The Lacquer Lady
Moonraker

MARY WEBB
Gone to Earth
The House in Dormer Forest
Precious Bane

H. G. WELLS
Ann Veronica

REBECCA WEST
Harriet Hume
The Judge
The Return of the Soldier

ANTONIA WHITE
Frost in May
The Lost Traveller
The Sugar House
Beyond the Glass
Strangers

Other VIRAGO MODERN CLASSICS

PHYLLIS SHAND ALLFREY
The Orchid House

SYLVIA ASHTON WARNER
Spinster

MARGARET ATWOOD
The Edible Woman
Life Before Man
Surfacing

DOROTHY BAKER
Cassandra at the Wedding

JANE BOWLES
Two Serious Ladies

KAY BOYLE
Plagued by the Nightingale

ANGELA CARTER
The Magic Toyshop

WILLA CATHER
Death Comes for the Archbishop
A Lost Lady
My Antonia
The Professor's House

BARBARA COMYNS
The Vet's Daughter

ELIZABETH HARDWICK
Sleepless Nights

EMILY HOLMES COLEMAN
The Shutter of Snow

ROSAMOND LEHMANN
Invitation to the Waltz
The Weather in the Streets

TILLIE OLSEN
Tell Me a Riddle
Yonnondio

GRACE PALEY
Enormous Changes at
    the Last Minute
The Little Disturbances of Man

STEVIE SMITH
The Holiday
Novel on Yellow Paper
Over the Frontier

CHRISTINA STEAD
Cotters' England
For Love Alone
Letty Fox: Her Luck
A Little Tea, A Little Chat
The People with the Dogs

**SYLVIA TOWNSEND
    WARNER**
Mr Fortune's Maggot
The True Heart

REBECCA WEST
Harriet Hume
The Judge
The Return of the Soldier

ANTONIA WHITE
Frost in May
The Lost Traveller
The Sugar House
Beyond the Glass
Strangers

If you would like to know more about Virago books, write to us at Ely House, 37 Dover Street, London W1X 4HS for a full catalogue.

Please send a stamped addressed envelope

Book Tokens

Give them the pleasure of choosing
Book Tokens can be bought and exchanged at most bookshops